His First
and Last

His First and Last

An Ardent Springs Novel

Terri Osburn

Montlake
Romance

Text copyright © 2015 Terri Osburn
All rights reserved.

No part of this book may be reproduced, or stored in a retrieval system, or transmitted in any form or by any means, electronic, mechanical, photocopying, recording, or otherwise, without express written permission of the publisher.

Published by Montlake Romance, Seattle
www.apub.com

Amazon, the Amazon logo, and Montlake Romance are trademarks of Amazon.com, Inc., or its affiliates.

ISBN-13: 9781477828786
ISBN-10: 1477828788

Cover design by Anna Curtis

Library of Congress Control Number: 2014957574

Printed in the United States of America

Chapter 1

The Nashville heat hit Lorelei Pratchett like a wet blanket, smothering her will to live. Not that she had much of one to begin with. The dream of becoming the next Meryl Streep, which she'd chased for more than ten years, remained so out of reach she'd have to launch herself into outer space to even get close.

And now she was back in Tennessee. The land of conservatives, camo, and country music. Freaking awesome.

Granny had said she was sending someone to pick Lorelei up at the airport, but she'd danced around the details, leaving her granddaughter clueless as to whom or what she should be looking for. A taxi from the airport up to Ardent Springs, sixty-five miles northwest of Music City, would cost more than Lorelei could afford.

To be fair, a cab ride to the end of the runway would cost more than Lorelei could afford.

Dragging two suitcases, which contained all of her worldly possessions, she shuffled over to the closest bench to remove her knockoff

Manolos and give her feet a rest. Her favorite suitcase, the black one with a smattering of cherries, fell over when a wheel popped off and rolled away.

"And we have a runner," she said to no one in particular. Lorelei didn't blame the little spinner. She'd make a break for it, too, if she had the chance. Correction. If she had the *choice.*

Before she could catch the wayward wheel, a handsome skycap snagged it off the sidewalk and returned it with a smile. "This one's trying to get away," he said, pearly whites gleaming, twang intact.

"Good thing you caught him before he hopped into a cab." If he thought she would tip him for retrieving that wheel, Mr. Skycap was sadly out of luck.

The sarcasm seemed to go over his head. "Do you need help getting it back on? I have a screwdriver over here."

"No help needed," she said, unzipping the front compartment of the suitcase and dropping the wheel inside. "But thanks for the offer. Don't let me hold you up. I'm sure you have skycappy things to do."

His smile faded as the man nodded and returned to his post. She probably shouldn't take her bad mood out on strangers, but her mouth had yet to get that memo.

"Still a charmer, I see," drawled a deep male voice from behind her.

Lorelei closed her eyes before turning around. Granny wouldn't be that mean. Maybe he was flying out, never to return.

Ha. As if Spencer Boyd would ever leave his beloved Tennessee home.

Turning slowly in her seat, Lorelei leaned back and looked up into her high school sweetheart's face. She blocked the waning sun with one hand, but could still only see him in silhouette. He looked broader than she remembered, but the hat was the same. In twelve years the man couldn't buy a new cowboy hat?

"Hello, Spencer," she said, employing every acting skill she'd ever learned to keep the surprise out of her voice.

"Lorelei," he responded with a nod. "This all your stuff?"

A sarcastic retort tickled the tip of her tongue, but she swallowed it down. "This is it. Please tell me you're parked close by."

With a head tilt to the left, he said, "Short-term lot right across the street here."

Lorelei replaced the yellow high heels, then rose to her feet. The move put her at eye level with her chauffeur, which put him around six foot two, since she was five ten and wearing four-inch heels. Broader and taller, Spencer Boyd had grown up while she was gone.

Not that he hadn't been handsome in high school. Quite the opposite. Every girl at Ardent Springs High tried to catch Spencer Boyd, but he'd only ever had eyes for Lorelei. Until she'd refused to accept a lifetime sentence in their tiny town popping out a passel of rug rats with the last name Boyd.

Back in the day, Spencer had been wiry and thin, with the potential for more, and he'd certainly fulfilled that potential. His broad shoulders were accompanied by a solid chest, narrow hips, and thighs that were made for denim. Lorelei had once known the body before her in the biblical sense, as Granny would say. Back when it was hard angles and so thin she could count his ribs.

There would be no rib-counting now, but she felt safe in the guess that a six-pack lurked beneath the button-down.

"You look good, too," he said. One side of his mouth tilted up in a grin that lacked any of the distaste she expected to see. The brown eyes held her blue ones, as if daring her to deny where her thoughts had wandered.

Lorelei pulled the yellow jacket tight across the front of her little black dress. "Shall we?" she asked, stepping to the edge of the curb, ignoring the suitcases at her feet.

"Allow me," Spencer said, a hefty dose of sarcasm dripping from each word. They'd always had that in common. "It's the gray Dodge on the right, two rows back."

After checking for oncoming traffic, Lorelei stepped off the curb and followed his directions. She didn't need the word *pickup* included with *gray Dodge* to know that's what she was looking for. That was a given. Males—and many females—in Ardent Springs had always driven pickup trucks.

Lorelei doubted that had changed in the last dozen years.

But she had forgotten another characteristic of Ardent Springs residents. They loved their dogs.

As she made the last step up to the passenger door, a large black beast hopped up in the truck bed and barked right next to her head. Lorelei jumped back, slamming her hip into the side mirror of the neighboring Honda.

"Holy crap! That thing nearly gave me a heart attack!" Her hip hurt like hell, but her pride was the real injured party. "You brought a stupid dog all the way to the airport?"

Spencer threw her suitcases into the truck bed, shoved his hat off his forehead, and shot her an angry look from the opposite side of the truck. "Champ here has a guaranteed ride home. You insult my dog again and you won't be so lucky."

Lorelei rolled her eyes. "Granny is so going to pay for this," she mumbled under her breath. Once Spencer unlocked the doors, she jerked hers open, but found climbing in wasn't so easy. She tried several angles, working to make sure her dress didn't slide up to her belly button, but nothing was working.

In her concentration, she hadn't noticed Spencer come around the back of the truck.

"In you go," he said, lifting her off her feet as easily as he'd tossed her suitcases through the air. Lorelei landed with an oomph on the bench seat, her dress high enough to reveal more than she was comfortable flashing her former boyfriend.

Thankfully, he'd been traipsing back around the vehicle and hadn't seen a thing. She hoped. Dress straightened and seat belt fastened,

Lorelei checked her reflection in the side mirror, dabbing a bead of sweat off her forehead and straightening her hair.

Spencer hauled himself into the cab using the steering wheel for leverage. Seat belt buckled, he opened the console and pulled out a dog biscuit.

"A snack for the road?" she asked, shooting him her most insincere smile.

The driver ignored her, slid the back window open, and waited. A large black head popped through the opening, took the biscuit, then popped back out.

"You want one, too?" He pointed to the slot in the console where the treat had come from.

With a curled lip, she answered, "I had six peanuts on the plane. I'm good."

"Suit yourself." Spencer started the truck, slid on a pair of sunglasses, and put the wheels into motion.

Lorelei noted the time on the radio and calculated how long the drive would take. If Nashville traffic was the same as it used to be at five thirty on a Friday, she had nearly two hours to enjoy the scintillating company of the cowboy beside her.

Snatching a pair of sunglasses from her purse, she opted for the cowardly way to handle the situation. She'd take a nap. Spencer paid the parking attendant, then rolled the truck onto Donelson Pike. As they drove toward I-40, she watched the sunset to her left.

Hard to believe less than twenty-four hours ago she'd watched that same sun set over the Pacific Ocean. A sigh escaped her lips, and she relaxed for the first time in weeks. Maybe months.

Lorelei hadn't expected this feeling of relief. As if she'd found her soft place to fall. Not even the scorching presence of the man beside her, the man whose ring she'd once worn, could dampen the feeling of home.

She may not have wanted to come back to her hometown, to face the demons she'd left behind—not that the demons she'd accumulated in Los Angeles were any better—but now that she was here, maybe things wouldn't be so bad. Maybe Granny was right—home was exactly what Lorelei needed.

The unexpected contentment made her sigh again, and then she turned her head to steal a glance at Spencer. The question tapped at her brain. *Ask him,* it said. *Ask him why he came to get you.*

The last time she'd seen him, a few days before she'd left for California, they'd reached an impasse. An obstacle too big for people their age to overcome with any kind of grace or tact. He'd refused to leave Ardent Springs. She'd refused to stay. Neither wanted a long-distance relationship since neither believed the other would change their mind.

Spencer had made it crystal clear that if she didn't love him enough to stay, then he never wanted to see her again. Unfortunately, he'd shared these feelings while they were strolling through the Main Street Festival, a summer celebration that rolled into the July Fourth festivities, with pretty much the whole town in attendance.

In a fit of temper, Lorelei had lashed out, declaring to every local within hearing distance that Ardent Springs was nothing but a two-bit town filled with small-minded idiots. Then she'd thrown Spencer's ring in his face and stormed off. The crying lasted three days, until the moment her plane landed at LAX.

But once that plane touched down, Lorelei vowed never to cry over a man again. And she hadn't. Until two months ago when she'd learned that the man she'd hoped to marry had reached the wife quota with the one he already had. The one Lorelei knew nothing about until Mrs. Maxwell Chapel had paid her a personal visit. A moment that set off a chain of events that threatened to land Lorelei homeless on the streets of Los Angeles.

Hence, her inglorious return home.

In twelve years, there had been no calls or letters from her high school sweetheart. Not even a hello passed through her grandmother. Nothing to make Lorelei believe Spencer's feelings had changed over time.

So she stuffed down the questions. They didn't really matter anyway. Whatever the answers were, they wouldn't change the past and would only bring more headaches for her present. Lorelei had enough of those already.

He couldn't believe she hadn't asked. She had to be curious why he'd been the one to drive all the way to Nashville to get her, especially since Spencer knew Rosie hadn't told her who the chauffeur would be. Not that he had much of an answer. The truth was, he went because Rosie had asked him to. And Spencer would do anything for Lorelei's grandmother. Lacking any real family of his own, he'd found a lifeline in Rosie Pratchett at one of the darkest moments of his life. Picking her granddaughter up from the airport was the least he could do.

But if he were honest, he'd admit he wanted to see her. He wasn't the boy she'd left behind anymore. The idiot who'd thrown a tantrum when his feelings got hurt, then tossed away the best thing he'd ever had.

Life went on. People changed. Except Lorelei.

He should have known. God, she looked as beautiful as ever. The blonde hair slightly shorter. The body that of a woman, not a girl of eighteen. There had never been any doubt Lorelei Pratchett would be gorgeous, but when he spotted her sitting on that bench, it was like taking a charging bull horns-first to the chest.

He'd hovered beside a column twenty feet down the sidewalk, buying time for his heart to settle back to a normal rhythm. He couldn't face her looking like a lovesick calf. If she knew how he felt, she'd chew him up and spit him out without a second thought.

Time may have passed, but he knew from experience that women possessed long memories. All women except his own mother, who couldn't even remember the name of the man who'd sired him. The sperm donor had taken off long before Spencer took his first breath.

"This is probably a stupid question," Lorelei said, tugging Spencer out of his reverie, "but anything exciting happen in Ardent Springs while I was gone?"

He couldn't help but chuckle. Just like her to believe nothing would happen in twelve years.

"Well," he started, wrinkling his forehead in thought. "The old Miller Tavern got bought out. Now it's Brubaker's."

"As in Harvey Brubaker? The grocery store owner?"

"As in."

"Huh," Lorelei said, watching the road ahead of them. "Why would Harvey buy a bar?"

"Because Mrs. Brubaker was spending a lot of time at Miller's and coming home real late smelling like other men." Spencer took the exit onto I-65 north. "Seems as good a reason as any."

"Oh." She remained silent for nearly a minute, then asked, "They were old when I left. They'd have to be pushing seventy by now."

"Yep," he agreed. "I do my best not to get a mental image on that one."

"Good idea." Lorelei nodded. "Anything else? I don't suppose there are any new shopping options? Something other than the Agri Co-op?"

He couldn't give her good news on that one. "Goodlettsville is still the only option for your kind of shopping. Nothing any closer. Yet."

"Lovely."

Silence loomed again. Spencer decided to fill it.

"So, are we going to keep ignoring the elephant in the truck, or are you going to ask?"

Lorelei turned around in her seat. "Elephant? Dude, that's a dog."

"Nice try, but I know you're not a dumb blonde, remember?"

She righted herself, tugging down her dress as she did so. Spencer could still see enough thigh to make his mouth water. Lorelei always did have great legs.

"I suppose that's a compliment." She sighed. "What question do you want me to ask? Why are you here? Do you still hate me? I don't need to ask if you're married. Granny kept me informed on that front."

Since she had yet to ask him anything, Spencer stayed quiet.

"Sorry about the divorce," she added. "Contrary to what you might think, I wasn't happy to hear about that."

Was that sympathy coming from the passenger seat? A friendly comment without a trace of sarcasm? Maybe he'd picked up the wrong woman.

"It wasn't fun," he said, gripping the steering wheel tighter than necessary. "Life goes on."

"Yes, it does, doesn't it?" He wasn't sure how to interpret that one. "You're being nice to me, so I'm guessing hate isn't the appropriate word anymore."

With complete honesty, he said, "I haven't hated you since a week after you left."

Lorelei nodded. "Right. I wasn't worth that kind of emotion."

Spencer shook his head in amazement. "You haven't changed a bit, Lorelei."

"You'd be surprised," she said. Her head leaned back on the headrest, and she shut her eyes. "As much as I'm enjoying all of this catching up we're doing, I'd really like to take a nap. Do you mind?"

"Nope."

"Thanks."

"Lorelei?"

"What?" his passenger growled, eyes still shut.

"I'll still be here when you wake up. And we're going to have to answer those questions sometime."

Her eyes were open now, glaring at him from beneath perfectly shaped brows. "I'll check my calendar. Maybe there will be an opening next year."

Spencer knew when he'd pushed far enough. "Thank you, ma'am."

A loud sigh was her only response. A minute later, soft snoring accompanied the radio.

Chapter 2

Lorelei woke up when her head smacked off the passenger door window as Spencer's truck bounced through the potholes in Granny's driveway. She'd been having a vivid dream that included Spencer, herself, and a hot tub. The memory of it hurt more than the bump on the head.

"You still snore," Spencer said. No *good morning sunshine.* No *you're pretty when you sleep.* Only a reminder that she snored. Jerk.

"Then I guess we're all caught up." Lorelei yawned, stretching her back as much as possible with the seat belt on. "I can't believe Granny hasn't fixed this driveway."

"We've filled in the holes a couple of times, but the rains wash it back out again."

We? What the hell did he mean *we*?

The truck stopped in front of the old garage, which looked freshly painted. Maybe *we* had painted that, too. As soon as Spencer slid the vehicle into park, Champ bolted over the side, barking his head off as if alerting the entire county to their arrival. Lorelei preferred to make a

quieter entrance, but she had to admit she *was* excited to see her grandmother.

It had definitely been too long.

By the time she'd climbed from her seat and crossed behind the
truck, Granny appeared on the porch. Lorelei gave in to the urge. Kicking her shoes off in two different directions, not caring one flying fig
where they landed, she followed Champ's example and bolted across
the yard, slowing enough not to knock the older woman off her feet.

Everything Lorelei needed was in that hug. Love, acceptance,
joy. Even the hint of sadness for more than a decade apart made the
embrace all the more honest. How long had it been since she'd felt honest contact with another human being?

Years.

"Step back and let me get a look at you," Granny mumbled against
her shoulder. Even without shoes on, Lorelei was half a foot taller than
the woman who'd raised her. "You were beautiful when you left here
all those years ago, but now you're absolutely gorgeous. As I knew you
would be."

"Granny," Lorelei said, "it's not as if I haven't sent you pictures."

"Pictures don't do you justice." A soft hand tapped Lorelei's cheek.
"I'm so happy you're home." Another tight squeeze around her middle,
and then the woman jerked back. "You must be starving. I've got the
chicken and dumplings in the Crock-Pot, but let's get you settled in first."

Granny stepped to the side, yelling, "Spencer!" only to find him
standing on the bottom step holding two suitcases. "You're such a good
boy. Would you mind taking those up to Lorelei's room? You know
which one it is."

Either Spencer had been given a tour of the upstairs in the last
twelve years, or all those nights he'd climbed the hickory tree to get in
her window, he could have come through the front door.

"No problem." Spencer wiped his boots on the worn welcome mat
as Granny held open the screen.

"You'll stay and have dumplings with us, too." Granny smiled at Lorelei, looking very satisfied with herself. After all these years, she couldn't think . . .

"Granny?" Lorelei crossed her arms. "Spencer and I aren't picking up where we left off. You know that, right?"

Tiny round glasses slid down a pert nose as her eyes went wide. "I never said you were."

She may not have spoken the words, but the message in those blue depths shone loud and clear.

"You stay here, Champ. I'll bring your food out in a minute." Granny tugged Lorelei inside, shuffling across the scratched hardwood floor to the kitchen. "I made a fresh pitcher of sweet tea for you. I know whatever they have out there in California doesn't come close to my sweet tea."

"No, it doesn't." Lorelei stared back at the beast breathing against the screen door. "Granny, did you say you were going to feed Spencer's dog?"

"Sure," she said, tittering about, grabbing a glass, then opening the fridge to fetch the pitcher and some ice. "Not that Spencer doesn't feed him, but when he works late, I make sure Champ gets his dinner." Granny reached for another glass. "I make sure Spencer eats, too. I swear, that boy would work himself to skin and bones if I didn't keep on him."

So now she was a dog sitter? And fed Lorelei's ex on a regular basis? Something smelled fishy in Farmville.

"Where exactly does Spencer live?"

"He didn't tell you?" Her voice went up an octave as if to show surprise, but Lorelei recognized bad acting when she saw it. Hell, according to critics, she was an expert at it.

"Come clean, old woman, and stop trying to con a con. Does Spencer live here with you?"

"In the house? No, of course not." A tall glass of tea was pushed across the large center island. "Drink up now. Before all the ice melts."

The half-dozen ice cubes chilling the tea would take longer than a few seconds to melt. Granny was dancing around something. Before Lorelei could press further, Spencer returned, setting his cowboy hat on the back of the couch before joining them in the kitchen. His light brown hair was cut close, with specks of blond scattered throughout.

Lorelei resisted the urge to run a hand through it to fluff where the hat had flattened it. She'd done that often when they were young.

"Bags are on the bed. Ginger was checking them out when I left, so they should be covered in white hair in no time."

Distracted from her living arrangement quandary, Lorelei asked, "You still have that cat?"

"I do. Ginger turned seventeen this year." Granny smiled with pride. "She's going to be so happy to see you."

"That cat hated me."

"She did not."

"She bit me. Twice. And I still have the scar on my arm from where she clawed me."

Pulling three large bowls from the cupboard, Granny moved to the silverware drawer. Everything was still in the same place, as if no time had passed since Lorelei left.

"You were always poking at her," Granny said. "You can't blame her for biting you when you provoked her."

"I never provoked that cat," Lorelei defended, choosing to stick with her selective memory. She might have poked. Once.

"You were always poking at somebody or something," Spencer piped in as he lifted the glass of tea to his smirking lips. "That was part of your charm."

Instead of coming to Lorelei's defense, Granny joined in the mirth. "That was your way of getting attention. My, you longed for attention. It's why I wasn't surprised when you ran off to become famous."

"I didn't run off to become famous," Lorelei corrected. "I left to pursue an acting career."

"You can't get famous doing that," Spencer mumbled, eliciting another cackle from Granny, who had the grace to smother the sound once Lorelei shot her a warning look.

"We're only playing with you, darling." The lid came off the Crock-Pot. "I expected you to grow a sense of humor over the years. You always were too serious for your own good."

Granny filled the bowls with chicken and dumplings, the smell sending memories bouncing through Lorelei's brain and making her mouth water. She wanted those dumplings, but she didn't have the strength to endure an evening of these two pointing out every one of her flaws.

"If you two don't mind, it's been a long day. I'd like to eat my supper in my room."

Spencer and Granny exchanged a look that said they both felt sheepish. Good. Lorelei may have been a class A brat, but she still had feelings. She carried her bowl and tea to the base of the stairs before remembering the mystery of Spencer's home address.

"Spencer?" she said, turning back toward the kitchen. "Where do you live?"

Another glance was exchanged. They were definitely up to something. Soft brown eyes met hers. "I rent the apartment over the garage."

That meant she could see his place from her bedroom window. And he could see her as well, if she left the curtains open. A shiver of awareness shot down Lorelei's spine, threatening to make her knees week. Flashes of teenage groping filled her mind.

Then again, there'd been no groping with Spencer. He'd always taken the time to make her feel special.

Lorelei shook her head to send the pictures back where they belonged—in the past.

"Right. Well. That explains it." Keeping her face expressionless, she smiled at the two people she'd loved and left. "Good night then."

Spencer watched Lorelei disappear up the steps. "You were right, Rosie. She's lost."

"I don't know what happened to her over there, but it changed her. Hurt her." Rosie carried her bowl to the kitchen table, where Spencer joined her. "I'm just happy to have her home, where we can help."

"The last thing she wants is our help," he said, pushing in Rosie's chair before taking a seat in his own. "That part is clear."

"What did she say on the way up here?"

"Not much." He shrugged one shoulder. "She didn't even ask why I was there to pick her up."

Just as she hadn't flinched at the news that Spencer lived over the garage. He'd been Rosie's tenant since shortly after his divorce five years ago. Having little to no relationship with his mother, and wanting nothing to do with her family, who were scattered around the back roads of the county, he'd been a bit lost when the life he'd built fell apart.

Rosie had been a sorely needed lifeline. Thankfully, she'd never blamed him for Lorelei's sudden departure all those years ago, and she offered him shelter when he couldn't afford anything else. In fact, she'd been more family to him than his own flesh and blood had ever been.

"You're kidding." Rosie slid a napkin across her lap. "I expected that to be her first question."

"Nope. She acted as if my being there was no big deal. As if nothing had ever happened between us." Which had hurt more than Spencer would ever admit. At least if she'd been angry, he'd know she still felt something for him.

"That's a bad sign." Concern etched the older woman's face. "She's worse off than I thought. But we won't give up on her. She needs us, and we're going to take care of her."

Spencer was more than willing to take care of the woman he'd never stopped loving, but revealing that fact too soon would put Lorelei's shapely bottom right on a plane bound for parts unknown. He'd have to wait her out. Keep a casual distance, but show her he was there when she needed him.

Lorelei had never asked for help a day in her life. Learning that she was on the brink of being homeless had taken all of Rosie's efforts, and then she'd only gotten her granddaughter to come home by promising to offer shelter and nothing more. If Lorelei thought for one minute they were plotting, making her sound like a fixer-upper project, the visit would end in the morning.

Time was what Lorelei needed. Which was good, since he had all the time in the world. Spencer couldn't rewrite the past, but he'd be damned if he'd let the past repeat itself.

Champ barked, pulling Spencer out of his thoughts.

"Oh, I forgot to feed him," Rosie said.

"No problem." Spencer fetched the dog's bowl from the pantry, then tossed in two scoops of the dry food Rosie kept on hand. "I'm surprised he's been patient this long." He added an extra scoop for good measure.

Setting the bowl on the porch, he gave the dog a pat on the head. "You came around eventually, didn't you, buddy?" Spencer had found Champ wet, scared, and hungry, cowering on the side of the road two years ago. It took an hour to get him in the truck, and another six months before the dog stopped flinching every time he tried to pet him.

"Lorelei will come around, too." He watched the dog eat. "I can wait."

The dream was more like a flashback. Eighteen-year-old Lorelei stood near the founding father statue in the town square wearing tattered Daisy Dukes and a faded Matchbox 20 shirt. Anger, fueled by a lethal combination of hurt, desperation, and pride, threatened to send her over the edge. Lorelei had just told Spencer she wanted to move to Los Angeles to chase her dream of being an actress, expecting him to share her excitement, lift her off the ground, and tell her how fabulous their life on the coast would be.

Only Spencer wasn't excited at all. He was obstinate, telling her she wasn't going anywhere because she was going to marry him and stay in Ardent Springs, where they belonged. How dare he tell her no, as if she were some petulant child asking permission? Lorelei shoved a lid on her temper and calmly explained that she could never be happy in their hometown.

The place where no one ever said anything nice about her. Where the church ladies tittered to each other every time she crossed their paths. Where her peers excluded her, acting as if she were somehow tainted and contagious.

But most of all, where her mother had been judged and vilified and taken from her much too soon.

"I need to do this, Spencer. Come with me," she pleaded.

He shook his head. "I'm not going anywhere, and if you loved me, you wouldn't be either."

Spencer's words flipped something in her brain, and her temper boiled over. Their raised voices had drawn a crowd of onlookers, providing Lorelei with the perfect audience. She'd tell these people what she thought of them. No one in this town had ever cared one ounce about Lorelei Pratchett, so why should she spare their precious feelings?

"This town is nothing!" she'd yelled, making sure everyone could hear her loud and clear. "You're a bunch of worthless, judgmental hypocrites, and you can all go to hell."

Turning on Spencer, she dragged the engagement ring with the almost nonexistent little diamond over her knuckle.

"You're no different than the rest of them," she accused. "I don't need you or your crappy ring." With that, she flung the piece of jewelry through the air, running in the opposite direction before it ever hit the ground.

And she kept running. Lorelei ran until her lungs burned and the lights of the town square had ceased to fill the night. Until she could see nothing in the darkness, but she could still hear them. The taunting voices tormenting her brain.

"Go, you little brat."

"We won't miss you around here."

"You'll never amount to anything, just like your mother."

The last voice jerked her from the dream, and Lorelei woke to the sound of incessant barking and what sounded like someone relieving himself outside her window. The dream wasn't new, but she hadn't experienced it in several years. She should have guessed coming home would bring it all back to the surface. Roused memories she'd spent twelve years burying in her psyche.

Wiping the sleep from her eyes, she waited for her heart rate to slow before throwing off the old wedding ring quilt Granny's granny had made and padding to the window seat.

What she saw made her wonder if she'd gone from dreaming about the ugly past to what life could have been if she'd stuck around.

A gorgeous man, wearing nothing but low-slung jeans and cowboy boots, pointed a garden hose straight up in the air, shaking drops of water from his sun-bleached hair and laughing as his dog danced in circles, trying to catch the falling mist on his tongue.

So this is what she'd given up.

Spencer had always been able to find pleasure in the simple things in life. What he'd ever seen in her, Lorelei didn't know. She'd certainly never earned his misplaced love. And whatever it had been, that part of her was gone now.

Lorelei's brain told her to leave the window, but her heart wasn't letting her go anywhere. She enjoyed watching them play, as if they didn't have a care in the world. Of course, the dog didn't. But how had Spencer stayed so happy over the years? He'd been through some rough times of his own. A failed marriage to some hometown girl Lorelei didn't know.

A lost child, though she'd never bring that up to him. Even *she* wasn't that heartless.

Besides, breaching such a deep hurt would open up an intimacy between them that Lorelei didn't want to encourage. Encouraging anything between her and Spencer would only lead to trouble. To more hurt when she once again caught a plane out of Tennessee.

Then again, if he knew what she'd become, that she'd been "the other woman" who'd destroyed a family, he wouldn't want anything to do with her anyway. Spencer deserved better than Lorelei Pratchett. He always had.

Sliding onto the cushioned bench, she pulled her knees to her chest and watched Spencer alternate between washing his truck and sending his dog into water-filled fits of joy. He'd make a good dad someday. She wished that for him. To find a woman who would give him the family he'd always wanted.

Knowing Spencer, he wished the same for her.

Though right now she wished he'd put a shirt on. Why couldn't he have developed a beer belly and gone bald? That might have made it easier to remember she wanted nothing to do with men, especially this man. Then again, Spencer would still be a sweet, generous, reliable guy regardless of his outward appearance.

He'd still be her Spencer.

Before Lorelei sunk too deep into pondering her high school sweetheart's positive qualities, the smell of Granny's nut bread drifted into the room. After a quick trip to the bathroom to brush her teeth and splash water on her face, she charged down the steps the same way she had as a girl.

Upon reaching the kitchen, Lorelei gawked at the spread before her. Breads, muffins, cloverleaf rolls, and an array of cookies covered every available surface.

How had she not noticed the smell before now? She would have loved to spend the morning baking with Granny, just like in the old days. The memory tasted almost as sweet as the treats spread out before her.

"Please tell me you didn't do all of this for me," she said, stepping up to the island. "I'm going to put on ten pounds the first week I'm here if you did."

Lorelei reached for a muffin, only to have her hand slapped.

"Don't get any ideas. These are for the bake sale tomorrow."

"Bake sale?" The church must be in need of new hymnals or something.

"For the theater," Granny said, slicing brownies and stacking them on a blue platter. "I'm sure I told you in my last letter."

The letters Lorelei had barely skimmed, if she read them at all. It wasn't that she didn't want to hear from Granny, she'd simply been too busy making a mess of her life to keep up with the gossip from Ardent Springs.

"Refresh my memory. Are we talking about the Ruby?" Lorelei sneaked a cookie, earning a scathing look from across the island. "Do they need a new concession stand or something?"

Granny stopped what she was doing. "You didn't read those letters, did you?"

"I might have skimmed." Lorelei popped a bite of cookie onto her tongue, sending a burst of pure pleasure to her brain. "I'd swear you put crack in these cookies. How did I ever live without them?"

"Good question," Granny replied. "Take another and you'll lose a finger."

Lorelei stuck out her tongue, revealing a mouth full of chocolate chip cookie.

Granny went back to her brownies. "The Ruby is falling down. Some on the city council want to knock it down, but we're trying to save it."

"Why not show special movies and charge more for concessions?"

"Lorelei, the place is nearly condemned. They haven't shown a movie there in five years, and the owners have ignored it since they closed the doors. It was already in disrepair then."

The Ruby was the place where Lorelei fell in love with acting. Where she'd spent countless hours dreaming of a glamorous life. She'd been ten when Granny started letting her go alone, and she'd spent nearly every weekend from then until she'd graduated high school basking in the glow of Hollywood.

The Ruby was where Spencer had put the ring on her finger that she'd eventually thrown back in his face.

As the credits rolled on *The Count of Monte Cristo*, he'd taken her hand as he'd done a hundred times before and slid the thin gold band with the tiny stone onto her left ring finger. She'd looked at him with eyes wide, but he never said a word. Just shrugged that one shoulder as if he'd done little more than shared a piece of gum.

That was Spencer. Understated to the end.

"If the place is falling down, what good is a bake sale going to do?" Lorelei asked. "Don't get me wrong. Your recipes should be available nationwide, but it's going to take more money to fix up a theater than you can make selling nut bread and cookies to the locals."

"I was hoping you'd say that." Granny placed the last brownie on the heap, then covered the dish with clear wrap. "I've signed you up for the Ruby Restoration Committee."

Chapter 3

"You did what?" Lorelei yelled, as Spencer walked through the front door pulling a T-shirt over his head.

"You loved that theater," Rosie answered. "When you agreed to come home, I signed you up. We need fresh ideas. Someone with youth and energy who'd be willing to fight for the theater."

"Morning, ladies," Spencer said, ignoring the tussle. He'd assured Rosie that Lorelei wouldn't appreciate being obligated to something without at least being asked, but that didn't mean he was stupid enough to join an argument between two stubborn women.

"Good morning, Spencer," Rosie said.

Lorelei barely spared him a glance, but said, "It's about time you put on a shirt," before returning attention to her grandmother. Spencer would have questioned the shirt comment if he hadn't been so distracted by how little she was wearing. "I'm not here to join a cause. The least you could have done was ask me first."

"If I'd have asked you, you would have said no."

"If you knew that, then why did you do it?"

"Because we need you and you need this." Rosie smacked the countertop. "You need something to do besides sit here feeling sorry for yourself, wallowing about all the things that haven't panned out in your life."

Lorelei's lip twitched. "Gee, Granny. Tell me what you really think."

She kept her chin up even as her eyes misted over. The woman had an iron will. Not a single tear slid down her face. Spencer had to bite his tongue to keep from defending her.

"I love you, Lorelei. More than anything on this earth. You're a fighter by nature, though heaven only knows where you got that trait. But right now, you need to stop fighting with yourself and put your energy into something more productive." Rosie let out the long breath she'd probably been holding all morning. "You loved that theater. Help us bring it back to life. You never know. You might bring yourself back to life in the process."

The argument was sound, filled with love and compassion, but Lorelei had always been the type who needed to come to things on her own terms, in her own time. There was nothing she hated more than being told what to do. Spencer waited in silence as the two women stared each other down, prepared to comfort Rosie when Lorelei walked away.

"I'll have to think about it," Lorelei said, surprising them both. "How much money are you trying to raise?"

Rosie glanced to Spencer, hope glistening in her eyes.

"We've raised three thousand," Spencer said. "We need seventeen thousand more before the owners will let us go in and make repairs."

Lorelei shook her head. "I should have known."

"Spencer is helping us map out the improvements," Granny said, following Lorelei into the living room. "He knows what we'll need and drew up the designs we presented to the council as well as the owners."

"Of course he did."

"This isn't about you and Spencer, Lorelei, and I don't appreciate this attitude. If anything, this is further proof that you need to learn that not everything is about you."

Rosie was really going for the tough love this morning. She'd told Spencer she had no plans to coddle Lorelei, but he hadn't realized that meant staging a full-frontal attack on her first morning home.

"Look," Spencer said, taking the chair across from Lorelei. "Check out the theater for yourself. If it seems like something you want to help with, then you're in. If you want nothing to do with it, then you're off the hook."

Rosie opened her mouth to argue, but Spencer motioned for her to hold silent. He knew what he was doing. The moment Lorelei laid eyes on the inside of that theater, memories would flood in from every corner. She'd not only join the fight, she'd demand a leading role.

Lorelei gnawed on her bottom lip, eyes cast down to the floor. Spencer could almost see the wheels turning. He waited her out, giving her the time she needed to weigh her options.

Rosie waited, too, but less patiently. She shifted from one foot to the other, slammed her hands onto her hips, then threw them in the air and charged back to her baking.

"I get to decide," Lorelei said so softly Spencer wasn't sure if she was talking to him or to herself. Then she met his eyes. "How bad is it?"

He pinched his lips and nodded. "Bad."

She sighed. "I need to take a shower first. I assume you're done washing your truck." The smile was subtle, but it sent his heart galloping around his chest. That explained the shirt comment when he'd walked in. She'd been watching him.

"I am and you do," he said, sharing a grin of his own. "You stink."

Lorelei threw a pillow at his head, which he ducked as he strolled into the kitchen. Snagging a muffin before Rosie could stop him, he said, "I'll meet you outside in thirty minutes. Wear something you won't mind getting dirty."

Then he walked out the door, letting the screen slam behind him.

Lorelei checked her hair in the mirror for the third time, while reminding herself for the fifth time that she was not trying to impress her old boyfriend. Nor did she care what anyone in this flea-bitten town thought of her. The locals weren't likely to have forgotten her little go-to-hell episode. Memories ran deep here.

Though her fellow citizens liked to call themselves good Christians, forgiveness was often in short supply. She'd learned that as a child when no one ever forgave her mother for getting pregnant off a one-night stand with a stranger.

As the child of that shameful behavior, Lorelei hadn't been treated with any more generosity.

So what? So she'd get some dirty looks and see folks whispering as she walked by. Lorelei had often enough been the topic of beauty parlor gossip in her youth. If anything, she was better prepared to handle it now.

Thirty-five minutes after Spencer had made his cowboy swagger exit, Lorelei stepped onto the front porch wearing cutoff denim shorts, a gray knit shirt thrown over a red tank, and a pair of white Keds.

"You're late," Spencer said as he leaned against his truck, cowboy hat pulled low, ankles crossed. If he'd once again been shirtless, he would have fit right into one of those Studs and Spurs calendars. Tipping up his hat, he asked, "Are those your getting-dirty clothes?"

Lorelei looked down. This was as casual as she could muster. What did it matter? It wasn't as if she were going off to dig ditches or something.

"What you see is what you get," she said, stomping around to the passenger side so she wouldn't have to see him looking so sexy. "And thirty minutes isn't nearly enough time to take a shower and get ready for anything, even something that involves getting dirty."

She heard the sigh followed by, "Lord, give me strength not to dump this woman on the side of the road." And then: "Champ, you stay here with Rosie. Maybe she'll let you chew on some of Lorelei's fancy shoes as a treat."

"If that dog so much as slobbers on my shoes—"

"Don't get your panties in a wad." Spencer climbed in and clicked his seat belt. "Champ would go for your underwear first. Your shoes are safe."

Lorelei was not about to discuss her underwear with Spencer, so she dropped the conversation altogether and focused on staring at the trees as the truck flew down Pratchett Lane. Not that they were flying very fast. Spencer seemed to have lost his teenage penchant for driving like a maniac.

Now he drove like Granny headed for Sunday church. Scratch that. Granny drove faster than this. At least he honored her desire to remain silent, forgoing any attempts at chatter until they'd reached their destination.

The Ruby Theater looked much as Lorelei remembered it. The marquee was empty, which reflected the lack of operation, but the red-brick front looked as sturdy as ever. The box office, centered between two sets of double doors, wasn't even boarded up.

Hadn't Granny said the building was nearly condemned? This looked more like the place needed a good dusting. Lorelei noticed the For Sale sign in the window.

"You guys didn't say it was up for sale." She stepped down out of the truck. "Why don't you wait until a new buyer takes over and let them fix it up?"

"No one's buying," Spencer said, joining her on the sidewalk in front of the box office. "The current owners keep the sign there, but it's pointless. They've agreed if we raise the funds to do the major repairs, they'll front the money for the smaller stuff and reopen the doors."

"I don't get it." Lorelei looked at Spencer, holding her hand over her eyes to block the blaring sun behind him. "Aren't they losing money by letting it sit empty like this? Why should anyone else have to pay for the repairs if they're the ones who didn't maintain it correctly in the first place?"

Spencer motioned for her to precede him to the entrance. "The building is paid for. All it's costing them is the taxes, and those are less than what it would cost to invest in renovations. The owners have enough other successful theaters to cover the taxes on this one."

As Spencer pushed open one set of doors, Lorelei expected the familiar scent of popcorn to fill her senses. Instead, she was hit by the smell of mildew and something rotten. "What the hell is in there?" she asked, remaining on the sidewalk.

"The better question is what *isn't* in there." Spencer flipped the stopper down to hold the door open. "Try not to breathe too deep. We're safe enough if we don't stay long."

Not sure she believed him, Lorelei pulled her shirt up over her nose and followed Spencer into the building. The interior stood in complete contrast to the outside. The front concession stand, which had been a fifteen-foot glass display case showing off everything from Jujubes to Whoppers, was little more than a metal frame with small shards of glass sticking up from the bottom every few feet.

Debris littered the floor, forcing them to watch every step they took. At one point, Spencer reached out his arm, pressing it against her stomach to stop her movement. He held a finger over his mouth, then pointed up.

Not sure what she'd find, Lorelei followed his directions, only to spot three sleeping bats hanging from the ceiling. She attached herself to Spencer's back and managed to scream only in her head. As he tiptoed to the doors that led into the screen room, Lorelei moved with him.

To an observer, they probably looked like a bad sketch from a Stooges film, but she was not about to get separated from him. If those bats woke up, or if God knew what other wild creature came at them, she was more than prepared to use Spencer as a shield. If something bad happened, it was his own fault for bringing her in here.

She'd expected the theater to be even darker than the lobby, but she had to blink several times when Spencer opened the door. Sunshine poured through holes of varying sizes in the roof. Water-damaged seats rolled out before her, some torn, others shredded to nothing, their burgundy velvet upholstery fallen victim to something with incredibly sharp claws.

Lorelei squeezed tighter to Spencer until he whispered over his shoulder, "Not that I'm complaining about this sudden longing to be near me, but you're making it hard to breathe."

Her arms loosened enough to let his lungs expand, but not enough to allow air between them.

"Thanks," he said, then led her down the left side aisle, stopping halfway down. "This is what we're looking at." He raised his face to the ceiling. "We've put tarps over the holes several times, but they either blow off, or the animals work at them until they slide over."

She couldn't believe what she was seeing. Couldn't reconcile this mess with the place she'd loved. The place that had served as her home away from home for so many years. The screen sported a dark stain along the left third and a deep gash in the upper right-hand corner. The curtains that had draped the walls lay on the floor as if someone had dropped them all at once, leaving exposed brick behind them.

The feeling hit too close to home. This structure reflected what had become of Lorelei's life. What she had let it become. For too long she'd ignored the signs of decay. Let outside forces tear at her self-esteem and batter her dreams. If she were forced to describe what it looked like inside her head, Lorelei could present a picture of her current surroundings with a one-word caption—*This*.

She asked the same question she'd been asking herself for months. "How did this happen?"

Spencer shrugged and shook his head. "Neglect. Apathy. Greed. Take your pick."

"Your committee really thinks you can fix this? Twenty thousand dollars would barely make a dent. You're fighting a lost cause."

A lost cause. Something Lorelei knew well.

"The twenty K is more a show of good faith. We have a written agreement with the Baler Group, owners of this theater and six other small movie houses between here and Memphis, that if we help raise the funds, they agree to do their part. They also agreed not to sell the building out from under us or this would all be a waste of time."

He pointed up to the balcony. "Believe it or not, things aren't as bad up there. The leaks are mostly by the screen, and the raccoons seem content to stay down here. The concession counter could be replaced with something used to start with. Popcorn machines aren't much."

Spencer had always managed to see the good in things. The possibilities. That was something she'd loved about him. No matter how moody or hateful she'd been, Spencer saw the good in her. Saw the potential of what she could be beyond the stubborn face she showed to the world.

"So?" he said, tossing a wet shingle out of his way. "You in?"

Staring at the wreck surrounding them, Lorelei knew nothing in this endeavor would be easy. But maybe she didn't need easy.

Maybe she'd gone down the easy road for too long.

"I'm in. I have my doubts, but I'm in."

When Spencer didn't respond, she turned to read his face. There it was. That twinkle in his eye he'd always gotten when Lorelei proved him right. He'd known she'd cave as soon as she saw the condition of the theater.

The idea of someone knowing her so well, better than she knew herself, made her stomach clench. Lorelei stepped back, putting more distance between them. She wasn't the simple teenage girl he'd once dated. There were open wounds Spencer knew nothing about.

"You ready to go?" Spencer smiled, but she could tell he knew she'd withdrawn. "My gut is telling me it's time for lunch."

"I'm not hungry." Lorelei's stomach chose that moment to make a liar out of her. To Spencer's raised brow she said, "Fine, but walk fast. If those bats wake up, I'm running you over to get out of here."

Spencer nodded. "Sounds fair." He kicked empty popcorn boxes and shredded seat cushions out of his way. "And Lorelei?"

"What?" she said, following the path he created.

He stopped, causing her to run into him. Staring into her eyes, his expression unusually serious, Spencer said, "I'm glad you're home."

Lorelei didn't have an answer, nor could she have spoken if she did, since all the wind rushed out of her lungs. As he leaned forward, she was certain he was going to kiss her. God, how she wanted him to kiss her.

Instead, he took her hand and said, "Now let's get out of here."

Chapter 4

He should have kissed her.

That was the only thought racing through Spencer's mind from the time they'd left the theater until they'd parked in front of Tilly's Diner. But doing so would have been a huge tactical error. Lorelei was already on the defensive. She'd had a chip on her shoulder back in the day. That chip seemed bigger than ever now.

Which made him wonder what had happened in the last twelve years. What had her life in LA been like? A new place where no one knew her should have given Lorelei the opportunity to start over without the parental baggage holding her down. Then again, maybe the crap from childhood tagged along no matter where a person ran off to.

Spencer wouldn't know, since he'd never felt the need to run. At least not any farther than out of the trailer park. He too knew something about parental baggage, but he'd been fortunate in that his mother had *always* been from the wrong side of the tracks. No one expected Paula Boyd to be any better than she was, and when she'd come up pregnant without a ring on her left hand, no one batted an eye.

In fact, where Lorelei was condemned for being a child of sin, Spencer had received little more than the occasional sympathetic glance. The double standard irked him, but he'd never played into it. Any respect his fellow natives had for him was solidly earned.

"Tilly's is still here?" Lorelei asked. "Nothing ever changes in this town."

"I wouldn't go that far." Spencer cut the engine and shot his passenger a smile. "We've got one of those twenty-four-hour pharmacies over on Cobbler Street, and the high school built a brand-new football complex three years ago."

"So the old folks can get their pills at three a.m., and the pigskin-obsessed have a new chapel." Lorelei dropped out of the cab. "At least their priorities are in the right place."

"Were you expecting a shopping mall with all your Rodeo Drive shops?" Spencer asked.

With clenched teeth, Lorelei said, "Struggling waitresses don't shop on Rodeo Drive."

"I thought you were a struggling actress?"

"So did I." Her voice dropped as she stepped out of the bright sunshine into the dimly lit diner. "Turns out we were both wrong."

"Hey, Spencer." The silver-haired waitress greeted them from behind the counter. "Have a seat, darlin'. I'll be right with ya."

"Thanks, Jeanne." Spencer led Lorelei to a booth along the left side wall. Before sliding in, she brushed a hand over the red vinyl, clearing invisible crumbs. The old Lorelei wouldn't have noticed a few crumbs.

"The burgers are still the best around," he said, pulling two menus from behind the salt and pepper shakers. "And if you're real nice, I'll splurge and buy you a piece of pie."

"I can pay for my own," Lorelei responded, sunglasses still perched on her nose as she perused the menu. "I'll have a salad."

The woman was skin and bones. If anyone needed a hefty dose of greasy calories, it was his tablemate.

"Since when do you turn down a hamburger?"

"Since I lost out on an underwear commercial because of love handles."

The sunglasses hid Lorelei's eyes, making it difficult to read her expression. But her voice made it clear she wasn't joking. Lorelei had always been confident about her body, which is why the confession put him off-kilter. This was the first time since seeing her at the airport that Spencer felt as if he were talking to a stranger.

With little else to go on, he followed his instincts. "Whoever was in charge of that commercial is a moron. And if I'd have been there, I would have told him so."

"It was a woman, and she was right." Lorelei crossed her arms and looked away from him. "And that white-knight bit is cute, but a waste of time."

Jeanne stepped up to the table before Spencer could respond. She'd been a staple at Tilly's Diner for as long as Spencer could remember. "Okay, folks. What are we having?"

"House salad," Lorelei said. "Separate checks."

"House salad for Lorelei," Jeanne said. Lorelei huffed as she removed the sunglasses, but the waitress ignored her. "And what to drink?"

"Water."

"Simple enough." Without asking, she said, "And a bacon cheeseburger with fries and a vanilla shake for Spencer."

"Yes, ma'am."

As the waitress walked away, Spencer chuckled. "Did you think the sunglasses would work?"

"Hoped, maybe." Lorelei continued to avoid making eye contact. "I suppose I have it coming, but I don't feel like facing it today."

"You have what coming?"

She shrugged. "I don't know. Open hostility. Public lynching."

"That would take some organizing," Spencer said. "Employing the phone tree to spread the word that you're back in town. Remind them to bring their pitchforks. I say you have another twenty-four hours before you need to start looking over your shoulder."

Lorelei finally met his eye. "I know better than most how far memories stretch in this town. And how unforgiving the general population can be."

"We're talking twelve years, Lorelei."

"That's like a nanosecond around here, and you know it."

Spencer leaned forward. "Has it ever occurred to you that maybe no one has given you a second thought since you left?" Almost before he'd finished speaking, a voice that could cut glass echoed from the diner entrance.

"Do my eyes deceive me, or has the infamous Lorelei Pratchett graced us with her presence once again?"

Becky Winkle strolled up to their table, her hair teased into its typical dishwater brown rat's nest. Leave it to Lorelei's high school nemesis to show up at exactly the wrong moment.

"Well, glory be, it really is you," Becky said.

Lorelei managed not to grind her teeth. Barely.

"Yes, Becky. It's really me."

Becky Winkle had been everything Lorelei was not in high school. Head cheerleader. Teacher's pet. Miss Popularity. All reasons to hate her on principle alone, but then Becky had made sure she and Lorelei would never be friends when, in the sixth grade, she took it upon herself to inform their classmates that Lorelei was a bastard. Yes, by the technical definition of the term, Lorelei certainly qualified. But sixth grade was also the year her mother had died, on Lorelei's eleventh birthday no less, making her both a bastard and an orphan.

There were two ways Lorelei could have gone that year. She could have curled into herself and attempted to become invisible, or she could have lashed out, burying the hurt under a mountain of attitude and spitefulness. Lorelei had never been the reserved type, and Becky's constant attempts to make her feel like a worthless speck of canned meat added fuel to an already angry fire. By the time they'd graduated high school, Becky and her friends had dubbed Lorelei "Hatchet Pratchett." A name Lorelei abhorred, though she would never have let them know it. Instead, she had smiled whenever they hurled it her way.

"Is this a brief visit?" Becky asked. "Or are you back to stay?"

With a smile, Lorelei said, "I don't really see how that's any of your business." She had no intention of staying in Ardent Springs any longer than it took to figure out her next move, but Becky didn't need to know that.

Becky's already thin lips flattened. "I see you still have the same attitude problem."

"I see you still dress in the dark."

"And we're all caught up," Spencer said. "Nice chatting with you, Becky." His facial expression managed to appear friendly and dismissive at the same time. A skill Lorelei had never mastered. Which probably should have been her first clue that acting was not her calling.

With narrowed green eyes locked on Lorelei's, Becky said, "It's a shame you haven't learned to tell the trash from the treasure after all these years, Spencer. Maybe one day you'll wake up and realize you can do so much better than this." The *this* was spoken with disgust.

"Since you're two up on me in the divorce count," Spencer said, "maybe you ought to take your own advice there."

Becky attempted to flip her hair over her shoulder, but not a lock moved. How much hairspray did that take? "I guess we all make mistakes now and then. You two have a nice lunch."

As Becky retreated across the diner, shooting Lorelei dirty looks as she went, Spencer ran a hand through his short hair. "That was uncalled for."

"Excuse me?"

"You've been back less than twenty-four hours."

"It's not as if I started that."

"Right," he said, his voice laced with sarcasm. "Asking if you were home to stay was an absolute provocation."

Lorelei couldn't believe he'd take Becky's side. "Have you forgotten how she and her friends treated me back in high school?"

"No," Spencer said. "But we're not in high school anymore, remember?"

Her mouth opened and closed twice, but Lorelei couldn't think of a response. So maybe she'd been a bit childish. Becky was wearing kelly green capris with an orange blouse she must have borrowed from her mother. Who could ignore that?

"I guess I'm not as mature as you are," she said, studying her menu as if they hadn't already ordered. "Sorry to disappoint you."

And she was. Which set her teeth on edge. Lorelei had believed she didn't care anymore what Spencer thought of her, but clearly she did.

Spencer sighed. "I'm simply suggesting you not start off this second chance by making enemies right away."

"Second chance?"

"Twelve years have gone by, Lorelei. Things change." He settled his hand over hers. "You can start over. Show them there's more to you than spite and attitude."

Lorelei removed her hand from his and crossed her arms on the table. "You think I'm staying."

"I didn't say that." His jaw tensed, which meant he might not have said the words, but he'd been thinking them. "Whether you stay for a month or a year, there's no reason not to make an effort."

"Let me be clear," Lorelei said. "I am not here to stay. This is nothing more than a layover until I figure out where I'm going next."

"And where *are* you going, Lorelei?" Spencer asked, his eyes boring into her, demanding an answer. An answer she didn't have.

"If I knew that, I wouldn't be sitting here arguing with you, now would I?"

With a smirk, he said, "Maybe that's your answer."

Before Lorelei could process that statement, Jeanne returned with their orders. As Spencer dove into his cheeseburger, she ruminated on his words.

Maybe that's your answer.

What? Like she was *supposed* to be here arguing with him? Just because sitting across from Spencer Boyd, deflecting his constant need to reveal whatever mushy core he claimed was hiding in her shallow inner depths, felt completely natural didn't mean a dang thing. Spencer and Ardent Springs had always been a package deal. She didn't want the second, which meant she couldn't have the first. But then she realized something. Why should Spencer get to ask all the questions?

"What about you?"

"What about me?" he answered around the three fries he'd shoved into his mouth.

"You live above the garage at Granny's. Is that your dream? Working construction and catering to an old lady?"

Pointing at her with a fry, Spencer said, "Rosie would have your hide if she heard you call her that." Then he ate the fry and wiped his hands on a napkin. Lorelei continued to stare, letting him know she expected an answer. "I don't work construction," he finally said. "I'm a carpenter, and I've taken some architecture classes. I hope to take more."

That she did not see coming.

"Really? An architect?"

"Don't act so surprised," he said. "Rosie told you I was helping with the plans to renovate the theater. Did you think they let any old construction worker do that?"

"I guess I didn't think much about it." Lorelei pictured architects as guys in suits in fancy, big-city offices. Not her old boyfriend who was still sporting T-shirts and a cowboy hat.

"Because we're a bunch of small-town hicks, our project wouldn't be professional?"

That was exactly how she'd thought of the Ruby project. Dismissing it as small-town and therefore small-time. Yet more faulty thinking on her part.

Not ready or willing to talk about her own misperceptions, she asked, "What do you want to do with the classes? Are you getting a degree?"

"That's the plan. But I'm taking it slow since I have to balance the classes around my work and helping Rosie around the house." He took a long draw of his milkshake before adding, "I'm also thinking about going into city planning. Nashville is expanding north, and we're close enough to attract those willing to commute. Ardent Springs could see serious expansion in the next five to ten years."

Lorelei had hit her limit of unexpected information. First, Spencer was working on a college degree. Then Ardent Springs as a suburb of Nashville? Their dinky little town expanding? And Spencer playing a role in that expansion?

"Wow," she said. "I don't know what to say."

"Again with the surprise." Spencer lifted his burger. "Don't you remember my obsession with old barns back in high school?"

"What do old barns have to do with any of this?"

"That was the beginning of it," he said, after swallowing a bite of burger and wiping his mouth. "I was fascinated by their simplicity and endurance. Then I progressed to churches, and eventually I did research on the old courthouse. Who built it. When. How they managed things back in the late eighteen hundreds, without the benefit of trucks, dozers, and cranes."

Without thinking, Lorelei swiped a spot of mayonnaise from the corner of Spencer's mouth with her finger. She froze, realizing what she'd done. As if a single second hadn't passed since they'd been together, happy and in love.

Wiping her finger on her napkin, Lorelei cleared her throat and asked, "How did they get the clock tower up there?"

Spencer didn't comment on her gesture, but his brown eyes danced as he answered, "The wings and tower weren't added until 1929, so they had more machinery by then." Swirling the straw in his glass, he added, "My research eventually led me to look into architecture programs, and now here I am. A college student at the ripe old age of thirty."

This was too important to let him make light. "This is a big deal, Spencer. I'm proud of you."

Lorelei had never doubted Spencer could do anything he set his mind to. She'd just been too self-involved to think about how far he might want to go. His reluctance to leave Ardent Springs felt like a lack of ambition to her wandering heart. Clearly, that assumption had been wrong.

In fact, the list of things she'd been wrong about was getting longer by the minute.

Leaning against the red vinyl behind him, Spencer stared with narrowed eyes. "I guess it's my turn to be surprised. I never thought college would impress you. If I remember correctly, you didn't think much of it back in the day."

"As you pointed out," she said, strangely pleased to have surprised him, "we're not in high school anymore."

A look she hadn't seen in a long time shone through his whiskey-colored eyes. The look that said she was special. A look that was far from accurate.

"There's hope for you yet, Lorelei Pratchett."

If only that were true. Hope was in short supply in her life these days.

Chapter 5

The next morning, Granny nudged Lorelei shortly after nine, ranting that they were going to be late for church. Since Lorelei's presence inside Ardent Springs Baptist Church was more likely to bring about a sudden lightning storm than do anything to save her long-lost soul, she grunted and pulled the covers over her head. Granny had tried again an hour later, but in the end abandoned the effort.

Not long after she'd heard Granny holler a farewell and close the front door behind her, Lorelei pulled the covers down and listened. Gone were the screaming neighbors, slamming doors, and endless sirens. There was no one living on the other side of the wall or under her feet. The stillness was almost unnerving, but she kept her eyes closed, enjoying the chirping coming from the trees outside her window.

Trees. Looming, lazy, listless trees with not a palm in sight. Lorelei had missed this place. Against her will and her own expectations, she'd missed the crickets and the frogs, the dirt roads and the dirt beneath her toes. She'd wanted sandy beaches and ocean waves, but sand invaded in places you didn't want it to reach, and the ocean waves were daunting, trying to suck you in and take you under.

Which described the majority of Lorelei's time in LA.

As the rush of failure threatened to drown out the quiet country sounds, something sharp and heavy pounced on Lorelei's foot, jerking her upright in bed.

"What the—?" she started, but Ginger followed the moving foot, her claws puncturing the quilt like a razor blade through toilet paper. "Get off of me, you crazy cat!" Lorelei pulled her legs up to sit cross-legged under the covers. The fur ball shifted, looking for its prey, then shot Lorelei an evil look before dashing out of the room. "Fine. I'm awake. And you're still evil," she said to the cat, who was long gone.

"And you're still not a morning person, I see."

The man was like a freaking rash she couldn't shake. "What are you doing up here, Spencer? I don't remember extending an invitation."

"Not lately anyway." His grin did funny things to her brain, which she hoped didn't show on her face. "I helped Rosie load up the baked goods, and she asked me to keep an eye on you." He moved into the room with the grace of a dancer, a quality she hadn't appreciated nearly enough in her younger days, and dropped onto the window seat. "The fund-raiser starts an hour after the service ends. As the newest member of the Ruby Restoration Committee, you're expected to be there."

"First off, I don't need a babysitter. It's not as if I'm a flight risk." She'd run away from home to chase a dream, then run from LA to save her sanity. This didn't mean there was a pattern forming. "And do they really need me to sit around selling cookies and muffins to the devoted?"

"You can't avoid the locals forever," he said. "Might as well face 'em and get it over with."

She hated how well he knew her. Facing Jeanne the waitress or even Becky Winkle one-on-one was bad enough. The thought of standing before a fellowship hall filled with the people who'd been judge and jury for both her and her mother made her reconsider the running idea.

"Don't you think my presence will do more harm than good?"

"Only one way to find out." Spencer rose from his seat and headed for the hall. "But then the locals might surprise you."

"Like they did yesterday?"

He stopped at the door, turning clear brown eyes her way. "Look at it this way. You got the worst encounter out of the way. And though you didn't exactly come through smelling like a rose, you proved that you're still as tough as ever." With a wink, he added, "You can do this, Lor. And Rosie and I will be there with you. Now get your butt in the shower."

Before he took two steps, Lorelei said, "You're more annoying than you used to be."

"Then at least one of us has changed," he said, ducking his head back in. "Rosie left four cinnamon rolls. I can't promise there will be any left by the time you get down here, so hurry up."

Lorelei hurled a pillow at the empty doorway, but she was laughing as she gathered her clothes for a shower.

He never should have gone up those stairs. Spencer told himself not to do it, but it was as if his feet had a mind of their own. Though if he were honest, he'd admit his feet were being ordered about by a different organ altogether. He'd been halfway up when she'd screamed, kicking his heart around in his chest and sending him sprinting the rest of the way. Fortunately, she'd been too distracted dealing with the feline to notice him arrive at her door in a panic.

She'd been beautiful when he'd found her on the bench at the airport. She'd been pretty in a pout at the diner the day before.

But Lorelei had been the sexiest thing he'd ever seen sitting up in that bed, blonde hair tossed and scattered around her face, blue eyes snapping, and the strap of her blue tank nightie falling off one delicious shoulder. His body was headed for the bed when his brain jerked the wheel in time to send him to the window seat. Keeping any distance between them was a struggle. Not crawling into bed with her had been the toughest thing he'd done since watching her pull away in a Greyhound a dozen years before.

His life hadn't been all that great while she was gone, so that was saying something.

To his surprise, she'd taken a shower and appeared downstairs in record time. For Lorelei, anyway. Dark denim made her legs look longer, if that were possible, while the blue button-down shirt matched her eyes. The outfit bordered on conservative compared to her usual attire, and he could only assume she'd dressed with their destination in mind.

After downing one of the cinnamon rolls with the claim that she was saving the other for later, she applied lip gloss while he cleaned up. Spencer worried she wasn't eating enough, fueled by her extra-thin appearance and her comment from the day before, but he let the subject slide for now. They rode to the church in silence, Spencer too busy picturing Lorelei looking like a sex kitten to keep up a conversation.

The almost-prim outfit did nothing to block out the sexier image of her sitting in the middle of a rumpled bed.

"Do I really have to go in there?" Lorelei asked as Spencer put the truck in park in front of the Ardent Springs Baptist fellowship hall.

He glanced her way to see fear in her eyes. His tough, screw-you-if-you-don't-like-me Lorelei was really scared.

"Like I said, you can do this." He unbuckled his seat belt. "Becky was never going to change, but give the rest of the town a chance."

"The question is, will they give me a chance?" she asked, her voice smaller and so unlike the girl he knew.

Resting his arms on top of the steering wheel, Spencer watched an elderly couple pass through the hall doors. "I guess that depends on which Lorelei walks in there."

"If you're suggesting I put on an act, there are two coaches and countless casting directors in California who would say you're wasting your breath."

"Lorelei, look at me." He waited for her to turn his way. "Twelve years ago, you were a driven eighteen-year-old desperate to break out of this small town. A town where your mother didn't have the best life, and that hadn't been all that kind to you because of circumstances outside your control."

Breaking eye contact, Lorelei slid her hands under her thighs. "When you put it that way, you make me sound like a victim. Like I didn't earn most everything these people thought about me."

"Everybody deserves a second chance. It's up to you how this one turns out."

An empty laugh escaped her lips. "Right. I'm in control. Wouldn't that be nice?"

"You can't control what anyone else says or does." Spencer tucked a wayward lock behind her ear. "But you *can* control how you respond to them."

Tapping her toes on the floor mat, Lorelei met his gaze once more, the fear less obvious. "Since when did you become a wisdom-touting guru? Is this the type of stuff they teach you in college?"

"I did some reading while you were gone."

"I knew if you didn't have me dragging you into trouble, you'd spend your life with your nose buried in a book." Her blue eyes sparkled, looking more like the Lorelei he knew.

Reaching for his door handle, Spencer said, "You did wreak havoc on my GPA once you got me in your clutches."

"And you enjoyed every minute of it," Lorelei said, laughing as she met him at the front of the truck.

Standing inches apart, Spencer put his heart into his smile. "That I did."

Darkened lashes lowered as Lorelei's gaze dropped to Spencer's mouth. He thought she might rise up on her toes and plant one for old times' sake. If for no other reason than to see if he still tasted the same. But then her eyes darted off toward the church. "You shouldn't flirt with me, Spencer. There's nothing but more of the same down that path."

"I wasn't flirting alone," he pointed out.

Tilting her head, Lorelei squinted from the sun as she met his eyes. "You knew the girl who roared out of here twelve years ago, but she didn't come back, Spencer."

"Then who did?" he asked.

With a shake of her head, Lorelei answered, "I'll let you know when I figure it out. Now let's go sell some cookies."

The only good thing about Spencer looking all sexy and kissable was that he served as an excellent distraction from the impending drama. If she was thinking about all the things she'd like to do to her ex-boyfriend, Lorelei couldn't obsess over all the ways the next few minutes could turn ugly. But then she reached the church hall doors and had to picture Spencer naked to suppress the panic. Which served two purposes.

One, she entered the church hall with a smile on her lips and a blush on her cheeks.

Two, the blast of icy-cold air that hit her in the face upon entering the hall was more welcome than startling.

"There's Rosie over in the corner," Spencer said, settling a hand on the small of Lorelei's back as he maneuvered her through the thin crowd. She considered shaking him off, but the extra support came in handy as she passed Buford Stallings, who'd been the Ardent Springs mayor while Lorelei was in high school. Buford had been present at the infamous street fair the night before Lorelei left town. Needless to say, she'd been angry at the time. And confused. And felt as if she were drowning and the only way to find air was to get on a bus and never look back.

Only now she *was* back and would have to account for her childish outburst. Possibly with blood. There was no way to tell.

The former town leader didn't look happy to see her, but then he didn't spit in her direction either. Better than she'd expected.

"There's my girl!" burst an unforgettable twang from across the hall. "Come over here and give me a big old hug, you pretty young thing."

Pearl Jessup, Granny's best friend from the time the two of them strolled into a kindergarten classroom, bounced across the bleached tiles in Lorelei's direction. Older, rounder, and grayer than when she'd last seen her, Pearl still had the beaming smile of a pageant queen and the energy of a two-year-old hyped up on red Kool-Aid.

"I told Rosie that you'd be even more gorgeous than ever, and I was right." The older woman wrapped Lorelei in a bear hug that threatened to pop a lung. Releasing her as quickly as she'd grabbed her, Pearl pushed Lorelei an arm's length away. "You could cut glass with those cheekbones, darling. And you're so thin I can practically see right through you." With a sigh, she added, "But she's still as pretty as ever, isn't she, Spencer?"

"Yes, ma'am. Almost as pretty as you are."

Pearl tapped Spencer on the arm as her cheeks turned pink. "Oh, go on now. You're only buttering me up so I'll save you some of my pineapple upside-down cake. But if you want you a piece, you're going to have to buy it like everybody else."

Spencer strolled forward with Pearl on his arm, the pair leaving Lorelei without a backward glance. "Been saving my cash for just that reason," he said. "Come on, Lor. Time to get to work."

"Right behind you," she said, telling herself she was not jealous of the older woman. And to be fair, Lorelei did remember Pearl's pineapple upside-down cake and wished she'd brought some cash of her own to get a piece. Maybe Spencer would share.

Remembering what Spencer had said in the truck, Lorelei passed through the crowd flashing a friendly smile at anyone who met her eye. It seemed to be working, as she received numerous smiles in return. Gloria Harper, who'd attempted to instill an appreciation of Shakespeare into Lorelei during tenth-grade English class, patted her on the shoulder and said, "It's lovely to see you again, Miss Pratchett."

Miss Harper had always referred to Lorelei as Miss Pratchett. She hadn't bestowed this honor on any of her other students, which made Lorelei feel as if she were different. Better in Miss Harper's eyes. It was nice to know she still had at least one ally in town, other than Spencer and Granny. And Pearl, she supposed.

"Are all of these people raising money for the theater?" Lorelei asked as she reached Granny, who was putting out bags of sugar cookies with five per bag.

"All of them," Granny said. "And it took some doing, but we got the church counsel to waive the fee for using the hall."

"How Christian of them," Lorelei said, counting the tables forming a U around three sides of the space. "Eighteen stands. Not bad." Squinting toward a table in the far corner, she asked, "What's that one over on the end? Did someone not get the baked goods memo?"

Granny looked in the direction Lorelei indicated. "That's Snow's Curiosity Shop. Her store sits on the corner of Fourth and Main, not far off the square. Lovely young woman. Claims she can't bake to save her life, so we let her bring whatever she wants so long as the proceeds go to the cause."

"Her name is Snow?" Lorelei didn't know if the woman behind the table was the Snow in question, but considering the giant ball of black curls surrounding the olive-toned face, the name would be ironic if it were.

"Snow Cameron. Been in town about a year, I guess." Granny looked up from her cookie arranging. "Is that right, Pearl? How long has Snow been here?"

Pearl looked up as if the answer could be found in the dingy ceiling tiles. "Snow rolled into Cooper's garage last June, so that's right. She's been here a year this month."

They made it sound like the woman dropped out of the sky. A sign of how infrequently newcomers strolled into town to stay, considering Pearl remembered it practically to the day.

"Wait. Cooper? As in Cooper Ridgeway?"

"You've got it," Spencer said, chiming in as he hefted a box of baked goods onto Pearl's table. "Cooper bought the garage when Tanner Drury's wife finally convinced him to retire. That was three years ago now."

Lorelei had no idea why she found the soap opera that was *As Ardent Turns* to be so interesting, but she couldn't help but be curious. "So Cooper now owns the garage where he worked when we were all in high school? So much for mechanics being a dead-end job."

"There's nothing wrong with good, hard work," Pearl said, slicing chunks of pineapple upside-down cake and placing them on paper plates for Spencer to then cover with cling wrap. "Cooper has been taking care of my Bessie for a decade now, and that pink Cadillac still runs like the day I bought her."

"And he's kept you in a car, too," Granny said, pointing with an oatmeal cookie. "So you should stop by and thank him sometime."

Lorelei blinked. "Granny, I don't own a car." She'd had a clunker in LA, but the ancient Chrysler had died six months ago.

"Sure you do. The Caprice is sitting in the garage at the house."

"You still have that boat?" Lorelei had learned to drive in the two-toned Caprice Classic, which was closer to a yacht than a car. She never expected the monstrosity would be waiting for her when she got home.

Granny crossed her arms in a huff. "Your grandfather wanted you to have that car, and I've made sure that wish was honored. You could show a little gratitude, young lady."

Adequately scolded, Lorelei apologized. "It's not that I'm not grateful," she said. "But I expected that car to be long gone by now. So I'm surprised. Having a way to get around on my own is going to be nice, though." She tried not to think about the gas and insurance that she wouldn't be able to afford anytime soon. "So thanks, to you and Pops."

"You're welcome." Granny returned to her cookies. "Insurance is paid through the rest of the year, and the tank is full. Keys are hanging by the back door."

Lorelei felt a weight lift off her shoulders. Now she could find work and not have to depend on Granny and Spencer to get her there. Not that she had any idea who would hire her, but Lorelei refused to curl up in a ball and give up, nor would she become a burden on her grandmother. There was always waiting tables—the only marketable skill she had—but the thought of serving the locals made her teeth hurt. Still, she'd do it.

The last twelve years had taught her many lessons, the biggest being that pride didn't pay the bills. Sadly, neither did acting. Waiting tables it would have to be.

Chapter 6

Spencer had a long list of things to do Monday morning, which meant he didn't have time to wait around and see Lorelei before starting his day. If he knew his former fiancée, she might be up by lunchtime, but there were no guarantees. He'd left the garage door open for her, in case she wanted to go somewhere. Though he'd oiled the track last week, on the same day he'd made sure the tank in the Caprice was full, the door was heavy, and he didn't want Lorelei fighting to get it open.

By midmorning, he'd measured Miss Hattie's kitchen for her new cabinets, put in an order for revised blueprints on the theater design, as he'd changed a few things based on feedback at the last meeting, and lined up two more kitchen remodels thanks to Mike Lowry recommending him. Mike was a native who'd moved to Nashville back when Spencer was still a bun in the oven to make it big in country music. Like Lorelei, he'd found not everyone gets their big break. After years slinging a hammer when he wasn't singing in the bars, Mike returned to Ardent Springs and set up his own construction business.

Luckily for Spencer, the man respected his work and mentioned Boyd's Custom Cabinets to clients looking for any kind of cabinetry.

Stepping through the entrance to Stallings Hardware, Spencer hesitated in order to let his eyes adjust to the dim interior. Once he could see, he headed for the counter. "Got an order for you, Buford," he said. "Miss Hattie wants the cherry, so I hope that's not still on back order."

"You're in luck," Buford responded. "Truck came yesterday."

"Perfect." Spencer dropped his clipboard onto the counter. "She also wants the satin, nickel-finish pulls from Sumner." Sliding a sheet of paper Buford's way, he added, "Fourteen doors and seven drawers. The item numbers are there, along with the rest of the order."

Surveying the list, Buford chuckled. "What are the odds old Hattie isn't going to change her mind again? I'd swear, the woman can't make a decision to save her life."

"She wrote a check and locked in an install date," Spencer said. "She's getting what's on that paper now, whether she likes it or not."

"You keep telling yourself that. I'll go put this order in and be right back." Buford disappeared into his back office, leaving Spencer to walk the store.

He'd had his eye on a new jointer for a while, and with Hattie's deposit on top of two more jobs on the books, he could afford it. Spencer was eyeing the nice little Steel City number when Grady Evans stepped up beside him.

"Finding a better use for that bake sale money?" the man asked, his voice like his brains, thick and slow. He wasn't a pillar of the community by any means, but Evans *was* a native, which meant he had enough of a voice in town affairs to be a nuisance.

Spencer kept his eyes on the power tool. "That money is for the theater, Grady."

"That piece of crap building needs to come down. Doesn't matter how many cookies y'all sell, you ain't gonna save it."

"You're entitled to your opinion, but we think differently." Which was an understatement where Grady was concerned. Spencer felt strongly that they needed to make Ardent Springs more relevant, which would in turn create prosperity and growth. Grady Evans would rather see the town fade into oblivion than join the twenty-first century. Heaven forbid they let in *outsiders*.

"This isn't your town, Boyd." Grady followed Spencer toward the front of the store. "We don't want you changing things. This town is fine the way it is."

Turning on his heel, Spencer glared at Grady. "This town is dying, Evans. You may be happy with that, but the rest of us aren't."

"Not everybody is with you." Grady stepped back as Spencer stepped forward.

"Not everyone," Spencer agreed, "but there are enough of us to make a difference, and that's all that matters."

Grady shuffled from side to side, the act of thinking of a comeback clearly straining his limited intelligence. "We'll stop you," he said, his voice less confident.

"What exactly are you afraid of, Grady?" Spencer crossed his arms as he leaned a hip against the counter. "Change? Is that it? Anything different than how it's always been has to be wrong?"

"Like I said, the town is fine the way it is."

"And like I said, you're entitled to your opinion, but I don't agree."

"Maybe I don't care if you agree or not."

"Then we have something in common."

Confusion crossed Grady's face, which didn't surprise Spencer. The man could barely read, let alone carry on a debate.

"Are you here to buy something, Grady, or harass my paying customers?" Buford asked, joining them from behind the counter.

"I pay!" Grady answered.

"Eventually." Buford stared down the cretin, who fidgeted under the scrutiny.

"I don't want nothin' from you, old man. There are other places I can spend my money."

"Then go bother them."

With a curled lip, Grady stomped toward the exit and attempted to slam the door behind him. The hydraulics at the top spoiled his plan, but the show was fun to watch.

"Sorry about that," Buford said.

Spencer waved the words away. "He isn't worth apologizing for."

"He isn't worth listening to either, but he's right. Not everyone agrees with our ideas."

"We don't need everyone to be with us," Spencer said. "We just need the ones who aren't to stay out of our way."

Buford handed over the receipt for Spencer's order. "You've lived here long enough to know that if enough folks get riled up, this expansion plan isn't going to happen without a fight. Talking change is how I got voted out of office, remember?"

"And we've been sliding backward ever since." Spencer was no politician, but he cared enough about this town to fight for what he felt was right. Some would let it die and go live somewhere else. He wasn't willing to do that.

"Winkle isn't too bad," Buford said with a sigh. "At least he's joined the Ruby committee. That's something."

Spencer's goals for Ardent Springs went far beyond saving one theater, but Buford was right. Any cooperation from city hall should be seen as a good thing.

"Speaking of, I should have revised prints by the end of the week." Spencer stuck the receipt under his clipboard latch. "I'll bring them by before the next meeting to see what you think."

"Sounds good."

With a tip of his hat, Spencer took his leave, but before he reached the door, Buford said, "I see Lorelei Pratchett is back in town."

"Yeah, she is," Spencer said, not sure if the man had a reason for bringing up his ex. "What about her?"

"Memories are long around here," the store owner said. "At the risk of stepping into your business, I hope you don't plan on getting involved with that again."

Stallings made Lorelei sound like a disease instead of a person. The need to stay on good terms was the only thing that kept Spencer from telling the man where he could shove his advice.

"Don't worry, Buford. I don't intend to let history repeat itself."

No. Things between him and Lorelei would end very differently this time.

Lorelei sat behind the wheel of the old car she once called Beluga, in deference to its size, of course, staring at the front of Tilly's Diner, feeling as if she'd faced a firing squad and lived to tell the tale. Barely.

She hadn't even gotten as far as filling out an application. As soon as she'd asked for one, Jeanne stated in no uncertain terms that Tilly's wasn't hiring. Odd considering the Help Wanted sign hanging in the front window. The waitress reaffirmed what Lorelei had told Spencer only two days before—that memories in Ardent Springs did not fade.

Which meant Lorelei was likely to get the same response from the other three food establishments in town. The pizzeria offered carryout or delivery only, so maybe they'd make an exception. She could take orders over the phone and no one had to know who they were talking to.

Oh, who was she trying to kid? By the end of her first shift, the entire town would know that Lorelei Pratchett was working the phones at Main Street Pizzeria, and business would dry up like burnt pepperoni.

Running her hands over her face, she tried to think of anyone in town who wouldn't have a grudge against her. Then she remembered the newcomer. The Snow person with a shop on the corner of . . . what was it Granny had said? Dammit, she couldn't remember.

Granny was at Pearl's for Monday morning bridge, and the ladies did not tolerate interruptions. That meant no calls for tiny details like the location of Snow's store. Spencer would tell her, but Lorelei didn't know where he was, and besides, she didn't have a phone or his phone number. So now what?

She could go back inside the diner and ask, but with her luck, Jeanne would call Snow and warn her that the scourge of Ardent Springs was coming her way. As Lorelei continued to debate her next move, feeling like an idiot sitting in a hot car not knowing what to do, she spotted Becky Winkle walking down the sidewalk from her right. When Becky turned her way, Lorelei leaned over the armrest out of view. Or so she hoped.

Then she realized what she was doing and sat back up. What was wrong with her? Bitchy Becky was not going to intimidate Lorelei into hiding.

Grow a backbone already, she mentally scolded.

But the ducking seemed to have worked, as Becky continued down the sidewalk like a woman on a mission. She crossed at the intersection and stepped into the store on the next corner. Lorelei looked up to see the sign over the door.

Snow's Curiosity Shop.

"Ask and ye shall receive," Lorelei said, rolling her eyes heavenward.

Now what? Did she wait Becky out and continue to melt in her metal box of a car, hoping her nemesis would exit the shop quickly? Or did she grow a set of ovaries and march inside with her head held high? As a bead of sweat rolled between her boobs, Lorelei knew what she had to do—get inside that store and hide behind something big until Becky left.

She considered the decision a compromise. Spencer suggested she not be mean to people, but Lorelei wouldn't be nice to Becky either. So she'd avoid her. Problem solved.

Hustling down the sidewalk hoping she looked intent on her journey and not like a soldier hopping from foxhole to foxhole, Lorelei reached the store, gave a quick glance through the glass door to make sure the coast was clear, then stepped inside and took cover behind an old curio cabinet.

The shop was dimly lit, or so she thought, until her eyes adjusted. The place appeared chaotic *and* organized at the same time. Lorelei spun to find a row of jewelry-covered shelves running the length of a wall. Her love for anything that sparkled took over. A necklace that looked like a tiny version of the construction paper chains she was forced to make in elementary school caught her eye first.

The chain was a muted copper color interrupted on one side by a beautiful mauve rose on a bed of leaves. The detail work was perfection, and Lorelei appreciated the craftsmanship that went into the piece. She'd roomed with a woman once in LA who made intricate pieces like this, so she knew the time and love that went into something so unique.

Flipping the little tag around to see the price, Lorelei bit her bottom lip. Though more than fair, it was well beyond anything she could afford. Then she wondered if Snow offered an employee discount. The downside would be that any money Lorelei made would end up right back in Snow's coffers. But on the upside, she'd own some to-die-for jewelry. Sliding her fingers lovingly over a string of gray pearls, Lorelei stepped to the left and her heart stopped.

Sitting on a cloud of black velvet was the most mouthwateringly gorgeous thing she'd ever seen in her life.

A perfectly round diamond rested at the center surrounded by star points of rubies. Around those were half circles of tiny diamonds that made the whole piece look like a glittering flower with petals made out of ice. Lorelei's hand shook as she reached for the delicate bauble, praying it would fit, while at the same time hoping that it wouldn't.

"I doubt you can afford it," said a voice from her left, startling Lorelei into jerking her hand back like a child caught stealing candy.

Turning toward the intruder, she saw Becky's smirk, satisfaction gleaming in her cold blue eyes. "The knockoff purse isn't fooling anyone, honey."

"I'm not your honey," Lorelei said, hugging the imitation Coach bag tight against her side. "And I was just looking." Not the greatest of comebacks, but Becky had caught her off guard. "Last time I checked, that wasn't a crime."

"Those shoes are the only crime going on in here." Becky lifted her nose an inch higher, making Lorelei want to punch her in it. What the hell was wrong with gladiator sandals?

"I would prefer you not harass and insult my customers," said the store owner, popping up out of nowhere behind Becky. Were these women ninjas or something? She hadn't heard either of them approach.

"I'm your customer, too," Becky said, as if this gave her permission to carry on insulting Lorelei all she wanted.

"And if this nice lady was insulting you, I would intervene on your behalf."

Lorelei assessed the woman taking up her defense. Thin, dark brows rode high over eyes the color of cognac, daring Becky to keep the confrontation going. She didn't know if the store owner would go so far as to throw the tacky dresser out to protect a complete stranger.

Becky snorted. "You're new around here, Snow, so let me give you a tip. No one in this town would describe Lorelei Pratchett as a nice lady."

"As far as I can see, she hasn't attacked anyone, unprovoked, as you have." The proprietor kept her patient, customer-service tone as she added, "And if she wasn't nice, she'd have told you by now that your entire outfit deserves a felony charge."

In that moment, Lorelei decided she wanted to be Snow when she grew up. Becky's mouth gaped and her eyes darted from her floral-pattern capris and mustard-yellow blouse to the two women standing before her.

"How dare you insult me?" she asked.

Snow didn't seem fazed by Becky's question. In fact, she ignored it, asking one of her own instead. "Did you come in to buy that Wagner waffle iron you've now visited four times?"

Becky huffed as she stomped her foot. The woman actually stomped her foot. Who did that?

"I wouldn't buy a thing from you, Snow Cameron. And don't think I won't tell my friends about this. You won't be seeing any of us in here ever again."

As the petulant child made her exit, leaving the heavy scent of bad perfume in her wake, Snow mumbled, "Thank God."

In shock from the entire encounter, Lorelei hesitated before speaking. When she did, she said, "You're my hero."

A husky laugh escaped full red lips. The woman smiled, but Lorelei was too busy wondering what brand of lipstick she was wearing to smile back.

"Do I have something on my face?" Snow touched her cheek as she spoke.

"Oh, no." Lorelei shook her head. "I'm sorry. That lipstick is the perfect shade of red. I was wondering where you'd gotten it."

"Believe it or not, it's called Red Lizard. I bought it last year in a store far away from here." The smile returned. "I'm Snow Cameron. I've heard a lot about you, Lorelei."

Great. They'd already gotten to her. "I hope you'll give me a chance to refute anything you've heard."

"No worries," she said. "Miss Jessup cleared up most of it."

Bless Pearl's biased little heart.

"Only most of it, huh?" Lorelei grinned, hoping to charm the newcomer into offering her a job. "The rest is probably true. I appreciate you chasing Becky off like that, but I feel bad if that's going to cause you to lose business."

Snow shook her head. "Her set comes in and looks around, but they never buy anything. Becky has done it so many times, I've taken to following her around to make sure she isn't sticking things in that ugly purse of hers. You never can tell with some people."

Lorelei liked this woman more and more by the second.

"Were you looking for something in particular today?"

"Uh . . ." Lorelei hesitated. The store wasn't overrun with customers, which meant it was unlikely Snow was hiring. But she had to try. "As much as I'd love to buy several pieces of this jewelry," she said, gesturing toward the shelf beside them, "I'm actually looking for a job."

"Oh." Snow's smile slipped. "I haven't thought about hiring anyone. I'm open six days a week, closing at five for the most part, so I can handle the hours by myself."

"That's fair," Lorelei said. She'd known this was a long shot.

"The Main Street Festival is coming up at the end of the month. I could use some help then."

Five days' worth of work at the end of the month. Not what she needed, and she couldn't turn down work elsewhere to be available for that one week, but it was something.

"I'd appreciate the chance." Something compelled Lorelei to be totally honest. "You should know that some people in town don't see me in the positive light Miss Jessup does. In fact, a lot of them have reasons not to think much of me. Seems only fair you know that before giving me a job. I'm serious when I say I don't want to cost you any business."

With narrowed eyes, Snow studied Lorelei. She looked to be weighing the pros and cons of the situation. If the scale came down on the side of the cons, Lorelei wouldn't blame her one bit.

"I appreciate your honesty," Snow said with a nod. "If you're available during the festival, the spot is yours. But in the meantime, if you have something I can sell, bring it in."

Lorelei blinked. "To sell?" Could she part with a few of her meager belongings?

"Sure," the woman answered. "Do you make anything? Jewelry, hats, crafts of any kind?"

She'd been called crafty more than once, but not the way Snow meant. "Afraid not. I used to sew back when I was in high school, but I haven't threaded a needle in a dozen years."

"Then maybe it's time to get back to it," Snow said as the bell over the door jingled. "Got a customer. Feel free to look around. Maybe you'll get an idea of something you could make. Fill a void, as it were." Without waiting for a response, the owner was off to help the newcomer.

Lorelei took the offer to wander around the store, racking her brain to think of anything she could make that Snow could turn into money. She'd dabbled in making a skirt or two in home ec, but she'd never been very good at it. Watching someone else make jewelry didn't mean she had the skill for it either, but then there was no lack of pretty baubles in this establishment.

The more she pondered, the more Lorelei realized the mistake she'd made chasing a worthless dream for so long. Her twenties were the decade she was supposed to find herself. To get good at something.

Lorelei had gotten good at one thing—slinging plates. And if anything, she'd lost herself instead of the other way around. This might as well have been her first day out of high school, and she had about as many answers as the clueless eighteen-year-old she'd been back then.

Maybe the pizzeria was still an option.

Chapter 7

Spencer pulled his truck up to the garage door, relieved the day was over. Between his run-in with Grady, faulty measurements on the Leeds house, and the missed delivery of semigloss varnish at the workshop, the afternoon had sucked. But it was nothing a cold beer and a happy dog couldn't cure.

Though some quiet time with Lorelei would be even better.

Imagining an evening with Lorelei tucked against his side put a smile on Spencer's face as he climbed the stairs to his apartment. He expected Champ to rush through the door, but when he pushed it open there was nothing but silence to greet him. That was strange. If Rosie had let the dog out early, Spencer would have been rushed by seventy-five pounds of black Lab as soon as he stepped out of the truck.

Concerned and confused, Spencer traveled back down the stairs and headed for the house. Halfway across the yard he spotted Lorelei sitting on the porch swing. She met his eye as he reached the top step.

"I think you've been thrown over for a pretty girl," she said, gesturing toward the black Lab leaning against her knee. She was scratching behind his ear, and the dog looked to be in ecstasy. Spencer tamped down the punch of jealousy.

"I don't blame him," he said, ambling down the porch. "I'd fall at your feet, too, if rubbed the right way."

Lorelei gave him a stern look. "Don't start the flirting already. I'm in a weakened state and don't know that I can fend you off."

That sounded positive to him, but her eyes told him she wasn't kidding. Looked like her day wasn't much better than his had been.

"Want to talk about it?" he asked.

Lorelei chewed her bottom lip, her eyes focused somewhere near her orange-tipped toes. "I tried to get a job at the diner," she said, her voice so quiet he had to strain to hear her.

He could see how well that went by the look on her face, but he asked anyway. "No luck?"

A heavy sigh served as her answer.

"Did you try anyplace else?" he asked as he settled onto the swing beside her.

"I considered the other restaurants in town, since waiting tables is my only marketable skill, but doubted I'd have better luck." Running a hand through her hair, Lorelei sat back. "Then I tried that Snow's Curiosity Shop, thinking maybe someone who doesn't know my history would give me a chance."

Seemed like a good idea. One he should have thought of for her. "No luck there either?"

She gave a noncommittal shrug, her eyes yet to meet his. "I didn't exactly get a no. She's willing to let me work the week of the Main Street Festival."

As Lorelei lost interest in Champ, the dog nudged his owner's hand, looking for more attention. Spencer obliged with a scratch under his chin.

"That's something. Maybe you'll do so well, she'll keep you on."

"She also suggested I bring in something she can sell, but we both know I don't have a crafty bone in my body."

Spencer turned in his seat to play with a lock of Lorelei's hair. "Depends on what you mean by crafty."

If looks could kill, he'd be choking for air. "Forgive me if I'm not in the mood to laugh. This is my life, Spencer. My screwed-up-beyond-saving life. Whoever said you *can't* go home again knew what he was talking about."

"Ah, Thomas Wolfe."

Now he had her attention. "You know who said that?"

"I suppose someone else might have said it before, but it's the title of a Thomas Wolfe book." He *was* a reader. She didn't have to look so surprised.

"What did you ever see in me?" she asked, taking him by surprise.

"Uh . . . What?" Several answers came to mind, but few he figured she'd believe. And most he wasn't willing to admit since he still saw them in her today. Though tarnished and dimmed in places, the Lorelei he loved was still in there. Whether she believed it or not.

"You're a genius compared to me." Lorelei pushed off the swing, sending it into motion so that Spencer was forced to put his boot down to keep the seat from taking off Champ's head. "Your background is as screwed up as mine, if not worse, and yet you have your life together. You have a job and you're going to school and people respect you. Maybe that's the one thing I did right," she added, storming off toward the front door.

Spencer caught her before her hand reached the screen. "What did you do right?"

"I took myself out of your life," she answered, rare tears dancing at the edge of her lashes. "If I've screwed up my own life this bad, imagine what I would have done to yours."

"Lorelei, you haven't screwed up your life." Out of instinct, he tried to pull her close, but Lorelei bolted away.

"You look at me and you see what you want to see, Spencer. You always did." She shook her head. "Open your eyes, because the woman standing before you is a mess. I have nothing to show for my life but the clothes in my broken suitcases. I'm thirty years old and I'm no better off than a child."

He wasn't about to encourage her pity party. "You're the one who needs to open your eyes. You have a grandmother who loves you and would do anything for you. You have two good legs and a strong back, and there's nothing wrong with that brain of yours except this delusion that life owes you something." Spencer took off his hat to run a hand through his hair, then slammed it back on. "You get what you give, Lorelei. You work hard and you earn the life you want."

"You think I didn't work hard in LA?" she asked. "I worked my butt off. I took classes and worked endless night shifts so I could run around auditioning all day, only to be told that I wasn't pretty enough or tall enough or short enough or stacked enough. Do you know what that's like? Do you?" she drilled. "No, you don't. So forgive me for wanting a break. For wanting something good to finally come my way."

"Getting a job waiting tables would be a break?" Spencer asked. "Really?"

Lorelei threw her hands up. "I don't know. It would have been something."

"It would have been more of what you hate doing." She needed to see that this was an opportunity to start over. "Take this chance to find something else. What did you love doing in the past that you'd want to do again? Something besides acting."

"I don't know what I could do in this dinky town."

"Forget the town. That's an excuse." Spencer wrapped his hands around the tops of her arms and gave Lorelei a gentle shake. "What did you love to do that you'd want to do again?"

Blue eyes darted around the porch as she struggled to find an answer. Then, out of nowhere, she said, "Baking."

Spencer stilled. "Baking?"

"Yes," she said, shaking him off. "The only thing I loved doing was helping Granny in the kitchen. There's a method to baking. You know, if you do A, B, and C exactly as the recipe calls for, you'll get it right." Lorelei's voice grew stronger as she continued. "And baking isn't like cooking, where you can throw in a pinch of this or take out a cup of that and the dish still turns out fine. Baking takes precision. There's no ambiguity to it."

"And the cookies and breads don't care if you're pretty enough or tall enough," Spencer said, leaning against the porch post. "They turn out the same so long as you follow the recipe."

A grin teased at the corners of Lorelei's mouth. "Yes. I guess that's a plus."

"Then there you go," he said, throwing an arm across her shoulders as he opened the screen door. "Lorelei the Baker is born."

Could she really do this? Lorelei stared through Beluga's windshield once again, gnashing her teeth over what to do next. In her brief perusal of Snow's shop, she hadn't seen anything edible. Not even candies near the register. So there was no reason to believe Snow even wanted to sell food. After all, breads and cookies had expiration dates. Jewelry and waffle irons did not. But that also meant Lorelei could provide an item that wasn't already in supply among the inventory.

Snow wanted something to fill a void, and that's what Lorelei could give her.

Before her confidence could wane, Lorelei marched through Snow's front door, pausing beneath the jingling bells to let her eyes once again adjust from glaring sun to dim interior. According to the sign in the window, the shop opened at ten. Lorelei planned her visit for 10:02, hoping she'd have a chance to talk to Snow without interruptions from shoppers. The one stipulation the store owner would have to agree to was that no one would know where the baked goods came from.

If the locals knew Lorelei supplied the treats, they were less likely to buy. So the source had to remain a mystery. Thankfully, Granny had agreed to keep her mouth shut, though getting her to swear not to tell Pearl had been no easy task.

"Hey there, Lorelei," said the woman she was there to see, appearing from the back of the store. "I thought I heard the bells go off."

"That was me," Lorelei said, her entire body filling with heat as she fought the urge to run. *I will not chicken out,* she thought. Moisture covered her palms, and she rubbed them on the front of her white denim skirt. "I've thought about what you said yesterday, about bringing in something you can sell."

"Really?" Snow's brows shot up as she leaned a hand on the glass counter. "Do you have something for me to look at?"

"Not exactly. It's more of a proposition right now."

Snow smiled as she crossed her arms. "I haven't been propositioned in a while. You have my attention."

Lorelei straightened her shoulders as she performed the speech she'd been rehearsing since the night before. "While walking around your store yesterday, I noticed that you don't sell any food items, and that might be by design, but you did suggest I fill a void and that's what I'm offering to do. Three days a week I could supply you with fresh, homemade sweets, including a variety of cookies, brownies, cupcakes, and breads. And I can come back at closing time and take whatever hasn't sold so you don't have to deal with it."

Her potential distributor tapped a manicured fingernail on the counter. "You're right. I did say fill a void, and that's something I don't have." Glancing around the shop, she added, "I've never thought about selling anything edible, but I don't see why it wouldn't work. I'd have to try some samples before saying yes, though."

"That can be arranged," Lorelei replied, her mind already running through which cookies to make. But she knew if this was going to work, she had to be up front with Snow about the need for anonymity. "There would be one requirement."

"What's that?"

"No one can know where the desserts come from," she said in a rush.

If anything was going to blow this deal, that was it. But Lorelei believed with all her being that if anyone knew she would profit from the baked goods, not a crumb would be sold. She needed to make money from this, especially since she didn't have a plan B. Heck, this *was* plan B.

"An odd request," Snow said with eyes narrowed, "but I've heard enough around town to understand why you wouldn't want folks to know it's you."

That was good *and* bad. "You're still willing to give me a chance? Even knowing my reputation?" Lorelei asked.

"Anyone who can tell an entire town to go to hell and then have the nerve to come back to it deserves a chance in my book."

Good to know the rumors were at least accurate.

"Miss Cameron," Lorelei said, extending her hand, "this might be the start of a very profitable friendship."

"If your cookies taste anything like your grandmother's, I'm sure it will be."

Chapter 8

Spencer tried to ignore Lorelei's fidgeting, but she kept crossing and uncrossing her legs, which caused her tight skirt to drift higher and higher up her thighs. If she kept it up, he'd kill them both due to failure to keep his eyes on the road.

"You need to relax," he said, his own body anything but. They were on their way to a Ruby Restoration meeting. The combination of his awakened libido and concern for how Lorelei would be received coiled Spencer's nerves tighter than the draw on a hunting bow.

"This isn't a good idea," she said for the fourth time in the last hour. "None of these people are going to want me on this project."

Her continued lack of confidence plagued Spencer. Lorelei had always been bold and brash, uncaring of what anyone thought. Now she was the total opposite. He'd go so far as to call her fragile. She'd fretted over the cookie samples for Snow, frustration and doubt causing her to burn the first batch. Then she'd declared the second not good enough and started over again.

This was not his Lorelei. Something she'd told him, but he didn't believe it until now.

"You were worried about the bake sale last Sunday, and that went well," he reminded her. "Give them a chance."

"A chance to chew me up and spit me out."

Spencer pulled into an empty space in front of the restaurant and slammed the truck into park. "Where is this coming from?" he asked, turning in his seat. "This isn't you. This isn't the Lorelei Pratchett who barreled through life on her own terms and to hell with everybody else."

Instead of meeting his anger with her own, Lorelei's eyes dropped to her lap. "That Lorelei got kicked enough times to change her attitude."

"Well, change it back."

She turned on him then. "If you think I like what I've become, you're wrong. But you take enough hits and it gets harder to get back up. I'm doing the best I can right now, okay?"

With that, she dropped out of the truck, slammed the door behind her, and stormed off toward the entrance. This was more than having to admit she was never going to be an actress. He didn't know what had happened to her out west, but someone as strong as Lorelei didn't break easy.

Feeling guilty for pushing her so hard, Spencer exited the truck and crossed the parking lot. He was surprised to find Lorelei waiting for him outside the front door.

Avoiding eye contact, she mumbled, "I can't believe you have these meetings at Lancelot's restaurant."

"They let us use the private room every Friday night for free," he explained. "Nobody else in town was willing to do the same." Spencer held the door for Lorelei to enter, then nodded at the teenager behind the hostess podium. "Hi, Tina. Is the room filling up back there?"

"Not yet, Mr. Boyd," the petite brunette answered.

As Spencer led Lorelei through the restaurant, she snorted behind him. "Mr. Boyd?"

"To a sixteen-year-old, thirty is ancient," he said over his shoulder. "Wait until they start ma'am-ing you."

Her voice turned serious. "I am not old enough to be called ma'am."

"You keep telling yourself that, darlin'."

Lorelei's huff was lost in the cacophony of voices that greeted them upon entering the private dining room of Lancelot's Family Restaurant. The room was lined with six coats of armor, each dustier than the one before it. The abundance of metal gave the room terrible acoustics, which made the nine people in the room sound like thirty. The majority of the noise was coming from Harvey Brubaker and Buford, who were in the middle of their usual argument.

"Earnhardt was the greatest driver ever, and anybody who can't see that is blind," Harvey bellowed.

"Earnhardt couldn't pop a pimple on Richard Petty's butt," Buford answered.

"Give it a rest, you old blowhards." The scolding came from Nitzi Merchant, who'd been the secretary at Ardent Springs High since Spencer's mother had been a student. Maybe longer. "Thank goodness you're here, Spencer," she said, waving a hand at the arguing men as she crossed the room. "You're the only voice of reason on this committee." With a smile that didn't reach her eyes, Nitzi turned to the newest member of the team. "Hello, Lorelei. You look as pretty as ever."

"Thank you, Ms. Merchant," Lorelei said, looking anywhere but at the woman addressing her. Leaning into Spencer's shoulder, she whispered, "I don't see Granny."

Rosie and Pearl had taken in their weekly Friday matinee down in Goodlettsville, but should arrive any minute. "They'll be here," he whispered back.

As if he'd conjured them with his words, the pair entered the room. "Sorry we're late," Rosie said. "Did we miss anything?"

"The usual," Spencer replied. He'd hoped the group would make a better first impression on Lorelei. How was anyone supposed to take them seriously when their own leadership acted like preschoolers on a playground?

"When will those two stop arguing about those silly race car drivers?" Pearl asked. "It's not as if they're ever going to agree."

"They're men, Pearl. They wouldn't know what to do with themselves if they weren't arguing about something." Rosie tucked her hand around Lorelei's elbow. "I'm so glad you're here, honey. Let's find our seats so Julie May can take our orders before things get started."

Rosie pulled Lorelei across the dining room, with Spencer following close behind, gauging the room for reactions to her arrival. Some didn't seem to have noticed, or pretended not to. Some looked unhappy but not openly hostile. Harvey and Buford were the ones to worry about. Pearl was right, the two rarely agreed on anything, but if they did agree on something, and that something was a no on Lorelei's involvement with the committee, Spencer would have a fight on his hands.

Once the ladies had put in their orders, Spencer added his own. He was half listening to Pearl's movie review when Jebediah Winkle entered the room. The mayor of Ardent Springs had a presence that could not be denied. Spencer had hoped he would be too busy to attend the meeting, as his mayoral obligations had kept him away before.

Of course, Spencer could not be that lucky tonight.

Lorelei felt herself grow smaller as Jebediah Winkle crossed the room. With his broad shoulders and heavy brow, he looked as menacing as she remembered. Becky Winkle had been Lorelei's nemesis, but her father had been her persecutor—a firm believer in the "sins of the father" philosophy. Only in Lorelei's case, it was the sins of the mother.

The woman had pulled the triumvirate of having sex outside of marriage, getting knocked up, and giving birth to a daughter who would no doubt turn out just like her. Regardless of the fact Lorelei had been an innocent child, Deacon Winkle never let her, or anyone else, forget where she'd come from.

Dark gray eyes sailed over her, assessing and dismissing in the span of a breath. In that moment, Lorelei knew she wasn't long for this committee. It would take an endorsement from the Almighty himself to win her a welcome, and that was certainly never going to come.

The meeting was called to order by Buford Stallings, and Lorelei wondered how he and Jebediah got along—the man who'd been mayor and the opponent who'd unseated him. Lorelei's knowledge of politics was minor at best, but she couldn't imagine being friendly with the person who'd taken her job away. Only losing an election was worse, because that meant the people you'd served had decided they didn't want you anymore. Stallings had been popular back in the day. What had Jebediah told the citizens to win their favor?

The minutes from the previous meeting were approved, and a treasurer's report was read, giving the amount raised to date minus expenses and including the profits from the bake sale on Sunday. Lorelei was impressed with the strict professionalism of the meeting, and the fact that a dinky little bake sale in a church hall could raise four hundred dollars. But the funds raised to date were under four thousand total, which left them far from the goal of twenty grand. According to Granny, the group hoped to reach that goal by Labor Day so they could begin repairs before winter set in.

There was no way that was going to happen without a massive fund-raiser. Something more than cookies and cakes and crochet purses for sale. Lorelei was contemplating ways to raise a significantly higher amount in less time when Spencer was called to address the room. He strolled to the front carrying blueprints and looking like a man who knew what he was doing. Even in high school, Spencer had been confident in who he was and what he wanted. That had been one of the reasons Lorelei was so drawn to him. He'd never been needy, and he'd never expected her to cater to him. They'd been the perfect match in every way.

Until they weren't.

Spencer used pins to hang the blueprints on the wall for the attendees to see. Then he adjusted the microphone and gave his spiel about the changes he'd made to the design and why. The biggest change had been to the roof for the purpose of ensuring the holes that had developed in the current structure wouldn't happen again, which made sense to Lorelei, so she didn't imagine anyone would disagree.

"How much more is that going to cost?" asked Jebediah, his voice less than supportive.

Spencer didn't falter. "There would be a slight increase, but the repair funds this would save down the road should balance out."

"You say 'should,'" the older man replied. "What if it doesn't?"

A muscle tightened along Spencer's jaw. Lorelei doubted anyone else noticed. "I can't guarantee a tornado won't rip through town and take the roof off, but as with any building, I can design the best plan to protect the structure going forward."

That seemed to appease the mayor, but two minutes later he chimed in again. Spencer was talking about the marquee, suggesting they save the current one instead of replacing it with something new, as had apparently been suggested previously.

"Isn't the point of this renovation to make the theater more modern so the public will want to use it?" Winkle asked.

"If we follow the plan, the theater will be equipped with the latest cinema technology, including a new digital projector. We're also upgrading the lobby, but there's no need to alter the facade of the entrance when the current marquee provides ample room to display all the information necessary for guests to know what movies are showing." Turning Jebediah's money concerns back on him, Spencer added,

"This is the perfect place to save funds that can be better spent elsewhere on the project."

"I don't remember these changes being discussed at a previous meeting."

"They weren't." Spencer's jaw tic became more noticeable with every question Jebediah asked. Not that the last comment had been phrased as a question.

"You seem to be making a lot of changes without discussing them with others first. Adding things that aren't wanted." As he said the last sentence, Jebediah's eyes cut to Lorelei and held, boring holes into her skull as if he were holding a blowtorch against her temple.

This was the reaction she'd expected, and boy, did Jebediah know how to project hate. She could feel it sliding over her in waves, as if he would smite her on the spot for doing little more than existing.

"Mayor Winkle," Spencer said, "as I recall, you joined this project nearly six months *after* its inception. And we welcomed you with open arms. Our goal here is to save the Ruby Theater, and I'm sure others will agree that we're happy to accept the help of anyone willing to offer their time and energy. However, if you feel you can no longer be a part of the process, feel free to remove yourself from this meeting. No one is expected to stay against his will, nor will anyone willing to join us be turned away."

Silence fell over the room as if the Grim Reaper had walked through the door. Even the diners in the main room seemed to have stilled their forks. Winkle transferred his gaze to Spencer, looking like a man about to call another out in a duel. Lorelei had no intention of being the reason this project imploded. She'd leave before letting that happen.

But when she moved to push her chair back, Granny stopped her.

After what felt like an hour, but was only seconds, Jebediah Winkle smiled. "By all means, anyone who wants to help is welcome. And if these changes to the structure that you propose will benefit the project, they need to be taken into consideration." Though he'd slipped on a pleasant, cooperative mask, the mayor's tone made it clear he wasn't conceding anything regarding the structural changes.

The mayor didn't spare Lorelei so much as a glance for the rest of the meeting. He may have backed down tonight, but Lorelei had no illusions about this being the end of it. If anything, this was only the beginning.

Spencer didn't feel like sticking around after the meeting. Normally, he'd stay and visit, talking one-on-one to make sure everyone was on the same page. But not tonight. Tonight he wanted to confront Jebediah Winkle and string him up by his balls. The mayor hadn't been man enough to come out and say what he really meant—that he didn't want Lorelei there. Thinking about the way he'd looked at her, as if she wasn't fit to scrape dirt off his shoes, had Spencer squeezing the steering wheel with enough force to snap it in half.

"I need you to stop doing that," Lorelei said, breaking the silence that had traveled with them for several miles. He realized she could have ridden home with Rosie, but she'd gone with him to the truck without question. A gesture that soothed some of his anger, until she said, "You have to stop defending me."

"Excuse me?" If she thought he was going to throw her to the wolves, she was wrong.

"You were right earlier when you said that I need to get back to the way I used to be." Her voice was calm, practical. "It's time I start defending myself."

"I didn't mean you had to face everything on your own." She had to know he'd have her back whenever she needed him. Not that she'd needed a protector in the past, but they'd always been there for each other. That wasn't going to change now. "Winkle is a jerk. No one else in there backed him up, and everyone knew what he was trying to say."

"The others didn't chime in because you didn't give them a chance."

"Lorelei—"

"Spencer," she said, cutting him off. "I appreciate what you're doing, but listen to me. I have to stand up against whatever this town throws my way. How they feel about me is my own fault. I don't deserve the hatred I saw in Jebediah's eyes, but I sure as heck didn't give the rest of them a reason to like me either."

"That was twelve years ago. You were a kid."

"A hateful kid with a chip on her shoulder and a burr up her butt." Spencer couldn't argue with the description. "I told them where to shove it, and they have every right to tell me the same thing. But if I'm going to be here for a while—not that I'm staying forever," she added, "I can't keep cowering behind other people."

Maybe Winkle's little demonstration had been what Lorelei needed. "I'm all for you fighting your own battles," he said. "And I'm glad to see a little of the old Lorelei coming through."

She shot him a droll look. "Don't do that."

"Do what?" he asked, holding back a smile.

"That," she said, poking him in the arm. "Yes, I'm saying that you were right earlier. Don't let it go to your head."

"I wouldn't think of it." Spencer slowed to make the turn into the driveway. "But, Lorelei?"

"What," she mumbled, shifting from side to side as he rolled through the potholes.

"I've got your back."

Lorelei reached for the door handle as he put the truck in park. "And my front if I'd let you." Hopping out, she straightened her skirt, tugging it down with little success. "We're not going there, so you can get the idea right out of your head."

That wasn't what he'd meant, and the fact that she dismissed his support as some kind of sexual play ticked him off. Spencer dropped onto the gravel and met her as she rounded the truck. "How do you know what ideas are in my head?"

"You're awake and you're breathing," she said, marching past him without so much as a glance.

Spencer watched her sashay across the yard. If she walked any faster, she'd be running. Then it hit him. She *was* running. If she didn't have the same ideas in *her* head, why was she in such a hurry to get away from him?

"I see there's one thing that hasn't changed," he said, catching up to her as she reached the bottom step. "You still want me."

"You're delusional, Boyd," she said, picking up the pace.

"Admit it, Lorelei." They stomped onto the porch at the same time. Spencer knew he was playing with fire, but without a push, she'd never admit the truth. "You still feel it."

"The only thing I feel right now is annoyed." She reached for the screen, but he slammed it shut, cornering her against the door. "Spencer, don't do this."

"Don't do what?" he asked, lost in the heat coming off her body. Lost in the headiness of being so close to the woman he'd never stopped wanting. "Don't stand so close? Don't smell so good?" His voice dropped when she licked her lips. "Don't kiss you right now?"

She made a noise somewhere between a plea and a purr. Though he was well into her space, she didn't push him away.

"I've missed you, too, Lorelei," he said before leaning in, turning his head left, then right, leaving nothing but a breath between them. He wanted her to come to him, and she did.

With a hard bite to his bottom lip.

"What'd you do that for?" Spencer asked, drawing back with his hand on his lip. He checked his fingertips to see if she'd drawn blood.

"You should have backed off when I told you to," she said, trying to look confident but her eyes gave her away. She may have won this battle, but the war still raged inside her.

Spencer would let her have the victory. Tonight.

"A simple push on my chest would have done the trick."

A car came up the drive, drawing their attention. The pair watched as Rosie pulled her sedan along the left side of the house.

"This isn't over," Spencer said, backing away.

"Is that a threat?" Lorelei asked.

Turning at the bottom of the stairs, he tipped his cowboy hat. "No, ma'am. That's a promise."

Chapter 9

Lorelei measured out the flour three times before she was satisfied it was right. She'd burned the first batch of oatmeal cookies, and somehow messed up the measurements on the chocolate chip ones, because they were tasteless when they came out of the oven. As much as she wanted to cry, Lorelei refused to give up. She sent up a rare prayer of thanks that Granny was still at church, because if she were home, she'd be soothing Lorelei and nudging her out of the way to take over.

But this was not Granny's responsibility. Lorelei had convinced Snow to sell desserts that *she* had made, not Granny. Besides, if Granny made them, everyone in town would know where they came from. Which was the reason Lorelei had pulled recipes off the Internet instead of using her grandmother's steno pad recipe books.

Anonymity was the key ingredient in these cookies.

"Something smells good in here," Spencer said as he stepped into the house. "Is that oatmeal?"

"Burnt oatmeal," Lorelei said, wiping her hands on the blue polka-dot apron covering her from shoulder to knee. "I mistimed the first batch."

"Good," he said, snatching a blackened cookie off the counter. "That means I get to eat them."

Lorelei had remained in her room doing recipe research all day on Saturday—some might have called it hiding, but whatever—so this was the first time she'd seen her former beau since the stunt he'd pulled on Friday night. She'd come so close to caving. Hell yes, she still wanted him. If her pride hadn't reared up and bit him, she might have dragged his Wrangler-clad bottom into the house and up the stairs.

But she'd shave her head before ever admitting so. And Lorelei was highly attached to her hair. It was one of the few good things her mother had passed on to her.

"I haven't decided if I'm talking to you yet," she said, smacking a cookie out of his hand. "I know I'm in no mood to feed you."

"Aw, come on, Lorelei. You can't stay mad at me." He reached for another cookie and, this time, was faster than she was. "You never could."

"I'm older and more bitter now. You'd be surprised what I can do."

The cookie paused halfway to his lips. "Now don't be teasing me like that. You're putting all sorts of ideas in my head."

She should have known she wouldn't win. Spencer had always been able to tease her out of a snit. "Just keep your sticky fingers off my cookies."

Spencer snatched an inedible-looking one, stuck it in his mouth, then said, "Okay," around the treat.

Lorelei rolled her eyes. She didn't really care if he ate the dang things. They were headed for the trash anyway. But that didn't stop her from flashing him a dirty look. He grinned as the timer on the oven went off.

"Oh, please let these ones be right," Lorelei said to herself and whatever higher cooking power might be listening. The scent of ginger filled the kitchen as she opened the oven door. The cookies looked exactly like the picture online, which she took as a good sign. Now if they only tasted good. "Come here, my little darlings." She transferred the cookie sheet to the stove top and closed the oven.

"That smells like heaven," Spencer said, creeping up behind her to look over her shoulder. "You're going to need a taste-tester to make sure they pass muster. Lucky for you, I'm willing to offer my services."

Lorelei spun around with a spatula in her hand. "Touch these cookies and you die."

Instead of stepping back as she'd expected, Spencer stayed where he was, one brow dancing precariously close to his hairline and his body entirely too close to hers.

"What are you gonna do with that?" he asked, his eyes darting to the utensil then back to her face. More precisely, her mouth.

"I'd say use it on you, but I doubt that will get the desired reaction." Her voice sounded breathy instead of stern. Dammit.

"Interesting choice of words." Spencer slid a finger inside each of the apron's pockets and tugged her forward. "What kind of reaction do you desire?"

Before Lorelei could answer, Champ started barking up a storm in the front yard, breaking the spell Spencer had cast around her.

"That dog better be dying or I'm going to kill him," Spencer growled, releasing Lorelei's pockets and exiting the kitchen.

Lorelei closed her eyes and leaned back on the stove, only to jump forward when the heat hit her bottom. A car door slammed outside, and she glanced out the window over the sink to see if it was Granny, though Champ didn't usually bark like that for someone he knew.

A man she didn't recognize was walking across the yard. From this distance, he looked like one of those men who aged well. His dark hair was dotted with bits of silver that caught the sunlight. She couldn't see his eyes, but he looked fit and wore a pair of jeans almost as well as Spencer did.

Curiosity carried her onto the porch as the two men shook hands. And as the pair drew closer to the steps, the stranger looked her way and stared as if he were looking at a ghost.

"Mike Lowry," Spencer said, "meet Lorelei Pratchett."

"I . . ." he started, then shook his head as if to clear it. "Sorry, you just look a lot like your mom."

"You knew my mom?" she asked. How did someone she'd never even heard of know her mother?

"Yeah," the man nodded. "Donna and I went to high school together."

Lorelei never thought of her mother aging beyond the point when she'd died, but this slightly graying man brought the reality to mind. Her mother would be pushing fifty right now, if she'd lived. But she hadn't lived. Lorelei did some quick math and realized her mother had been thirty when a drunk driver had run a stop sign and killed her on impact.

The same age Lorelei was now. For the first time ever, she truly understood how short her mother's life had been cut. The revelation sent her swaying on her feet.

Spencer charged up the stairs to steady her. "Lorelei?" he said. "Baby, what's wrong?"

"Don't," she said, shaking him off. "I'm fine. It's nothing."

"Are you sure?"

She wasn't sure of anything except the fact that every day she woke up was one more than her mother had been given.

"Yes, I'm good," Lorelei said. "I haven't eaten is all." Which was true. She'd been so nervous about the baking, she'd skipped breakfast.

"From the looks of things, I'd have thought you were making breakfast right now." Mr. Lowry nodded toward the spatula Lorelei had forgotten she was holding.

"Oh." She stared at the secret-revealing utensil. "No. Um . . . I was emptying the dishwasher." Lame, but plausible.

"No, you—" Spencer started, but Lorelei cut him off with a swat on the arm.

"Can I see you inside for a second?" she said, dragging him by the sleeve toward the door. She'd forgotten to tell Spencer about the strict secrecy of this project. Mr. Motormouth was going to blow her cover before she'd made her first delivery.

"Excuse me for a minute, Mike," Spencer said over his shoulder. Then he whispered into Lorelei's ear, "What is wrong with you, woman?"

"You can't tell him what I'm doing," she hissed once the screen slammed behind them and she'd pulled him far enough away to not be overheard.

"What's he going to do? Report you to the burnt-cookie authorities?"

She smacked him again for the sarcasm.

"If you do not stop hitting me—"

"No one in town can know these cookies come from me or they won't buy them."

"What?" he said, brow furrowed. "That's ridiculous."

"I need this, Spencer. I can't take the chance of someone finding out. Not right away." She hated it, but Lorelei edged closer to begging. "Don't blow this for me with your infernal need to tell the truth all the time. Please."

He hesitated, as if fighting with his conscience, before caving in. "Fine. If you don't want people to know, then they won't hear it from me."

"Good," she said, glancing over her shoulder to see the man outside. "Now who is that? Did you know he knew my mother?"

"I had no idea," Spencer answered. "Mike moved to Nashville after high school and worked a lot of construction. I think he went down to be a country singer, but it never panned out. About a year ago he came back and started his own construction business. He gives me a lot of work putting in custom cabinets."

That statement won her full attention. "You build cabinets?"

"That's my business. Boyd's Custom Cabinets." Spencer raised a brow. "Where did you think I went all day?"

"I don't know." She hadn't thought about it. She knew he had a job—seeing as that fancy truck didn't pay for itself—but it never occurred to her that he owned his own business.

"I'm going to try not to take your lack of interest in my life as an insult." Spencer snatched the spatula from her hand and tossed it on the island. "Now step outside and try to act normal." He looked down her body. "And you might want to take that apron off. The flour is a dead giveaway."

"Well, shoot," Lorelei said, untying the apron strings and gently tugging the ancient material over her head. Granny never threw anything away, which was why Lorelei was wearing the same apron Granny's mother had cooked in nearly a hundred years ago.

Spencer held a hand out for her to take. When it remained empty, he turned around. "What are you waiting for?"

"I don't need to hold your hand to walk onto the porch." Lorelei stepped up beside him. "You have to stop acting like we're picking up where we left off."

"Where we left off was you throwing a ring at my head and telling me to go screw myself," he said matter-of-factly. "We're picking up someplace else."

"We're not—" Lorelei started to argue, but Spencer stepped through the door before she could finish. She followed, pasting on a friendly face for their visitor. It wasn't until she reached the rail that Lorelei questioned why she had to return to the porch at all.

"Sorry about that, Mike. Lorelei got a spoon stuck."

Such a freaking jerk.

"Not a problem." Mike scratched his head. "Are we going to discuss the job sitting out here?"

"The job?" Lorelei asked. Why did she need to be out here to talk about cabinets?

"The kitchen isn't totally clean, so Lorelei would prefer to do this out here, yes."

Lorelei would prefer to do what out here?

"Fine by me. Should we sit?" the older man asked.

"Of course." Spencer carried a white wicker rocker down the porch. "Lorelei and I will sit on the swing, and you can sit here," he said, indicating the rocker for their guest.

Lorelei shuffled across the wood planks before Mike could join them. "What are you doing?" she whispered. "Why am I even out here?"

"Trust me," he said out the side of his mouth, then pulled her back to plop down on the swing next to him.

"Well, Lorelei," Mike said, rubbing a hand along his clean-shaven chin. "I can only offer part time right now, but it sure would help me out of you're willing to do it."

Was this some kind of a joke? Had she blacked out and missed the first half of this conversation?

"Mike," Spencer spoke up, squeezing Lorelei's knee as if in warning. Of what she didn't know. "I'm afraid Lorelei's in the dark about this. I didn't get a chance to mention it yet."

"Oh, sorry about that. No wonder you look so confused." Mike laughed, and Lorelei drove her thumbnail into the back of Spencer's hand. It took three full seconds, but he finally let go. "My construction business is taking off, and I need someone to answer the phones in the office three days a week. It's mostly taking messages and relaying them to me at the job sites. Some of it is checking schedules and then light clerical stuff. Filing invoices. Entering payments in the accounting software."

"Accounting software?" Lorelei sent Spencer a panicked look. Not only had he thrown her into this awkward situation with no warning whatsoever, now she was going to have to admit that she knew nothing about clerical stuff, as Mike had called it.

"It's an easy system. If I can learn it, anyone can," he said.

She'd used computers at various restaurants over the years, but that was only to key in orders on a touch screen system that a chimp could have mastered. "I suppose I could give it a try." Wait, did she just agree to work for this person? She needed time to make the cookies. What was she doing? "But I'm not sure I can do this. Did you say part time?"

"That's right. Monday, Wednesday, and Friday is what I'm looking at right now. If business improves, the position could turn full time, but that's likely a ways off."

Lorelei could feel Spencer watching her. She turned to see him making a weird face, trying to communicate something with his eyebrows, but she had no idea what. Monday, Wednesday, and Friday were the days she'd deliver the cookies to Snow. But she'd have to make them the day before, which if she took this deal, she'd have off. In fact, if she were working somewhere on the days the new treats showed up, then it couldn't be her supplying them.

Suddenly, she understood the eyebrows.

"Did you have a salary in mind?" she asked. Since nothing he'd say could be lower than what she'd made waiting tables, the question was merely a formality. Not asking would have appeared desperate, which she was, but this potential new boss didn't need to know that.

"I can afford minimum wage to start, but I'm willing to give increases as the business grows," he answered. "And based on performance, of course."

Definitely a step up from waiting tables. But this meant Spencer had gotten her a job. Lorelei might not be able to afford it, but she still had some pride left.

"One more question." This was the point when she needed to stick a sock in it, but that had never been her style. "Did you create this job for me as a favor to Spencer, or are you really looking for an assistant?"

Mike smiled. "You don't just look like your mother, you got her guts as well."

Lorelei never considered her mother a gutsy person. If anything, she remembered her as the total opposite. If she'd had guts, she might have gotten out of bed once in a while, faced life head-on, and not hidden under the covers leaving her daughter to fend for herself. But this man remembered Donna Pratchett in a positive light. That was enough for Lorelei.

"When should I start?" she asked. She could see Spencer smiling in her peripheral vision. He was going to take credit for this, which meant she'd have to bow and scrape in gratitude or never hear the end of it. Eh, she'd survived worse.

"Tomorrow morning would be great." Mike rose from his seat, and Lorelei and Spencer followed suit. Her new boss was almost exactly her height, something she hadn't noticed when he'd been on the stairs and she up on the porch. Again that feeling of familiarity hit her. Maybe he was one of those people who had a twin somewhere on the planet. Someone she'd met in LA. "Spencer has the address, and the dress code is casual. Come in at nine and we'll get started."

"I appreciate the opportunity," she said, taking the hand he offered. "And I'd love to hear more about my mother sometime." The words were out before Lorelei knew she was going to say them. She never talked about her mom, not even with Granny. But the draw of hearing about her from someone who remembered her fondly was too much to pass up.

He gave her hand a squeeze. "I'd be happy to share some stories." After exchanging a brief shake with Spencer, Mike Lowry made his exit, leaving Lorelei dazed and Spencer looking very happy with himself.

As the burgundy pickup with Lowry Construction emblazoned across the tailgate disappeared from sight, Spencer said, "That should at least get me a couple cookies."

"Yes, it does," she sighed. "Let's go see how those gingersnaps came out."

Chapter 10

Spencer was sliding his boots on when the cell phone went off. The caller ID showed the call to be from Rosie's house, and when he answered, the voice on the other end was so muted that at first he thought someone had butt dialed him. Except who butt dialed from a landline?

He finally heard what he thought was Rosie's voice say, "Get down here quick." Then the line went dead.

His first thought was that someone was in the house, but Champ would have sounded the alarm if a stranger had dared to step on the property. And Rosie would surely call 911 before calling him. Jamming his foot in the other boot, Spencer trucked it down the stairs, trying not to trip on the untied laces. When he reached the porch, he heard Lorelei's voice through the screen door.

"I don't know what I was thinking," she was saying. "No one is going to want these ugly cookies. There are too many."

"Those are not ugly cookies," came Rosie's voice. "Lorelei, calm down."

"What if there aren't enough?" Lorelei asked, her voice more frantic than before. "What if this isn't what Snow expected?"

"Then you'll make more the next time." Before he could knock, Rosie jerked the door open and said, "It took you long enough."

How did she know he was there? And he'd gone as fast as he could.

"What's going on, ladies?" Spencer asked, walking into the kitchen as if it were any ordinary day. Except on an ordinary day, he didn't get summoned to the house before work.

"Lorelei is a little nervous," Rosie said, sliding up to the counter and lifting a coffee mug to her lips. Over the rim she gave Spencer a wide-eyed *do something* look.

"Well," he stalled, rubbing his hands together, "that's normal. First day of something, two somethings, really, is always a bit stressful."

"Don't patronize me. And Granny shouldn't have called you, especially not when she created this mess."

Spencer shifted his gaze to Rosie, who continued to sip her tea, but there was guilt in her downcast eyes. "What does she mean, Rosie?" He didn't mind coming to Lorelei's rescue, but stepping into a family argument was a different story.

"I didn't do a thing," the older woman defended.

"She doesn't like the idea of me working for Mike Lowry, though heaven only knows why. You'd think she'd be happy that her freeloading granddaughter is on the precipice of having not one but two sources of income." The younger Pratchett woman threw her hands in the air and propped her bottom on the back of the couch. "I can't win around here."

Waiting for Rosie's explanation, Spencer joined Lorelei on the back of the sofa.

"Now don't you two go ganging up on me," Rosie said, setting her mug on the counter. "Baking three days a week and working another three at some office is a lot to jump into, that's all I'm saying."

"In other words, she thinks I'm going to screw up. Again."

"Don't be putting words in my mouth, missy."

"Let's all step back a second here." Spencer put himself between the two women. "Lorelei, do you think you can handle the baking and working for Mike?"

Lorelei gnawed on her pinky nail as she stared at the floor. "I pulled fourteen-hour shifts sometimes seven days a week in LA. But I didn't make the food, and I sure as heck wasn't running any software programs. I never even made supervisor. Maybe Granny is right."

"I never said you can't do this, Lorelei." Rosie stepped around the island. "But do you have to work for Mike Lowry?"

That took Spencer by surprise. What did Rosie have against Mike?

"Why shouldn't I?" Lorelei asked. "Does the man have some deep dark secret that I should know? Or are you really afraid I'll screw up his business and make yet another enemy in this town?"

"I'm not worried you'll screw anything up. It's just that . . ." There was something Rosie wasn't saying, though Spencer couldn't imagine what.

He'd worked with Mike for nearly a year and had nothing but good things to say about him. And unless he'd missed it, there was nothing in the local gossip to change his opinion.

"What?" Lorelei said. When Rosie didn't answer, she pushed herself off the couch and into the kitchen. "I can't keep arguing. I'm going to be late."

"What do we need to do? This stuff needs to get to the car, right?" Spencer checked the clock over the stove. "You have an hour before you need to report for work with Mike, and two hours before Snow's store opens. How is the delivery set up?"

He hadn't thought to ask before, but if Lorelei wanted her role as cookie supplier to remain a secret, she couldn't exactly be seen walking them through the front door of the shop.

Lorelei tightened a loose corner of plastic wrap. "I told Snow I'd deliver them around eight thirty. She's going to take them at the back door so no one sees me."

"Great. That leaves plenty of time to reach the construction office out on Mount Hope." He picked up a tray and expected Lorelei to do the same, only she didn't. Instead she stared at the treats as if they were going to leap off the island and dance. "What's the problem?"

"The problem is, now I'm all worried," she said, waving her hands over the treats. "What if these are awful? And what if I crash this simple software thing that Mike mentioned yesterday? What if I delete all of his files and he can't get them back?" Her teeth bit down on the pinky nail again. "I don't even know if I'm wearing the right thing."

The denim clinging like a second skin to her long legs looked new or close to it, and the purple top had the normal buttons and a collar. She was wearing a pair of tan flat shoes that looked professional and comfortable. All of which he would expect to find on the secretary at a construction office.

"You are not going to crash anything, but if you do, Mike probably backs up his files. Whatever might be lost, I'm sure he can get back."

"See!" Lorelei yelled. "I don't even know that much. Granny is right. This is a bad idea."

He'd had enough.

"That better be the last time I hear you say those words," Spencer said. "We're going to put these trays in the car, you're going to deliver them, and then report to the job you agreed to take yesterday." Stopping beside Lorelei, he leaned close to her nose. "You're a grown woman with more than average brains. These cookies are awesome, which I should know since I ate enough of them, and you will figure out the office stuff. Now open the door."

His outburst seemed to have startled her, as Lorelei blinked twice, then scurried to the door without argument. If he'd known acting like a caveman was the way to shut her up, he'd have done it years ago.

But what was more surprising than her silent obedience was what happened at the car.

"I owe you," she said, coming up behind him with a tray of cookies in her arms. After sliding it onto the backseat, she turned to face him.

"I doubt this will be my last meltdown, but I'm working on it. And I know you went out on a limb to get me this job. I won't embarrass you."

"I never thought you would." He wanted to give her a kiss for luck. The kind of kiss that would stay with her all day and have her looking for him come sundown. But Spencer had learned the hard way that Lorelei wasn't ready for that yet.

Still, this was progress.

"I don't know why you have so much faith in me." Lorelei tilted her head to one side and smiled. It was a replica of the smile she'd given him the first time he ever asked her out sophomore year. The one that sent his heart into his throat and made him want to promise her anything. "Maybe someday soon I'll earn it."

"You don't have to earn anything with me," he said, holding eye contact. "You should know that by now."

In true Lorelei style, she ignored the sentiment, instead turning toward the house. "We need to get the rest of these loaded."

She had to give him credit. Spencer was persistent. He was also hotter and harder to resist than he'd been twelve years before. And with every encounter, she felt herself weakening. But Spencer had also turned out to be a really decent guy. A guy who deserved a girl who wouldn't drive him crazy, have a mood swing every forty-five seconds, or break his heart.

All of which Lorelei was destined to do if she took him up on what he was offering.

Not that she knew exactly what he was offering. He'd been quick to remind her how they'd ended, with enough resentment in his voice to show she may have been forgiven but nothing was forgotten. So what did he want? Sex? If she believed for a second they could do a little mattress dancing without either of them getting hurt, Lorelei would be the first one in the bed.

And as much as she'd like to pretend she could love him and leave him, the little promise she'd made to stop lying to herself nipped that thought in the bud. She'd take the hit if her heart was the only one on the line, but Lorelei wasn't about to hurt Spencer. Not again. She may have been a failure and an involuntary home wrecker, but he'd experienced real loss. And as had been the truth twelve years before, Spencer deserved better than anything she could give him.

As Lorelei stared out the window of Lowry Construction, twisting her mind around the man who'd gotten her this job, the phone rang, jerking her out of her reverie. Thankfully, the calls had been few and far between since Mike had left her around eleven. It was now lunchtime, and after taking yet another message that sounded like a foreign language to her, she realized she hadn't brought anything to eat.

If she went out, she could drive over to Snow's to see how her baked goods were selling, but Lorelei didn't know how to lock up the office, and Mike hadn't said anything about her leaving before he came back. So she was stuck. For half a second, she entertained the idea of calling Spencer and asking him to bring her something, but she still hadn't asked for his cell number.

By twelve thirty Lorelei was desperately searching the drawers of her tiny desk for someone's forgotten candy bar, when she heard the office door open and close. If that was Mike bringing her a sandwich, he'd just won boss of the year.

"Hello," trilled a high-pitched voice accompanied by the sound of heels clicking along pale floor tiles. "Anyone home?"

Mike had assured her no one ever came into the office unless they had a meeting with him, and those were usually conducted elsewhere. Maybe one of the guys' wives needed something.

"Can I help you?" Lorelei called to the visitor.

To her surprise, Becky Winkle stepped around the corner. She looked as startled as Lorelei, if the height of her painted-on brows was any indication. "What are *you* doing here?"

The question sounded more like an accusation, lined with displeasure and a hefty dose of venom.

"I work here," Lorelei answered. "What are you doing here?"

Becky's mouth flattened as she spoke through a clenched jaw. "I brought something for Mike," she said, holding up a white bag. "Where is he?"

Lorelei knew exactly where Mike was, since he'd made sure she had his full schedule reflecting where he intended to be throughout the day. But she wasn't going to share the information.

"He's working," she said in way of answer, which wasn't an answer at all. What did Becky have to do with Mike Lowry? And why would she bring him something? Then Lorelei noticed the extra button undone on the blouse and the fresh lipstick. She couldn't really be after . . . no way, Lorelei thought. That was gross. The man was old enough to be her father.

"I realize that he's working," Becky snapped. "I want to know *where* he's working."

"I don't have permission to share that information," Lorelei said, using what she hoped was her professional assistant voice. "If you'd like to leave him a message, I'll pass it along."

Right into the trash.

Becky crossed her arms, nearly smashing whatever was in the white bag. "I assure you Mike would want you to tell me where he is."

If that were true, Lorelei would lose total respect for her new employer.

She reached for the pink message pad on her desk. "Sorry, but until I hear that from him, you'll have to settle for leaving a message."

The bimbo stomped her foot. "This is ridiculous," Becky said, smacking the message pad from Lorelei's hand. "I demand you tell me where he is."

If Lorelei hadn't been so startled, she might have heard the back door open again. But anger made her deaf to the new visitor as she ripped into her current opponent. "You have exactly three seconds to pick up that notepad, place it back in my hand, and get out of this building before I rip your face off."

"Looks like I've arrived in time for a show," Spencer said. Becky jumped at the sound of his voice, but Lorelei didn't take her eyes off her adversary.

"Your time is running out," she growled.

"You won't touch me," Becky said, but the quiver in her voice revealed her doubts. "You wouldn't dare."

Lorelei took a step forward, but Spencer stepped in front of her. "She isn't worth it, Lor."

"She crossed a line, Spencer. Get out of my way."

"You always did need a keeper," Becky quipped, drawing Spencer's attention.

"Get out before I let her have you," he said.

Becky ignored the order. "I wonder why she won't tell me where Mike is. Maybe she wants to keep him for herself."

Lorelei rolled her eyes. That one wasn't even worth a response.

"Leave," Spencer said. "Now."

Becky gave one last hateful look before prancing toward the exit. Her perfume was still hanging in the air when Spencer said, "What was that all about?"

"You heard her," she said, dropping into her chair. "I won't tell her where Mike is."

"Why not?" he asked. Surely he didn't think . . .

"Because if he wanted Becky Winkle to know where he was, he'd make sure she had a way to reach him. I'm here to relay business messages, not personal ones." Snatching the memo pad off the floor, she asked, "Anything else you want to know?"

"Nope," he said, pulling over a desk chair and sitting down. "Except if you're hungry?"

In her anger, she'd missed the bag in his hand. "Starving. What do you have?"

Spencer pulled two BLTs from the satchel. "Lunch."

She should have known he'd come through. "That reminds me," she said. "Give me your number."

The sandwich stopped in midair. "Why? Do you want to call and breathe heavy in my ear? Or maybe send naughty text messages?" He stuffed the sandwich in his face, then wiggled his brows in her direction.

"You need help," she said, holding the sandwich over a napkin as she pushed a wayward tomato back in. "Twice now I've needed to call you for something and didn't have your number. And I don't have a cell phone, so there will be no texts, naughty or otherwise."

"That's the other thing." Leaning to one side, he pulled a cell phone from his back pocket and tossed it on the desk beside her napkin. "Rosie asked me to give you this."

Lorelei stared at the phone as if it might grow legs and crawl away. "Where did that come from?"

"I told you," Spencer said, wiping a dot of mayo from the corner of his mouth. "Your grandmother."

"But I didn't ask for a phone." And she couldn't afford to pay for it. Lorelei had no intention of mooching off her grandmother any more than she had to. She couldn't afford to pay rent, or even contribute much in the way of groceries right now. The only reason she could make her first delivery to Snow was because the ingredients were already in Granny's pantry. Anything that went beyond "need to live" was something she'd have to do without.

"I'm nothing more than the delivery guy on this one."

She was torn. Having a phone *would* give her a modicum of independence. Turning the device over, she pressed the button on the bottom and the screen lit up. The background was a picture of Spencer and Champ.

Delivery guy, my tuckus.

"I suppose all new phones come with this picture?"

He leaned forward to look at the screen as she held it up. "I wouldn't be surprised. That's a good-looking pair right there."

Lorelei shook her head. "What else did you put in here?"

"My number, Rosie's number, the number to Snow's store, the number here, and, of course, the house phone. That should get you started."

Get her started? That was everyone she'd have any reason to call. She touched the contacts icon, and as he'd promised, all of the mentioned numbers popped up. Next to Spencer's name was a picture of his smiling face, a selfie from the looks of it, with a gold star in the corner.

"What's the star for?"

"Hm?" he mumbled.

She shoved the phone in front of his nose. "There," she said, pointing to the little star. "What's that for?"

"Oh." Spencer took his time wiping his mouth and hands. "That means I'm one of your favorites."

Lorelei struggled not to laugh. "Assuming a lot there, aren't you?"

He flashed a hurt expression. "Are you saying I'm *not* one of your favorites?"

"If you mean favorite pain in my butt, you're certainly at the top of that list."

"Number one. I'll take it."

She did laugh then. The man was incorrigible. And if Lorelei wasn't careful, all of her best intentions where Spencer was concerned would go right out the window. Along with her panties. And maybe her heart.

Chapter 11

Spencer hadn't bothered to tell Lorelei that he'd stopped by Snow's place to see how the cookies were selling. Thanks to a plate of samples that Snow said she couldn't keep filled, the little treats were selling at a steady stream. It had been early in the day though. Once word spread, she'd likely sell out.

Which was good. He wanted to see Lorelei succeed. He also wanted her to find something of her own that would keep her in town. She'd reminded him more than once that she wasn't back in Ardent Springs to stay, but that didn't mean she wouldn't change her mind for the right reason.

"Hi there," said a voice from behind him as he waited for his gas tank to fill. Spinning around, he was greeted by the half-smiling face of his ex-wife.

"Carrie," he said, ignoring the punch of heat in his gut that always surfaced with these run-ins. "Um . . . How are you?"

"I'm good, Spencer. How are you?"

She looked good. Still thin. Her hair a little shorter. Darker. The blue eyes, a lighter shade than Lorelei's, were still sad.

"I'm good, too," he answered.

Silence fell between them, as it had six years ago when they'd both lost so much.

Carrie's eyes dropped to the ground, then off to the distance. "I heard Lorelei is back."

Of course she had. Lorelei had been home for more than a week. Plenty of time for the news to run from one end of the county to the other. "Yes, she is."

"And you've been spending a lot of time with her."

You had to love the local gossip. No detail left out. And likely a few added to enhance the truth.

"How is Patch?" Spencer asked, reminding Carrie that she had another man's ring on her finger now. A man she'd slept with long before removing the ring Spencer had given her. All of which meant who he spent time with was none of her concern anymore.

His ex-wife crossed her arms tight across her chest as if trying to hold herself together. "He's okay. Found some work over in Gallatin. The drive isn't great, but the pay is good."

"Things are looking up then." Patch wasn't Spencer's favorite person, for obvious reasons, but that didn't mean he couldn't wish them well. A loud click sounded, signifying the truck's tank was full. As he slipped the nozzle back into the pump, he said, "It was nice seeing you," and reached for his door handle.

"I'm pregnant," Carrie said, jolting him to a halt.

Spencer turned slowly, his eyes landing on watery blue ones. Her bottom lip was quivering, and she'd somehow folded further into herself.

"Only a couple months along," she said, her voice cracking on every other word. "I wanted you to hear it from me."

He nodded, acknowledging the exchange of information, but his brain didn't seem capable of forming a verbal reply. What was he supposed to say? That he was happy for her? That he hoped this one would make it? That this conversation was easy and he never thought about the child they'd made, who never got the chance to take his first breath?

Opening his door, Spencer said, "I hope everything works out for you." It was the best he could do. And it was the truth. He'd never wish for Carrie to go through a repeat of what had happened to them. Spencer wouldn't wish that on his worst enemy.

His door was nearly shut when Carrie surprised him by putting herself in the way. "I want you to know that this baby isn't a replacement for ours. Jeremy will always be my firstborn. No matter what." The words spewed out of her as if she needed to say them as much as she needed to breathe.

Her eyes told him the words were sincere. No matter how ugly their ending had been, he and this woman had once made something beautiful.

"Thank you," he said, brushing a knuckle along her cheek. "I really do hope this time turns out better."

A tear rolled down her cheek as she nodded and backed away. Spencer pulled out of the gas station with dry eyes and a heavy heart. The past couldn't be changed. Unfortunately, it couldn't be forgotten either.

By the time four thirty came around, Lorelei was ready to crawl out of her skin. Not for lack of duties, as she'd spent the day organizing Mike's filing system, which could best be described as willy-nilly. From what she could tell, the system made perfect sense to its creator, but she doubted anyone else would comprehend his methods. Materials were filed together by vendor instead of job, which made billing nearly impossible to keep straight. Though he seemed to have created some sort of batching coordinates, they made as much sense to Lorelei as filing the concrete vendor under "Heavy Equipment."

Meaning no sense at all.

But while her brain tried to focus on back-ordered rebar and lumber inventory, all Lorelei could think about was how her treats were selling at Snow's. Which was why she practically ran into the store at five minutes to five. Unfortunately, Snow was waiting on a customer at the counter, requiring Lorelei to act casual until the transaction ended and the patron took her leave. Casual wasn't easy when she spotted three empty plates on a table near the entrance. Behind them was a sign that read Sold Out—New Stock Coming Wednesday.

Did the sign apply to her stuff? Crumb-covered plates had to mean yes. Unless selling dirty plates was a new trend she'd not caught in the latest *Martha Stewart* magazine. Not that Lorelei read *Martha Stewart*.

As Snow handed the customer her bag full of goodies, another patron walked through the front door. Jebediah didn't see Lorelei standing near the jewelry as he stormed toward the counter like a man on a mission.

"I understand you've branched out to selling food goods, Ms. Cameron. Is this true?" Jebediah asked upon reaching the counter.

He didn't even offer so much as a howdy-do in greeting. What a blowhard.

"You've heard correctly, Mayor Winkle," Snow answered, unruffled by the man's arrogance and lack of charm. "I'd let you taste a sample, but the goodies were gone before two o'clock."

Lorelei did a mental happy dance at the news.

"Where did these *goodies*, as you call them, come from?"

"I have a local supplier. Why?"

"I need to make sure these items are safe for our citizens," the mayor replied.

Lorelei almost outed herself by yelling, "Bull!" What did he think? That Snow was selling brownies laced with PCP?

Snow flashed a friendly smile. "I can assure you that these baked goods are totally safe, except maybe to the waistline."

The mayor tapped a finger on the glass countertop. "Ms. Cameron, forgive me, but I'm not sure your word is enough to settle the matter."

The friendly smile vanished. "Did someone file a complaint with your office? Or has the clinic been overrun with locals complaining that a cookie they bought in my store made them sick?"

The man answered through gritted teeth. "No complaint has been filed, nor have I heard of anyone getting sick. At least not as of right now."

"Then maybe you should tell Harvey Brubaker that my selling cookies and breads three days a week isn't going to cut into his local grocery monopoly." Snow delivered the suggestion with a head tilt and one raised brow. "If there's nothing else, I'm going to have to ask you to leave. It is closing time."

Lorelei could practically see the steam shooting out of Jebediah's hairy ears. Served the man right for butting his nose in where it didn't belong.

"If those cookies are made in someone's home, that needs to be made clear so patrons are aware that the supplier isn't licensed or inspected."

"Duly noted," Snow said, stepping out from behind the counter. "I'll add a sign saying so to the display. Now I do need to lock the door behind you." She swept an arm toward the exit as if to say, "After you."

Jebediah Winkle's twitching jaw indicated loud and clear that the man wasn't used to being dismissed, let alone virtually thrown out of an establishment. Especially not in the town over which he ruled. As Lorelei ducked behind the same armoire that had shielded her from his daughter the week before, the older man stomped through the exit, sending the jingling bells overhead into a cacophony of noise.

Flipping the lock into place, Snow turned in Lorelei's direction saying, "I really don't like him."

"Then we definitely have something in common." Lorelei stepped into the light. "Thanks for not outing me."

"Even if you wanted people to know, I wouldn't have told him where the stuff came from." The store owner pushed up the sleeves of her sweater.

"Jebediah Winkle has been trying to bully me since the day I opened this place. He even referred to me as a foreigner at a council meeting."

"I was born in the city limits and he's never liked me either," Lorelei said. "If that makes you feel any better."

"What did you do that was so awful?" Snow asked.

"I was born on the wrong side of the blanket."

"And that was somehow your fault?"

"Apparently," Lorelei said with a shrug. "But enough about ancient history. So the treats sold out?"

"They sure did. As soon as anyone tried a sample, they were hooked." Snow paused with the shade pulled halfway down the door as she glanced from side to side at the spaces in front of the building. "Where's your car?"

"Parked over on Margin. Everyone in town knows the two-toned monstrosity as mine, so I left it near the post office."

"That's two blocks away," Snow said. "It's over ninety degrees out there."

"Which is why I'll need my second shower of the day before dinner." But Lorelei didn't want to talk about the weather or the unattractive odor floating from her armpits. "They really liked the cookies? How about the breads? Not too dry?"

Snow chuckled. "Geez, woman. Did you bake them or give birth to them?"

How could Lorelei explain how important a few batches of cookies were without sounding like a complete loser? And how did she tell this near stranger that she'd never accomplished anything substantial in her life, let alone made something with her own two hands that had any value? At least not to anyone but herself.

She couldn't. Which meant turning down the dork-o-meter.

"I'm looking for feedback to see if the next shipment needs any changes."

"The only thing that needs to change is the quantity," Snow said, hopping back around the counter and pressing a button that opened the cash drawer. "Here's your seventy percent of the sales, and I'll need double the amount of product on Wednesday."

Lorelei stared at the money in her hand, which wasn't much, but it would go a long way toward replenishing the ingredients she'd used from Granny's pantry. "Did you say double?"

"I did," Snow said, sliding the drawer closed. "Oh, and I gave you a name. Hope you don't mind."

"A name?" Lorelei was too busy calculating how she was going to bake twelve dozen cookies to follow the topic change.

"The first customer wanted to know where the cookies came from, and I panicked and said Lulu's Home Bakery. It was the first thing that came to mind."

The mention of the nickname Lorelei's mom had given her when she was a little girl set off a herd of stampeding butterflies in her stomach. Snow couldn't possibly have known the connection. She wasn't even sure Granny would remember.

"You hate it," Snow said, concern etching lines around her hazel eyes. "You can change it to something else. If anyone asks, I'll tell them they heard me wrong or something." She shoved a slender hand into her curls. "Maybe you can pick something that sounds close to Lulu?"

"No," Lorelei said. The perfection of the name calmed the butterflies and put a genuine smile on her face. "Lulu is great. Really."

Snow didn't look convinced. "Are you sure?"

"Yes. I'm sure." In fact, she hadn't felt this sure about anything in a long time. "You can add the name to the sign that lets customers know the treats are baked in a scary non-licensed and non-inspected kitchen."

That elicited a laugh from her distributor. "Consider it done. I have a little experience with graphic design. How about I work on some logos and you can pick one Wednesday morning?"

Her first profits, a business name, and now a possible logo all her own? Lorelei felt something akin to pride swelling in her chest. An experience with which she was wholly unfamiliar. "That would be amazing, thanks."

"Consider it done." Snow checked her watch. "Shoot. I have some-place to be by six. You mind if I set the trays outside the back door so you can bring your car around to get them?"

Lorelei had forgotten about the trays. "Oh, sure. Don't let me hold you up." She'd been considering asking Snow to join her for dinner, but she should have remembered that other people had lives. "I'll see you Wednesday morning then."

Snow followed her to the door, presumably to lock it behind her. "And I'll have a shiny new logo ready to go."

Lorelei stepped onto the sidewalk, but turned before the door closed. "Thanks again for giving me this chance, Snow. I really do appreciate it."

"No thanks needed. You came up with a product I can sell. That's good business." As Lorelei turned to leave, Snow said, "Hey, do you want to grab dinner sometime?"

The sun gleamed off the bells hanging over the door as they swayed in the breeze. The effect threw a golden glow around Snow's curls, and the chimes carried an angelic tune. Lorelei smiled at the image. "I'd like that a lot," she said, nodding her agreement.

"Good," Snow said. "We'll talk about it on Wednesday."

The wild-haired woman closed the door and gave a wave through the glass before pulling the shade back into place. Lorelei all but floated up Fourth Avenue toward her car. She hadn't expected to make a new friend in the hometown she despised, but oddly enough, that's exactly what she seemed to have found. The name of her business played through her mind. Lulu's Home Bakery. Lorelei couldn't have picked a better name if she'd tried.

Chapter 12

Lorelei stood next to the garage debating whether or not to go up the stairs. She knew Spencer was up there. Granny said she'd invited him for dinner but had been turned down, which was odd enough to make her grandmother worry. Lorelei wasn't worried at all, or so she told herself. Spencer was a big boy, and the fact that he'd taken a night off from trying to get under her skin was a welcome change.

Except she was dying to tell him that the desserts were a success and show him her first tiny bit of profit. Lorelei even planned to give him a cut. Spencer had helped in the kitchen, getting the treats secured on the trays, and then aided in loading them in the car. It was silly, but the man deserved to be paid for his time and effort. Ten dollars wasn't much, but it was a third of her earnings from the day.

Still, going up those stairs would be entering dangerous territory. It was one thing to resist Spencer on her own turf. The little apartment over the garage was just that—little. One large room as far as Lorelei remembered. A large room that would include her ex-boyfriend, his belongings, and his bed. Right there. Probably looking all tossed and inviting.

Or maybe that's how Spencer would look. Tossed and inviting.

"This is stupid," she murmured, stomping off in the direction of the house. She made it five feet before the voice in her head whispered, *Coward.* That stopped her in her tracks. Lorelei was not a coward. There was no reason she couldn't walk into that apartment, share her good news, hand over the cash, and walk right back out.

"You're not walking into a den of iniquity, Lorelei," she berated herself as she climbed the wooden stairs. "It's only Spencer. You can handle Spencer."

But as soon as he opened the door, she knew she'd made a mistake. A big, fat, holy-lickable-abs mistake. His hair was wet and spiky, his feet were bare, and his jeans rode low and unbuttoned.

Lorelei nearly swallowed her tongue at the same time her libido put on a party hat.

"Hi," Spencer said, looking less than happy to see her. "Is something wrong?"

Brain function was slow to return. She managed a quick shake of her head, but nothing audible.

Champ barked, drawing Lorelei's attention away from the incredible body standing before her, which seemed to kick things above the neck back into gear.

"I didn't mean to bother you, but I wanted to share my good news." *And a shower,* the tramp in her brain whispered. Her body tightened as a result of the visual that brought to mind.

"Um . . ." Spencer glanced around the space behind him. A small table held a large pizza box and an empty paper plate. Farther in was a coffee table holding a longneck beer and an open laptop while a news program glowed from the television. "Come on in," he said, pulling the door open wider before moving the pizza box and plate to the counter, then doing a spin in the tiny kitchenette space. "I was just working on some homework. Do you want a beer?"

Spencer appeared to be off his game, which aided in tamping down Lorelei's unwelcome response to his appearance. He wasn't acting like the lovable charmer he'd been at lunch. Or even the confident quiet storm he'd been at the airport.

Something was wrong, and heaven help her, but Lorelei felt a strong desire to beat the crap out of whoever had put that touch of sadness in his eyes.

"I'll take one, sure." Stepping inside, she closed the door behind her. Champ butted her with his head, which got him a stroke behind the ear. While Spencer had his head in the fridge, she considered her options.

Getting Spencer to discuss whatever had happened since they'd last seen each other would take a casual approach. She needed to let him think talking about it was his idea. "I like what you've done with the place," she said, taking in the sparse furnishings. Behind the coffee table was a brown couch and matching chair, both overstuffed and likely secondhand. But they were clean, as was the ivory linoleum and beige carpet that covered the floor.

Thankfully, there was no bed in sight. The kitchenette was L-shaped, with a wall that shot out along the right-hand side and ended maybe eight feet into the space that hid the bedroom area.

"It isn't much, but it's better than anything I had growing up." Spencer had never been one to talk about his childhood. His mother hadn't been a mother at all, preferring cigarettes, booze, and random men to nurturing her only child. His father had never been in the picture. His mother's family was scattered around the area, but not much better from what she knew. Most of his formative years had been spent in a trailer park not far from downtown—a place he'd longed to escape as soon as high school was over.

All of which contributed to Lorelei's failure to understand why he ever wanted to stay.

While they'd been together, the plan had been to get their own place, a real house, and make it a home. Except the thought of settling down and popping out kids scared the biscuits out of Lorelei, and sent her running for a westbound bus. Not that she'd been averse to having kids, she just didn't want to have them in this town and expose them to the same treatment she and her mother had endured.

But Ardent Springs was home for Spencer and always would be. Even in high school he'd talked about what the town could be. Lorelei didn't share his optimism or his devotion to the people around them.

On the rare occasions she'd wondered where Spencer ended up, Lorelei would shake him out of her mind. And like a bad penny, he'd pop back up again. Though she never asked anything about him, her grandmother mentioned him often in her letters. Lorelei blamed those letters for not allowing her to forget him.

So maybe that's what the problem was. Maybe he'd run into his mother. "I haven't asked about your mom since I've been home. How's she doing?"

He popped the top on the longneck and passed it her way. "About the same. Miserable, angry, and playing the men in town like a bad poker hand."

Now Lorelei knew there was something wrong. "Have you seen her lately?"

He leaned back on the edge of the counter and crossed his ankles. "Not in a couple months. So what's your good news?"

So much for the mom angle. Lorelei motioned toward the living area with her beer. "Can we sit?"

Spencer chewed the inside of his lip as his eyes narrowed. He wanted to ask her to leave. She could see it in his face. But manners won out. "Yeah," he said, pushing off the counter. "Have a seat. I'm going to grab a shirt."

She was tempted to tell him not to bother, but clamped her mouth shut and made her way to the couch. She sank deeper than expected, which forced her to extricate herself from the cushion. Lorelei scooted to the edge to keep from sinking in again. Champ crawled up beside her and dropped his head on her thigh.

"Is he allowed on the furniture?" she asked, giving the black beast a pat on the head.

"He's not going to hurt that hand-me-down," Spencer said. Lorelei turned at the sound of his voice and spotted him pulling a brown T-shirt over his head. Behind him sat a large bed covered in a rumpled gray comforter and black sheets. Only one side of the bed was turned down. The other looked untouched.

She could give him a reason to mess up the other half.

"I don't mean to be rude," he said, closing the computer as he took the empty chair, "but I'm not up for being social tonight. So what's the news?"

So much for the casual approach. "I noticed pretty quick that you had a stick up your butt about something." Lorelei pulled the cash from her back pocket and dropped a ten on the table. "The treats sold out at Snow's today. That's your share of the profits, since you helped with the packing and carrying."

"That's your money, Lorelei. I don't want it."

"Well, you've got it. Feel free to shove it where the sun don't shine." She was off the couch and halfway to the door before he stepped in front of her.

"I'm not taking your money," he said, trying to put the ten-dollar bill back in her hand.

"You earned it." She refused to open her hands, resorting to hiding them behind her back. Not the best idea since Spencer reached around her, putting them entirely too close together. "Stop being so freaking stubborn," she said, the struggle making her breathless. That's the reason she wanted to believe anyway.

Spencer clamped his arms tight, ending her ability to move. "You're the stubborn one," he said, his words coming out breathless as well. "I ate enough cookies to more than pay me for my time. This is your accomplishment, Lor." Serious brown eyes stared into hers. "You earned that money. You should keep it."

They stood there, pressed together, for what could have been seconds or hours, with neither saying a word. Spencer's arms relaxed, but he didn't push away. Nor did she. Instead, her hands slid up his torso until one rested flat over his heart. She could feel it beating beneath her palm. Warm and alive and in time with her own.

"I wanted to share this with you," she whispered. But she didn't mean the good news or the money. And Spencer knew it.

He couldn't have resisted Lorelei even if he wanted to. Especially when she looked at him that way, as if she'd give him anything he wanted. And tonight, he needed her. Needed something he couldn't name or explain, but he knew whatever it was, the woman in his arms was the only one who could give it to him.

Spencer leaned close, tilting his head to the right. Lorelei's head tilted the opposite way as their breath mingled together. The heat from her hands on his chest seared him through the thin cotton as he slid his own higher, one resting on the small of her back, applying a gentle pressure to pull her closer. He desperately wanted to taste her, but was afraid she'd reject him again. That she'd bolt away and ramble more bull about how different she was now. How he needed to keep his distance.

There was no distance between them now, and when Lorelei leaned forward, Spencer took what she offered.

The kiss was slow and gentle, skittish and tentative with closed mouths. Then her hands went around his neck and her lips opened and Spencer was lost. Or maybe he was found. Lorelei tasted like apples and cinnamon and home. Like everything he'd ever wanted and all the things he thought he'd never have. Similar but different. He lifted her off the ground, and long legs wrapped around his hips as she whimpered deep in her throat. Spencer spun them both and pressed Lorelei's back against the front door.

His hands slipped under purple satin and met hot skin smooth as silk beneath. He cupped a breast, and Lorelei nipped at his bottom lip. As his mouth trailed over her jawline to the spot at the base of her neck that had always driven her crazy, she pressed hard against him, making him burn behind the constraining denim. He wanted to be inside her. To ride away the night, letting Lorelei wash all the hurt and pain away.

But some stitch of sanity stepped forward with the understanding that driving into Lorelei wouldn't drive away his demons. If anything, having sex with her now, like this, would do more harm than good. His head was in the past, swirling in betrayal and loss. When he made love to Lorelei, it would be about her. About them. Not some consolation sex to make him feel better.

Spencer broke the kiss, but held Lorelei steady against the door. She tried nipping at his lips, but he pulled back, sliding her hair out of her face with shaking hands. "We need to take a breath," he said, watching desire pool in her eyes and struggling not to give in to his own. "I'm going to let you down."

She was shaking her head no as her feet hit the floor. "I don't understand."

The part of him that was still straining against his jeans didn't understand either. Spencer took a step back once he was sure that Lorelei could stand on her own. "This isn't the right time." Spencer ran his hands over his face. When he looked up, he noticed Lorelei's cheeks had been rubbed pink by his scruff. "I'm sorry," he said, rubbing his thumb along her delicate skin. "I shouldn't have done that."

Dark blue eyes lightened as they narrowed. "Shouldn't have done what? I made the move, Spencer. *I'm* the one who climbed *you* like a stripper pole." One finger poked him in the chest. "I thought this was what you wanted. You've tried to kiss me twice now. What changed?"

He hadn't expected the anger. If anything, Spencer thought she'd be glad he stopped them. If she'd wanted to be kissed, she sure as heck had an odd way of showing it.

"What changed with you?" he parried. "You've kept me at a distance since you got back. So what's different about tonight?"

"You looked sad," she said, then threw a hand over her mouth.

"I looked what?"

"Forget it," Lorelei stammered, her eyes dropping to the floor. "You're right, this was a mistake. I never should have come up here."

Spencer trapped her against the door with an arm on each side of her head. "Are you saying you were about to have pity sex with me? Is that what this was?"

"I didn't come up here to have sex with you!"

"No, that idea came after you saw how sad I looked, right?" For no rational reason he could name, Spencer was livid. "I don't need your pity."

"And I don't need to be barked at," she answered, pushing against his chest. "Excuse me for caring."

This time he backed off and let her open the door. "I told you I wasn't going to be good company."

"Understatement of the year," Lorelei said, storming down the steps. "Go to hell."

He watched her stomp across the yard, and though he couldn't hear what she was mumbling, Spencer had no doubt he was being insulted in varied and colorful ways. All of which he'd earned. She slammed the front door hard enough to shake the windows on the old place, and he remained in the doorway waiting for the light in her bedroom to come on. Which it did seconds later. The jeans hit the wall first, and then the purple top went flying before she disappeared out of sight.

Spencer had royally messed up this time. Whatever ground he'd gained was gone. All because he couldn't forget the past. Deep down, he knew stopping had been the right thing to do, but turning down a woman like Lorelei wasn't something a man did without consequences. He'd dinged her pride tonight. That ding would cost him.

Returning to the couch, he stared at the muted weatherman standing in front of a map that showed nothing but thunderstorms for several days to come.

"You don't know the half of it, Mr. Weatherman," he spoke aloud, as Champ joined him on the ancient brown sofa. If only he hadn't run into Carrie today and been reminded of the one thing in his life he could never change. Maybe then tonight would have turned out differently.

"Winning her back is going to be even tougher now, buddy." The dog rolled over for a belly rub, failing to show the proper concern for his owner's troubled love life. "We'll start over tomorrow. Or whenever she agrees to talk to me again. Lorelei can't avoid me forever, right?"

The dog flopped back onto his stomach and dropped his chin onto the cushions with a doubtful look on his face.

"Your confidence in me is overwhelming, my friend," Spencer said, opening the laptop before unmuting the TV.

Chapter 13

Lorelei had managed to avoid Spencer for the rest of the week by staying in her room when she wasn't at work or turning out baked goods. Except for the night before, when she'd had dinner with Snow Cameron. Not until after the meal did she realize that Snow had kept Lorelei talking the entire time, which resulted in her dinner partner sharing almost nothing about herself. Either Lorelei was more stuck on herself than she knew, or Snow Cameron had perfected the art of not discussing her past.

But tonight was the next Ruby Restoration meeting, and that meant breaking her silence where Spencer was concerned. Was she glad he'd thrown on the brakes before they did something stupid? Of course she was. Did her pride still smart from the fact that he was able to be the rational one while she'd been lost in lust? Hell yes. Would she ever admit as much to her sexy ex-boyfriend?

Abso-friggin-lutely not.

She would also never admit that her dreams for the past few nights had been filled with images of Spencer's body, slick and hot, hovering above hers while she all but begged him to take her. Her subconscious apparently didn't care much about pride. And to make matters worse, her jeans had gotten tighter. She'd been suffocating her ramped-up sex drive with the sweets she could now make without referencing the recipes. Lorelei even had to bake an extra batch of chocolate chip cookies the night before because she'd tossed so many of the things into her own mouth.

"And that's the last of them," Mike said, sliding the final payroll check her way. Lorelei had been dropping the checks into window envelopes as he signed them. As of this, her third day on the job, she had yet to encounter anyone else who worked for Lowry Construction, but Mike assured her they'd all be in around lunchtime to pick up their paychecks.

"Do I need to verify IDs?" she asked. "Make sure they are who they say they are and I don't give a paycheck to the wrong person?"

Boss Man, as Lorelei had begun calling him, scratched his chin. "I don't think that'll be necessary, but if it makes you feel better, you can have them sign something when they take the check."

"Sign something?"

"Sure. Create a log and have them sign next to their name."

Had to love how he assumed she could create a log out of thin air. "I'll see what I can come up with."

Mike shot her a smile as he picked up his cowboy hat from the shelf behind his desk. "Your enthusiasm is one of the things I like best about you, Lorelei."

Sarcasm. How cute.

"I bet it's tough to fit a hard hat over that cowboy number," she said, flashing her boss an unrepentant smile as she ripped a piece of Scotch tape without looking. The fact that she could poke him a bit made Mike one of the cooler bosses she'd ever had. Once Lorelei figured out that she amused him and that he could take a joke, their encounters had become more fun.

"That's why I had one specially made," he said, circling his desk, then perching on the front corner. "Cost a pretty penny but worth it to protect the Resistol."

"Resistol?" Lorelei asked. "What is that?"

"Only the finest brand of cowboy hat you can buy." Mike flipped the black felt with two fingers, making it land atop his head. "George Strait wears Resistol hats."

Lorelei remembered what Spencer had said about Mike trying his luck at stardom down in Nashville. Which meant they had more in common than both having ties to her mother.

"Did you ever meet him?" she asked, truly curious.

"Who, George?" Mike shook his head. "I had one of those 'friend of a friend knew a merch guy' connections, but it never panned out."

"Then it must be true what they say about LA and Nashville being so alike. What's the lyric?" Lorelei searched her memory banks for the song she was thinking of. "Something about LA being Nashville with a tan."

A grin split her boss's face. "Sounds about right."

"I forgot to tell you that Becky Winkle showed up here on Monday looking for you." Twisting a rubber band around the paychecks, she added, "She was quite put out when I refused to tell her where you were."

"I appreciate that." Mike's cowboy hat rose as he scratched his head beneath it, the silver hair at his temples catching the light. "She's been after me for months. I keep telling her I'm too old, but the girl is determined and I have no idea why."

Lorelei considered her employer. He had probably qualified as hot in his younger days. Which made her wonder if, back in the day, her mother had ever chased Mike the way Becky was chasing him now. In fact, was Mike's connection to her mother what had Granny so against him? Maybe Mike had broken her mother's heart and Granny never forgave him. She was tempted to ask, but the question seemed a little too personal.

"You're an up-and-coming businessman in the community," Lorelei explained. "Becky was always a social climber. So now she wants to climb you."

He gave her a stern look. "There will be no climbing of me by Becky Winkle, social or otherwise."

"Good to know," Lorelei said with a nod. If Mike had been interested in the hateful blonde, her respect for him would have taken a major hit.

With a glance at his watch, Mike said, "I'll need to leave for my eleven o'clock appointment soon. Are you all good here?"

"I am." Lorelei couldn't think of anything she needed, except for an excuse to skip the restoration meeting that night. "I don't suppose you need me to work over, though? Until, say, ten or eleven tonight?"

Mike's expression turned tense. "Please tell me that's not some weird way of asking me out."

"What?" That was so not what she meant. "No. That's gross."

"I'd normally take being called gross as an insult, but in this case, I'm glad to hear you feel that way."

"I have one of those Ruby Restoration meetings tonight, and I'm dreading it." Lorelei shot a paper clip across the room using a rubber band as a slingshot. "Jebediah Winkle sends me evil vibes across Lancelot's tacky back room, while the rest of them drone on about car washes and bake sales. They're never going to raise enough money that way."

"Then what do you suggest they do?"

She paused with paper clip number two ready to fly. "What do you mean, what do *I* suggest?"

He stared at her expectantly.

"What?" she asked.

"You joined the committee of your own free will, I assume."

Lorelei didn't like where this was going. "Kind of."

"That means you agreed to help raise the money. So help."

"How? No one on that committee is going to listen to me." Lorelei shot the paper clip, eliciting a *dink* as it bounced off the window. "I'll work whatever booth they put me behind, or handle a hose to scrub down a line of pickup trucks in the Brubaker's parking lot. I'm sure that's all they expect me to do."

Boss Man swiped the next paper clip before she could load it in the slingshot. "Who cares what they expect from you? If you don't like their ideas, come up with better ones."

That sounded like something Spencer would say. "You're being very bossy."

"I get to do that because my name is on the door. Now I suggest you spend a little time this afternoon, after you organize the inventory sheets, of course, coming up with fantastic fund-raising ideas that will blow that committee's collective socks off."

"Fine," she said, tossing the rubber band on the desk. "But when they laugh in my face, I'm going to let them know how you've agreed to join the committee."

Mike was nearly to the door when he yelled back, "I can't secure the construction work if I'm on the committee. Conflict of interest. Now get back to work before I start docking your pay for all those paper clips you keep shooting behind the file cabinet."

In her most mature fashion, Lorelei stuck her tongue out at her boss. Something he couldn't see since he'd already exited the building. How was she supposed to solve the fund-raising problems in one afternoon when the entire committee hadn't come up with anything viable in a year? Whatever they did, it had to be bigger than anything they'd done so far. But what? They could have a big gala and charge a hundred bucks a seat, but no one in town would pay that.

They could sell something. What were the rules against putting the statue of some old founding father on eBay? There was a perfectly good one standing in the town square doing nothing but collecting bird crap.

Nah. Someone would probably get their panties in a bunch. Lorelei cogitated for another minute or two, and then she spotted the flier on her desk about the Main Street Festival coming up next week. What if they had a shorter fall festival to raise money for the Ruby? Instead of five days of carnival rides and parades, a two-day event with lots of food and entertainment that would bring folks in from miles around. But what would be the draw?

Maybe Mike had connections in Nashville they could use. Bring in a moderately big name, someone up-and-coming, or better yet, old and on the decline. At least then people would know who he was and maybe come out to see an old has-been before he rode off into the sunset for good.

The more she thought about it, the more she could see the options in her mind. Lots of elements would need to be donated to limit the overhead costs from eating up all the profit, but the committee had enough merchants on board to make that happen. A Restore the Ruby Festival. They could hold it in the fall when the weather would be cooler. If they pulled it off, work could probably begin on the Ruby by Christmas, as they'd hoped.

Lorelei's first inclination was to call Spencer and run it past him, but she needed to have a real plan before pitching the idea. Mike had told her to plot, and plot she would. Then, tonight, she'd have something real to offer at the meeting. How triumphant it would feel to watch Jebediah Winkle have to agree with something she'd suggested. Such sweet revenge for how he'd acted the week before.

Dragging a yellow legal pad out of her top drawer, Lorelei made a list of potential sponsors and participants, mapped out the area around the Ruby where the festivities could be held, and even drew up where the stage would be. Leaning back, she stared at the diagram.

"This could work," she mumbled, excitement bubbling in her chest. "By damn, this could really work."

Four days felt like forever.

Rosie hadn't invited Spencer in for dinner, and other than catching glimpses of Lorelei out his window, racing in or out of the house, he'd had no contact with her since the argument on Monday. The plan had been to give her a couple days to cool off. Considering how she'd been acting since her return, Spencer knew she wasn't upset that they hadn't had sex. What she was mad about was that *he'd* called it quits before she did.

And women said men were the ones with fragile egos.

By Thursday, he expected to find her lingering on the porch, waiting for him to saunter up and charm her into a smile. But she wasn't even home when he'd gotten in from work. Maybe she *did* intend to avoid him forever.

Which left Spencer with a dilemma. Tonight was a Ruby Restoration meeting. Should he expect her to show up without prompting, or knock on the door and offer to give her a ride? Would she refuse to stay on the committee because of him, or continue to take part while also continuing to give him the cold shoulder?

"Are we going to this meeting or are you going to sit up here twiddling your thumbs all night?" came a voice through his screen door.

Spencer spotted Lorelei standing on the other side, brows up expectantly.

"I guess that's my answer then," he said, grabbing a ball cap off the coffee table. Champ jumped off the couch, but Spencer waved the dog back. After snagging his keys off the counter, he stepped onto his tiny porch and pulled the door shut behind him. Lorelei was already at the truck.

Spencer pressed the button on his key fob to unlock the doors. "I wasn't sure you were coming."

"Well, I am." The long blue dress she wore made climbing into the truck look like an agility test, but she was in and buckled before he slid the key into the ignition. "Look," she said, turning his way as far as the seat belt would allow. "Let's not make a big deal about this. You were a jerk. We both lost our minds for a minute. It won't happen again."

He'd argue two of those points if he hadn't already decided this wasn't a battle he'd insist on winning. And if she wanted to believe what sparked between them wouldn't catch fire again, Spencer would let her have her delusions. For tonight anyway.

Still, he couldn't resist one tiny poke. "I accept your apology," he said, turning the truck onto Mill Avenue. Lorelei huffed, and though he couldn't see her face as she glared out the passenger window, Spencer had no doubt she'd rolled her eyes. "So are the treats still selling well?"

He'd made a point of stopping into Snow's shop around midafternoon both Wednesday and today, so he knew the answer was yes. That didn't mean he wouldn't give her the chance to brag.

"Sold out every day this week," she said. "We doubled the amount after Monday, but we'll leave the quantities at the current level for now, then increase them for festival week." Lorelei sounded like a true businesswoman, and he was happy to see her finding a niche. Something she could be proud of.

Of course, if he spoke as much aloud, she'd find some way to deflect the compliment. So he kept the thought to himself.

"Sounds like a plan. And the job with Mike?"

Again, Spencer had asked Mike that morning how Lorelei was working out. The man had nothing but glowing praise for his new office assistant. And she'd been worried about learning the software.

"I like him." Lorelei leaned an elbow on the passenger door. "He doesn't seem to mind my relaxed version of being professional. And he doesn't look at me like I'm going to screw something up at any minute, which is nice."

"Good." Spencer didn't like that she'd talked about the man instead of the job, but he ignored the ping of jealousy that felt like a hot poker between his ribs. "I'm glad."

Lorelei sighed. "Go ahead. I know you're dying to say it."

For once, he didn't have a clue what she meant. "I'm sorry?"

"You know you want to rub it in that you convinced me to find something I liked to do, which got me baking, and then landed me this job with Mike. So go ahead," she said. "Gloat."

The woman was impossible. "Lorelei, you came up with baking all on your own. Then you found the recipes and made the sweets." He leaned her way. "Again, *on your own*."

"Fine," she huffed. "But you got me the office job."

"No," he corrected. "I introduced you to someone who had a job opening I thought you could fill. You got the job, and you're the one making it work."

Spencer glanced her way and watched her mouth form a straight line. "I know the phone was your idea," she said.

"Yes, the phone was my idea," he confessed. "I take full credit for getting you the same techno-leash the rest of us have. You happy now?"

"I thought about calling you today." The words were spoken so softly, Spencer thought he'd heard her wrong.

"Am I hearing things or did you just say you thought about calling me?"

"Don't return to jerk-dom," she scolded. "I think I have an idea for how we can raise a lot of money for the theater."

And he'd thought Lorelei showing up at his door had been a surprise.

"That's great," he said, keeping his enthusiasm in check until he'd heard the details. Since she hadn't been on the committee long, he was concerned she might suggest something they'd already tried. "How?"

She held silent, causing him to look her way. Lorelei was chewing on her bottom lip, staring out the windshield as if the answer was somewhere in the distance.

"Lor?" he said. "Come on. Tell me."

"I'd rather wait and tell you when I tell everyone else."

Now she'd really shocked him.

"Tell everyone else?"

"Last week during the meeting there was a point when Buford asked if anyone had new business. I figured when that question came up this week, I'd raise my hand."

Last week she'd been too afraid to walk into the room without him. Now she wanted to stand up in front of the entire committee. What a difference a week made.

"Okay," he said, drawing the word out to three syllables.

"I want you to be honest. If you think it's a stupid idea, you have to say so. In the meeting."

"I'm sure it isn't stup—" he started.

"I'm serious, Spencer. The only way they're going to know that I'm not on this committee solely because you're coddling your ex-girlfriend is for me to put this out there and take the hits. If they come." She ran a hand through her hair. "Which will suck, but at least I'll know I tried."

They rode the next mile in silence, until Spencer said, "I'm proud of you, Lorelei. I'm really proud of you."

With another eye roll, this one clearly visible, she muttered, "There's no need to get sappy."

But the smile in her eyes said she appreciated the comment.

Chapter 14

Her tongue was as dry as the LA River, and her hands tingled as if they'd lost circulation. That's all Lorelei needed, to have a panic attack right before putting herself on the gallows.

Well, the gallows was a tad dramatic, even for her, but the thought of standing up in front of this committee felt like setting herself up for a public flogging. What if they didn't like her idea? Maybe they had too many festivals already. Though there were none in the fall. That she knew of. Crud. She should have run this whole thing past Spencer when she'd had the chance.

But then it wouldn't be her idea. And she wanted this one. Lorelei wanted to prove to her enemies that she was more than the rebellious, attention-seeking teenager they remembered. If nothing else, she could use this temporary return to town to win some respect. And to give something back as her own apology for being such a hotheaded brat in her youth.

The meeting had been shorter this week, and Jebediah Winkle was nowhere to be seen. Which helped calm Lorelei's nerves.

"Does anyone have any new business to discuss?" Buford called from the podium. Silence loomed as everyone present exchanged empty glances. This was it. This was her chance.

"Okay, then—" Buford continued.

"Wait," Lorelei said, bolting to her feet. Her stomach dropped to her knees as all eyes turned her way.

"Yes?" the former mayor said, surprise and suspicion clear on his face. "Did you have something to say?"

Lorelei nodded, her vocal cords temporarily out to lunch.

The faces around her watched with varying degrees of interest. Granny looked worried, while Spencer gave her a nod of approval.

"I have a suggestion for a fund-raiser," she said, her voice timid.

"You'll have to speak up," Stallings bellowed.

"Sorry," she said, speaking louder. "I said I have a suggestion for a fund-raiser. I think we should have a street festival around the theater. This fall. The parking lot is big enough to hold a stage and still have room for a good-sized audience. We could maybe bring someone in from Nashville who would draw a crowd."

The mumbling started immediately, but no one shot the idea down. Or laughed her back into her seat.

"Local restaurants could set up booths. Actually," she said, the idea growing as she pitched it, "any business willing to donate their time would be welcome. Churches. Window salesmen. Anyone who could benefit from interacting with the public." The mumbling turned to nods of agreement, boosting her confidence. "We'd charge a small entry fee, run it over the course of a weekend, and so long as the majority of supplies are donated, make a hefty profit that would go toward the restoration."

"A festival?" Buford asked. "Like the Main Street Festival?"

"Sort of." Lorelei walked from her seat in the back corner toward the front of the room. "Only this would be called the Restore the Ruby Festival, and everyone would know that it's a fund-raiser. We could set up games, have a kid section, and with enough food and entertainment, I think we could draw people from neighboring counties." She turned toward her ex. "Or even Nashville. Show them what our small town has to offer."

Spencer's face beamed with pride. Lorelei ignored the nausea churning in her midsection, enjoying the feeling that she'd done something right for a change.

While she was busy giving herself a mental high five, the rest of the room finished ruminating.

"That sounds like a lot of work," Harvey Brubaker said. It didn't take a genius to know that a grocery store would not be the kind of business to partake in what Lorelei was proposing. And if there was live entertainment in the Ruby parking lot, his bar and any band he'd hire would take a hit.

Nitzi Merchant chimed in. "Anything we do is going to take work, Harvey. I like this idea." The vote of confidence was accompanied by a wink in Lorelei's direction.

"Harvey is right," Buford interrupted. "Ms. Pratchett, are you willing to chair this endeavor, or were you only throwing out the suggestion and expecting others to handle the heavy lifting?"

Lorelei considered telling Stallings where he could shove his heavy lifting, but she'd come too far to let her inner child ruin this. "It's my idea. I'm fine heading up the planning." What the hell did she know about planning a street festival? Absolutely nothing, that's what. But until Monday, she'd never run an accounting software system either. She'd figured that out, and she could figure this out, too.

"I make a motion that Lorelei Pratchett create a full presentation for the Restore the Ruby Festival and present it to the committee,"

Spencer said. The motion was seconded and passed before Lorelei knew what hit her.

"Ms. Pratchett, we'll expect the full presentation in two weeks." Turning to Nitzi, Buford added, "Make sure that's on the agenda."

"Got it," Nitzi said, taking notes with an extra flourish.

"Two weeks?" Lorelei asked.

"That's right," Buford nodded. "Main Street Festival is next weekend, so we'll be taking next Friday night off."

"Oh," she said, still stunned from this new development. "Right."

Minutes later, the meeting was adjourned and Lorelei was surrounded by members offering their own suggestions. She hadn't expected so much enthusiasm.

"Nice work, Ms. Pratchett," Spencer whispered in her ear as he passed by behind her. She turned to say thanks, but Nitzi surprised Lorelei by pulling her into a bear hug.

"Brilliant, my dear." The older woman released her as quickly as she'd attacked. "I've been saying for months that we need to think bigger, and now here you are with this wonderful idea. Simply brilliant."

Lorelei appreciated the vote of confidence, especially from someone who hadn't been her biggest fan before this meeting, but the people circling her were tossing around big names in the world of country music. Some were tittering that this could be the event that would hit their goal and then some. Expectations were growing, and Lorelei had only made the suggestion minutes ago. Now she had to deliver, but the bar was being raised by the second.

Way to go, big mouth, her inner demons chided. *The perfect opportunity to fail once again. Good luck not screwing this up.*

Granny chose that moment to pull Lorelei from the crowd. With misty eyes she said, "I'm so proud of you, honey. I knew this would be good for you, and you're good for it. You're going to make a difference."

"Thanks," Lorelei said, but her doubts were growing stronger. A good difference or a bad difference? What had she done? And how was she going to get out of it?

Spencer couldn't have been more proud of Lorelei in that moment. He watched her receive a pat on the back from one member after another, each filled with more enthusiasm than he'd seen in months. When Buford had first called for new business and Lorelei held her tongue, he'd worried she'd chickened out. But even knowing she might have been crucified for speaking up, she did it. And she did it with style, blooming right before his eyes. There was a hint of the old Lorelei in there. The girl who knew her own mind and had a wicked imagination was finally using that spark of creativity to do something good.

And once the kudos had run out and she was walking his way, he saw fear in her eyes.

Not good.

"I need to get out of here," she said as soon as he was close enough to hear her.

"We need to tell Rosie that we're leaving."

"She'll figure it out." Lorelei charged out of the room and through the restaurant, bursting through the front door like a woman running for her life. Since he refused to run, Spencer lost sight of her until she came into view pacing next to his truck. He wasn't sure, but it sounded as if she were mumbling a hefty dose of profanity.

"You want to tell me what's going on?" he asked.

Lorelei jerked on the door handle that was still locked. "Let me in."

"Not yet," he said, leaning on the front grille. "You may have saved this entire project. So what's with the panic attack?"

"I'm not having a panic attack," she said, continuing to pace and shaking her hands as if they'd fallen asleep. "And I didn't save anything. I made a suggestion, that's all."

"It's a good suggestion."

"But I didn't think they'd make me run it," she admitted. Of course the idea of taking responsibility for something would scare the hell out of her. She'd come back to town after years of being responsible for little more than delivering plates and finding her next meal. Now she was running a budding baking business, helping manage a small construction office, and looking at coordinating a major community effort for the town that already had a grudge against her.

For once, he couldn't blame her for being freaked out.

"Come here," he said, taking her by the hand and dragging her to the back of the truck.

"What are you going to do, beat some sense into me?"

Spencer stopped in his tracks. "Do you believe I'd ever lay a hand on you?"

"Sorry." She shrugged. "Stupid question."

He dropped the tailgate and turned her way. "Have a seat."

Lorelei did as ordered and crossed her arms with a huff.

"You're not going to have to run this all by yourself," he said.

"That's true." She picked at her cuticles. "Winkle will probably be here next time. He'll shoot it down in flames, and then I'll have nothing to worry about."

"Winkle doesn't have that kind of power." At least not on this committee, Spencer thought.

"Someone should tell him that. I don't think he knows." Lorelei sat up a little straighter, kicking her feet forward and back. "This is Mike's fault."

"How's that?" Spencer asked.

"He told me if I didn't like the ideas everyone else had, I should come up with a better one."

Spencer smiled. Good old Mike. "And you did."

Lorelei snorted. "What I did was set myself up for a crash of epic proportions."

With a roll of his eyes, he said, "That's not melodramatic at all."

"What can I say?" she asked. "Overacting is what I do."

When she shot him a half smile, he realized she'd made a joke. "Cute. Now tell me what's really going on here."

Leaning back on her hands, Lorelei raised her face toward the sky, closed her eyes, and breathed deep. "I got so carried away thinking about how much money we could raise with this festival that I didn't think about me being responsible for any of it."

"And being responsible for it would be a bad thing?"

She leaned close enough to bump shoulders. "That's the million-dollar question."

He bumped back. "I think it would be a good thing."

"That's because you're completely blind to my faults."

"Now you've gone from dramatic to delusional." Spencer threw an arm around Lorelei's shoulders. "If anyone is aware of your faults, it's me. The difference is, you hate yourself for them, and I choose to like you in spite of them."

Slipping her hand into the one dangling over her left shoulder, Lorelei whispered, "I can't decide if that makes you a sap or an idiot."

"I'm a man, Lorelei," he said, staring into moonlit blue eyes. "A man who likes what he sees, faults and all."

She didn't have a comeback for that one, and he was fighting the temptation to lay her down in the truck bed and take advantage of her lowered defenses. But since he didn't feel like going another four days getting the silent treatment, Spencer followed a different instinct.

"You can do this," he said, squeezing her hand. "I have complete faith in you."

"Now who's being delusional?"

Ignoring her question, he hopped off the tailgate. "I know what we'll do."

"What?" Lorelei asked.

Spencer held out a hand. "How long has it been since you went dancing, Ms. Pratchett?"

After a brief hesitation, she shook her head. "Oh, no."

"Oh, yes." He pulled her off the truck to stand pressed against him on the gravel. "I'm taking you two-stepping, woman. This night calls for a celebration."

Lorelei had thought walking into that first restoration meeting had been hard. Ha! That was nothing compared to walking into Brubaker's Bar. At least at the meetings, people were on their best behavior. Social cuts were subtle, and no one made a scene. Put her in an Ardent Springs crowd loaded up on beer and bravado and all bets were off.

Which was why she clung to Spencer's arm like a money-strapped bride holding on to the last Vera Wang at a fire sale.

Spencer stopped not far inside the front door and glanced around as if looking for someone he knew. The place wasn't as packed as Lorelei had expected, but then it wasn't even eight o'clock yet. The real party wouldn't start until closer to ten, she assumed.

"Over there," he said, yelling over the volume of the band. "In the corner."

Lorelei craned her neck in the direction Spencer indicated, but the only thing she saw in the corner was the back of a man with broad shoulders wearing a sleeveless black-and-green flannel and a ball cap turned backward on his head. Before she could ask who it was, Spencer was cutting a path around the dance floor, pulling her along behind him.

"Heya, Coop," he said in greeting, drawing the attention of the flannel wearer. The first thing Lorelei spotted was a substantial bicep with a tattoo that looked like . . . Were those tire tracks?

"Boyd!" the man exclaimed, doing the guy-hand-grab-and-pat-on-the-back thing. Turning in her direction, he said, "Hey there, Lorelei. You're looking as good as ever."

This person knew her? What had Spencer called him? Coop? The name sounded familiar, but it took several seconds before the revelation came. "Cooper Ridgeway?"

The mechanic had at least two inches on Spencer, and his arms looked as if he'd spent the last twelve years bench-pressing cars instead of fixing them. The Cooper she remembered was a scrawny kid with greasy hair and the perpetual black under his fingernails. His hands still showed signs of years working with his hands in grease, but the hair looked clean, if shaggy, with brown curls swirling around the brim of his hat. Green eyes twinkled as he flashed her a genuine smile, revealing the dimple in his chin.

"The one and only," he said, giving her a half hug and dropping a kiss on her cheek. "How you doing, lady?"

Lorelei was so stunned by the show of affection, she struggled to produce verbal communication. "Good," she managed. "I'm good."

"Spencer says you're working out at Lowry Construction. You liking it?" Spencer was deep in conversation with a brunette on the other side of the tiny cocktail table, making Lorelei want to kick him. Even if they weren't there as a couple, he didn't have to pick up another woman while Lorelei fended off the boy-mechanic-turned-hunk.

In response to his question, she nodded, keeping a smile pasted on her face. Though Cooper had been part of their high school group, he'd been more Spencer's friend than hers. She wasn't even sure they'd ever held a conversation. But here he was, chatting as if they were old buddies catching up. So this was the difference more than a decade could make. Everyone acting like grownups. Lorelei couldn't decide how she felt about that. She sure didn't feel like a grownup.

"You want a beer?" Cooper asked.

"I've got it," Spencer said, patting his friend on the arm. "Put the order in just now." So maybe he hadn't been trying to pick up another woman. He'd still left her to fend off Cooper. "Time to give Lorelei here a dance floor refresher course."

Before she could argue, Lorelei was facing backward on the edge of the dance floor. Spencer turned his ball cap around, presumably so the brim wouldn't poke her in the forehead every time she looked down at her feet. The change made him look younger. And hotter. Damn him.

"You ready?" he asked.

"I don't remember how to do this, Spencer."

"Sure you do. It's like riding a bike." He took her right hand in his and tossed her left onto his right shoulder. "Step back with your right and follow my lead."

With that instruction, he moved them onto the floor, and by some miracle, Lorelei's feet did exactly what they were supposed to do. The shuffle step that started with the right foot, then a step with the left. Shuffle step, then left. They did two turns around the sawdust-covered floor with her body pressed tight against Spencer's frame. She knew dancing so close made it easier for her to follow, but it was also making it difficult for her to think. Good thing her feet were operating independently of her brain.

Just when she was feeling lulled into a daze, he leaned down to whisper in her ear. "You ready for a spin?"

"I'm barely staying upright," she answered, panic clear in her voice. Spencer wasn't fazed. "You trust me?"

The answer yes came too quickly to mind. "Is that a trick question?"

Instead of responding, he pushed gently on her left hip while applying pressure with his left hand. Lorelei did a full turn, landing back in Spencer's arms and on the correct step. The move happened so fast, she wondered if maybe she'd imagined it.

"You can fight it all you want," he said, his lips touching her left earlobe, which sent a shiver down to her toes. "But your body still follows my lead."

Leaning back to look him in the eye, she said, "You're enjoying this, aren't you?"

"Yes, ma'am," he said, winking as he twirled her into another spin.

Chapter 15

Lorelei had agreed to take a turn around the floor with Cooper, who wasn't nearly the skilled dancer Spencer was. The man could rebuild a '55 Chevy with his eyes closed, but he had the rhythm of a three-legged water buffalo. Spencer watched them fade into the crowd around the far corner, then emerge again with Lorelei laughing at something Cooper had said. Or she was laughing *at* him. Either was possible.

Spencer liked to watch her like this. He'd never been a jealous man, which turned out to be a fatal flaw when it came to his marriage, but with Lorelei he never doubted. She wasn't a saint, by any means, but even in grade school she'd had a strong code of ethics that she stuck to no matter what. Part of that code had been loyalty and never taking what belonged to someone else.

He remembered back to a time during sophomore year when one of their friends had thought it would be funny to snag some candy bars from Puckett's Pharmacy. Old Puckett wouldn't have missed a few bits of chocolate, but Lorelei wouldn't do it. And it wasn't because she worried about eternal damnation of her soul or going to jail. She simply believed in wrong and right, and you didn't take something you didn't earn or pay for.

The same went for people. When they'd been together, she'd been loyal to a fault. Lorelei took commitment seriously, and in that way she'd spoiled him. Made him believe everyone lived life by the same standards. Learning he was wrong, and in such a humiliating fashion, had been a dark day in his history. Spencer didn't trust easily anymore, but he'd trust Lorelei to the ends of the earth.

His mission now was to get her to trust him back, because there was still a mess of baggage she was hauling around. If she'd let him, Spencer was ready and willing to help lighten her load.

"And I appreciate your efforts," Lorelei was saying, as the pair returned to the table.

"It was my pleasure." Cooper snagged his longneck off the table and held the cold bottle to his sweat-covered forehead.

"Did you come back with all your toes intact?" he asked Lorelei, gaining an irritated glare from Cooper.

She took a drink of her own beer before answering. "Yes, I did," she answered. "Not everyone can be a twinkle toes like you."

Cooper did a spit take, then offered Lorelei a fist bump, which she accepted. "I also thanked him for keeping Beluga running all these years. As much as I hated that old boat, it's nice to have something to drive that isn't going to leave me stranded on the side of the road."

"That's why you should always make friendly with your mechanic," Cooper chimed in, adding a brow wiggle for emphasis.

"Is that Haleigh Rae over there?" Spencer said, leaning over Cooper's shoulder.

"Where?" the big guy said, jerking around so fast he nearly knocked Lorelei over.

"Whoa, there!" she cried, trying not to spill beer down the front of her dress. Cooper continued to search the crowd, and a hint of guilt settled in Spencer's chest.

"I was kidding, dude. She isn't here."

When Cooper turned back around, he looked as if he'd been punched. His guilt got stronger.

"That's not cool, man."

"What am I missing here?" Lorelei asked.

Spencer hadn't intended to be mean. He'd had a gut reaction to Cooper flirting with Lorelei and lashed out in a way he knew would get the man's attention.

"We have to be talking about Haleigh Rae Mitchner. Is she still in town?"

"Nah." Cooper shook his head. "She moved to Memphis."

"Then why would you think she was in the bar?" Lorelei asked.

"She comes home every year for the Main Street Festival," Spencer answered, sparing Cooper the need to explain. Though Lorelei could probably guess how their friend felt about the former schoolmate by his reaction seconds earlier.

With a slow nod, she said, "Oh." There was more enthusiasm in her voice when she said, "Then she'll be home soon. Maybe we can all hang out?"

Lorelei didn't have a lot of female friends in high school, but as Haleigh wasn't a cheerleader or one of Becky's followers, they'd spent some time together. Not best friends doing the slumber party thing, but they shared some classes and hung out at a bonfire or two. The fact that Lorelei was trying to find a way for Cooper to spend time with Haleigh took Spencer by surprise.

"That's a good idea," he said.

"Haleigh Rae is a doctor now. She won't be interested in hanging with a grease monkey." Cooper took a swig of Bud Light and kept his eyes on the swirling dancers passing by.

"You make her sound like a snob," Lorelei said, tapping him on the arm. "I don't remember Haleigh being that way at all."

Instead of responding to Lorelei, Cooper rose on his toes to peer at something across the room. Spinning around, he said, "Farmer. Five o'clock."

Not what Spencer wanted to hear.

"Did he say there's a farmer at five o'clock?" Lorelei asked. "What does that mean?"

"Not *a* farmer," Cooper clarified. "Patch Farmer. The asshole who took Spence's wife."

And that was not how Spencer would have preferred to answer her question.

"He took your wife?" Lorelei's voice rose an octave on the last word. "Like, kidnapped her?"

"No," Spencer said through clenched teeth. "She went willingly."

"The rat bastard," Cooper growled.

Spencer appreciated his friend's support, but this wasn't a subject he wanted to discuss, nor was he interested in making a scene.

"Do you want to leave?" Lorelei asked, her hand suddenly in his. "I don't mind."

With a shake of his head, Spencer said, "This place is big enough for the both of us. It's been five years. We've run into each other before."

Cooper tapped his nearly empty bottle on the table. "I don't know how you've never knocked his head off."

"What's done is done." He could have let pride win out, but in the end, Patch had done Spencer a favor. If Carrie hadn't slept with the factory worker, it would have been someone else. Spencer was better off without her.

Lorelei squeezed his hand. "Are you sure?"

Giving her a reassuring smile, he said, "Yeah, I'm sure."

"Okay then. I think Cooper needs another beer, and I need to visit the little girls' room."

The overpowering urge to keep her with him shot down Spencer's spine. He pushed the weakness away. "Go on then. Do you want another beer, too?"

She yawned before answering. "I better switch to Coke or I'll be asleep on a barstool soon." Staring hard as if to reassure herself he was okay, she hesitated before turning toward the bathrooms. "I'll be right back."

Yes, she would. And maybe by the time she got back, Spencer would have tamped down the urge to ask her never to leave him. He hadn't even won her back yet and already the thought of losing her again made him sick to his stomach. This was a stupid side effect of knowing Patch was around. Of having history thrown in his face. Screw history, Spencer thought. It was time to focus on the future.

A future with Lorelei.

Lorelei couldn't believe that Granny never told her Spencer's wife had cheated on him. How stupid could a woman be? And who in her right mind would leave Spencer?

That stopped Lorelei in her tracks a few feet from the ladies' room entrance. *You did, you idiot.* Right. Still. Lorelei would never cheat on anyone.

And that stopped her again, this time less than a foot *inside* the bathroom. She hadn't cheated on anyone, but she had been an accessory to the crime. So to speak. How would Spencer feel if he ever learned what she'd done? That she'd been the other woman once upon a time? Would he believe her when she said she hadn't known the man was married? Would that even matter?

"You're Lorelei, aren't you?" The question sounded more like an accusation, and Lorelei looked around to see who had spoken the words. The only other person in the bathroom was a slip of a woman with dishwater-brown hair, who looked as if she needed a cheeseburger and a makeup tutorial. The pink lip shade was totally wrong for her skin tone.

"Yes, I'm Lorelei," she answered. "Do I know you?"

"Not personally. I was a couple years behind you in school."

Lorelei hadn't made much time for underclassman. "Right. Go Wildcats."

"I'm also Spencer's ex-wife," she said. "I'm Carrie."

"So you're the one." This wasn't the girl she would have imagined for Spencer. Meek. Soft-spoken. Her opposite in every visible way. But then again, maybe that made sense. "I understand your Farmer dude is out there somewhere. You should probably go join him."

"I guess Spencer hasn't said very nice things about me."

"Spencer doesn't talk about you at all," Lorelei said. Spencer may not be willing to confront the man who'd slept with his wife, but that didn't mean Lorelei would make friendly with the woman who'd hurt him.

"Funny," Carrie said. "He talked about you all the time."

Stepping toward the stalls, Lorelei said, "I doubt he spoke highly of me back then."

Carrie stepped with her. "On the contrary. He couldn't speak highly enough."

Lorelei didn't believe for one minute that Spencer spent his married years talking about the girl who'd gotten away. That wasn't his style. The woman had to be lying.

"Do you know what it's like to lay next to a man, all the while knowing he wished you were someone else?"

"You're the one who cheated," Lorelei said, stepping close enough to see the bruise her adversary had tried to cover with makeup. "If you were dumb enough to trade Spencer Boyd for the man who put that mark on your face, that's on you, not me."

"You were always there," she said, a tear sliding down her cheek. "I couldn't compete with the ghost of Lorelei."

"You couldn't compete with a woman who was two thousand miles away? You had him," she said. "He was right there next to you, and you threw him away. For what?"

The younger woman turned away. "I don't have to explain myself to you."

"I didn't start this conversation, Carrie. Don't dump your laundry in my lap, accuse me of breaking up your marriage, and then act like *I'm* accosting *you*." Lorelei stepped into a stall and slammed the door. Fading footsteps indicated the woman was leaving, but then they stopped.

"If I could have kept him, I would have," she said. "But he was never mine." Carrie's voice wavered. "He was always yours."

Lorelei tried to block out the bitterness and hurt laced through Carrie's words. She tried not to think about what it would be like to be with a man who wanted someone else. To have him look at you but see another woman in your place. Whatever had happened between Spencer and his wife had nothing to do with her. Or so she kept repeating over and over in her mind. A marriage was between two people, not three. Though she certainly had experience being the third wheel.

Had Maxwell thought of her when he was with his wife? Or worse, pictured his wife when he was having sex with Lorelei? Just thinking about either scenario made her shiver with distaste. And feel like even more of a moron for not realizing he was married before the truth came knocking.

"Dammit," she muttered, saying the word aloud unintentionally.

"What is it?" Spencer asked.

She'd requested he drive her home shortly after the encounter with Carrie in the bathroom. At first, Lorelei intended to tell him about the run-in with his ex-wife, hoping he'd clear her conscience by declaring the demise of his marriage had nothing to do with her. But fear that he'd admit Carrie was right kept Lorelei silent. Part of her didn't want to know. There were only so many marriages a woman could shatter before ignorance could no longer be an excuse.

"Did you forget something at the bar?" he asked when she failed to answer the first question. "We can go back."

"No." The last thing Lorelei wanted was to go back. "I was thinking about something else. It's nothing."

Spencer gave her knee a squeeze. "You aren't still worried about the festival stuff, are you?"

The fund-raiser was as good an excuse as any. "It's a big job. Wouldn't take much to screw it up."

"I told you." He patted her knee this time. "You won't have to do it all alone. We'll create a festival committee and split up the duties."

Lorelei shook his hand off her knee. "That's a good idea. Maybe you should give the presentation." Hours ago she'd wanted this win for her own. Now she wanted to drive to the nearest bus terminal and buy a ticket for someplace far away.

"You're not getting out of it that easy." He chuckled. "Your plan. Your presentation."

"Right." She fell silent, desperate to be home. There were too many voices in her head. Too many demons ready to throw accusations and insults her way.

Humming along with the tune on the radio, Spencer let the subject drop. But not for long. "Are you sure there isn't something else bothering you? You've been acting strange since before we left the bar."

"Were you happy?" Lorelei asked, the words coming out without thought.

"Was I happy when?"

"I don't know," she said, shaking her head. "At any point in the last twelve years."

He fell silent, but his grip tightened on the wheel. The change was so slight, Lorelei would have missed it if she hadn't been staring at his hands to keep from looking at his face. She was afraid of what she'd see there. She was afraid of how he would answer.

Which would be worse? If he said yes, or no?

"There were moments," he said, the carefree tone gone. "Some good moments."

"Life should be more than that, don't you think?" Lorelei really wanted an answer. Her whole existence felt like a futile attempt to reach some happy destination, and no matter what she did, it either remained out of reach or slipped through her fingers before she could enjoy it.

Or worse yet, she'd messed up someone else's happiness.

Instead of answering her, Spencer said, "What about you? Were you happy in the last twelve years?"

Possible answers swirled in her mind, blending and melting together, each contradicting the next.

"Does it count if you believe you're happy, but nothing going on in your life is what you think it is?"

They passed two mile markers without a response from Spencer. She didn't blame him. It was a crazy question. Was anything in life ever what you really thought it was? This was why it sucked to be the kind of person who could never live in the moment. Lorelei was always too busy looking ahead, anticipating some far-off windfall, to pay attention to what was going on around her at any given second. When she'd finally felt as if that windfall had come, her life had ended up being one giant illusion.

"Yeah," he said, startling Lorelei out of her pity party. "It counts. Happiness is like the rainbows of life."

Lorelei blinked. "I'm pretty sure speaking that sentence means you lose your man card."

"I'm serious." Spencer removed his ball cap to run a hand through his hair. "Rainbows aren't real. You can't walk up and touch one. It's a trick of the light. That doesn't mean you've never seen one. And I bet every time it's happened, you smiled." Slipping the hat back on his head, he added, "So anytime you feel happy, it counts. Whether it's five minutes or five years. You felt it and no one can say you didn't."

She couldn't have said why or how, but his answer made Lorelei feel better. Yes, Maxwell had lied to her. Yes, he'd humiliated her and turned her into something she never wanted to be. But for those few months, before she knew the truth, Lorelei was happy.

And the first day she'd taken the cookies to Snow's and they'd sold out. She'd been happy that day.

And two nights ago, when Granny had made Lorelei's favorite—peach cobbler—and they'd watched *Casablanca* together with the lights turned low and Ginger purring on the back of the couch behind them. That was two hours of happy.

Maybe life wasn't about some sustained level of bliss. What if all you had to do was enjoy the moments when the urge to smile outweighed the desire to scream or cry or curse at the wind? The concept sounded too simple to be right, but then again, Pops had always accused Lorelei of making things more complicated than they needed to be.

"You still with me over there?" Spencer asked.

"Yeah," she answered, "I'm with you."

Taking her hand, Spencer dropped a kiss on her knuckles. "Good."

Instinct told her to pull away, but in the back of her mind, Lorelei imagined a rainbow hiding among the stars. So for once, she smiled and enjoyed the moment.

Chapter 16

Spencer woke Sunday morning to a text from his mother saying she needed to see him. There was only one reason Paula Boyd ever wanted to see her only child, and that was to hit him up for money. Another one of her temporary sugar daddies must have left her high and dry.

Dry meaning without food, cigarettes, or booze.

Thanks to an impromptu grandmother-granddaughter shopping trip to Goodlettsville the day before, Spencer hadn't seen Lorelei since leaving her at the front door on Friday night. He'd hoped to crash the kitchen today, sneak some cookies, and keep the momentum of his charm offensive moving forward. Dealing with his mother had not been on his agenda.

Unfortunately, if he ignored the message, his mother would hunt him down and likely make a scene when she found him. It was best to pay a visit to his boyhood home, hand over some twenties, and be on his way. If he knew his mother, she'd find a new man by the end of the month, and Spencer wouldn't hear from her again until fall at the earliest.

All of which was the reason he found himself staring at a dilapidated porch that leaned precariously against the front of a small, blue-and-white single-wide trailer he'd rather set fire to than ever enter again. Careful where he stepped, for fear of falling through the rotten wood, Spencer crept to the front door and knocked.

"About damn time," came a gravel-filled voice from inside before the dingy white door was yanked open. "I sent you that message two hours ago."

Refusing to argue, he ignored the greeting and stepped inside. The place was a disaster, as usual. The faded blue recliner looked to have a few new burn holes in it, while the ashtray beside it, a pedestal glass number that had been with his mother for as long as he could remember, overflowed with ash and butts. He could feel the stench of smoke already clinging to his clothes.

"How much do you need?" he asked, more than ready to get this over with.

"Who said I wanted anything?" she asked, talking around the cancer stick dangling out the side of her mouth.

Spencer fought to hold on to his patience. "You did. In a text, remember?"

She removed the Marlboro from her mouth and used it to point at him. "I said I needed to see you. That don't automatically mean I want money."

"Really?" His mother always did have a selective memory. "Then why am I here?"

"I got some news." The woman who looked close to twice her age pulled a ratty robe closed over her threadbare nightgown. Her bloodshot eyes pinged around the room, looking anywhere but in Spencer's direction. "Came in a letter from your aunt."

As far as Spencer knew, his mother hadn't talked to her only sister in more than ten years. "Why is Aunt Trish writing now?"

Hesitating long enough to take another drag off her cigarette, she answered, "Not that aunt."

If she was trying to confuse him, his mother was doing an excellent job. "I don't have any other aunts."

"Yes, you do," she barked. "Your father's sister."

That news hit hard enough to send him back a step. "You've always said you didn't know who my father was," he argued. "What game are you playing here?"

As a little boy, Spencer had asked over and over when his father was coming home. By middle school, he'd figured out there would be no father-son reunion, but he'd still wanted to know something about the man who'd contributed to his existence. Finally, in the middle of his freshman year, she'd confessed that she didn't know who his father was. That he'd been nothing more than a drifter passing through town and she couldn't have picked him out of a lineup if she had to.

A childhood that had been anything but positive had shattered into a million pieces that day. The only dream that had kept him going, that his father would someday take him away from the messy floors, empty cupboards, and occasional backhands across the face, died with his mother's hateful words. From that point on, Spencer knew he would have to get himself out, and that's exactly what he'd done.

"Do you really think that I would have a kid and not know who his father was?"

"What else was I supposed to think when that's exactly what you told me?" He growled the words, vibrating with the urge to grab this sorry excuse for a mother and shake the truth out of her.

Snatching a bottle of beer off the tiny counter, the woman who'd made his life miserable dropped into the scarred recliner. "His name was Crawford. Doug Crawford."

Hearing his father's name should have felt like a gift, but Spencer was too numb to feel anything at all. Then the tense of her statement hit him.

"Did you say *was?*"

She nodded. "That's the news. He died last month."

Employing every ounce of strength he had, Spencer stayed upright. His thoughts seethed like a pack of wolves in a feeding frenzy. A month ago, he could have shaken hands with his father. He could have looked him in the eye and maybe seen his own image, only older, staring back. Now he'd learned his father's name and lost him in the same breath.

"Where?" he asked. "How?"

"Texas," she answered, her voice devoid of emotion. "Somewhere around Dallas, I guess. Lung cancer got him." She took a long drag after the last statement, completely unaware of the irony in the action. As if lung cancer were a criminal that randomly killed innocent bystanders and had nothing to do with the chemicals she was sucking down her windpipe.

And then, when Spencer didn't think she could shock him any further, she pulled an envelope from beside the cushion of her chair and held it out to him. "There's a picture. I thought you might want it."

Unable to lift a hand to take the offering, he stared at the crumpled paper. "You thought I might want it? Did you ever think that I might have wanted it twenty-five years ago?"

Shaking the missive, she said, "You gonna take it or not?"

Spencer swiped the letter from her hand and turned to leave. If he stayed one second longer, he would not be held responsible for his actions.

"Did you say you brought me some money?" she had the nerve to ask as he stepped through the door. Without answering, he walked to his truck, started the engine, and put it in gear.

Lorelei hummed along with the radio, enjoying her new kitchen utensils and mixing bowls more than she'd have expected. As soon as she'd seen the ad that the kitchen supply store down the interstate was having a going-out-of-business sale, she'd begged Granny to go with her, promising they could eat anywhere the older woman wanted.

Knowing her grandmother's love for Cracker Barrel, and constant disappointment that Ardent Springs lacked the establishment, Lorelei knew where they would end up. The menu didn't feature many light and healthy options, but she'd made do, and it was worth the extra calories to see such simple joy in the older woman's eyes.

In fact, Granny must have still been running on the carb high that morning, since she hadn't once pestered Lorelei about going to church. She'd dropped a kiss on her cheek, warned her not to set the new pot holders on fire, and bid a toodle-oo. An hour after her departure, and five minutes into Lorelei's first batch of peanut butter cookies being in the oven, Spencer stormed through the front door like a man running from a horde of zombies.

"I can't believe she could be so mean," he said, one hand holding an envelope in a death grip. He didn't look at Lorelei as he spoke, but paced the space between the kitchen and the living room, his eyes unfocused and surprisingly moist.

Spencer never cried. This had to be serious.

Lorelei left the cookie batter on the counter and wiped her hands on her apron. "What's wrong?" she asked, trying to catch him by the arm, but he paced away. "You're scaring me, Spencer. Calm down."

He spun, waving the envelope in the air. "She said she didn't know who he was."

"She who?"

"That bitch who calls herself my mother, that's who!" His voice reached a volume Lorelei didn't know was humanly possible. Ginger skittered up the stairs, and Champ whined at the front door. "It was all a lie," he snarled, his cheeks a deep red that said his blood pressure was reaching dangerous levels. "All of it."

She'd never liked Spencer's mother, and the feeling had always been mutual. There wasn't a maternal bone in the woman's body, and the fact that Spencer had turned out to be such a sweet guy was the closest thing to a miracle Lorelei had ever seen. That she'd lied about something was no surprise, but what she'd lied about was still unclear.

"You need to calm down, hon. Let's sit on the couch." She led him into the living room, but Spencer wouldn't sit.

"All this time, she could have told me. Given me a name." The pacing resumed. "But no."

The only name Spencer had ever wanted was the one that belonged to his father. Even Paula Boyd couldn't be that horrible, to know all these years and keep the secret.

Putting her body in his way, Lorelei cupped Spencer's face in her hands, forcing him to look at her. "I can't help you if you won't tell me what happened," she said, holding eye contact until his pupils started returning to normal. And then he clasped her wrists and laid his forehead on hers.

"My whole life, she knew who my father was," he whispered, pain and betrayal making his voice crack. "She never told me, and now he's dead." Spencer rolled his head from side to side against hers. "He's dead and it's too late."

Tears filled her own eyes, and all she could do was hold him. Lorelei pulled his head down to her shoulder as his body shook. Spencer's arms squeezed the air from her lungs, but she held on without complaint, giving him as much support as she could. Having never known the identity of her own father, Lorelei understood the longing for information. The emptiness of never knowing where you came from. Never knowing if there was something you could have done to bring him back.

To finally get answers when it was too late would be devastating. Like being given the world and having it yanked away before you could even get your hands on it.

Once the shaking subsided, Spencer pulled back, wiping his eyes on his sleeve and the hem of his shirt. "I'm sorry," he said, which was so like him.

"You have nothing to be sorry for," she said, dabbing at her own eyes. The letter was still in his hand, crumpled and bent. "What's in there?"

"She says it's a letter. From his sister." Spencer loosened his grip and tried to smooth out the paper. "There's a picture inside."

"Have you looked at it?" she asked as he stared at the envelope as if it held the eighth wonder of the world. And for him, it did.

A shake of his head was the only response.

Rubbing his arm in a desperate need to comfort, she asked, "Don't you think you should?"

This time he gave a nod of affirmation.

"We need to sit down for this." If he fell apart again, Lorelei wasn't sure she could hold him up. In all honesty, she wasn't sure she could hold herself up, considering what was in that envelope.

Spencer turned and dropped to the couch, never taking his eyes off the letter. Lorelei plopped down, too, pulling up a knee and turning her body so she was facing him.

"His name is Doug Crawford," he said, then corrected himself. "Was. Was Doug Crawford."

"That's a good name," she said, completely out of her depths for an appropriate response when someone told you his long-lost father's name for the first time. "The return address says Annie Ramirez. So that's your aunt?"

"Yeah. That's what Mom . . ." His voice cut off. "That's what she said."

"Okay. You have an aunt named Annie. And she's still alive. Obviously."

"Yeah," he said, making no move to open the letter.

Lorelei laid her fingers over the envelope. "Do you want me to open it for you?"

He began to nod yes, but changed his mind. "I can do it." With shaking fingers, he lifted the flap and withdrew a long yellow sheet of paper folded into thirds. Setting the envelope down as if it might break, he opened the letter and a small picture fell into his lap.

They both froze as if someone had pulled the pin on a grenade and tossed it between them. Neither reached for the photo.

"That's him," Lorelei said, speaking the most obvious statement of her life. The picture had fallen image side up onto Spencer's thigh, revealing a large man wearing a black cowboy hat, a Western shirt with a bolo tie, and a smile identical to Spencer's.

With the look of a little boy getting his first baseball glove, Spencer picked up the picture, slowly lifting it to eye level. Brown eyes studied the man staring back at him as if he wanted to memorize everything about him. "He looks like me," he said, his voice cracking again.

Leaning her head on his shoulder, Lorelei said, "I think *you* look like *him*."

"Yeah." He rubbed his cheek against the top of her head. "I think you're right."

Chapter 17

An hour later, Spencer sat on the porch swing staring at the letter he'd read four times already. He couldn't make himself put it down. So many mysteries solved in this small collection of sentences. Questions answered. The pain of losing the man before he ever had the chance to meet him still lingered close to the surface, but with every pass of the letter, a dim light inside his chest grew brighter.

Ms. Boyd,

I believe you know my brother. His name was Doug Crawford, and he died three weeks ago.

When Doug was diagnosed with lung cancer, the disease had already taken over most of his body, and he knew he didn't have long to live. Unfortunately, he had less time than we thought. Six weeks ago, Doug told me he had a son with you. A son he never met. My brother made a lot of bad choices during his lifetime, and *he made it clear that abandoning his son was at the top of that list. Doug asked me to arrange a meeting, so he could at least apologize to the young man before he passed away.*

As I said, Doug didn't have as much time as we'd hoped, and he was gone before I could find your address. I don't know how you feel about my brother, but I hope you'll pass this on to your son. Doug Crawford was a good man. Not the best by any means, but still a good man. This picture was taken less than a year ago. Doug would have wanted his son to have it.

Respectfully,
Annie Ramirez

The letter didn't give an abundance of information, but it proved that the man *did* know about him. Which meant he could have contacted Spencer years ago. After the first reading, Lorelei had noticed the postmark on the envelope was nearly two weeks old. So the inestimable Paula Boyd had kept his father from him an extra two weeks. No doubt she'd debated telling him at all. When Spencer considered how close he'd come to never knowing, the anger grew red-hot again. He'd already ground his teeth enough to wear off a solid layer of enamel.

Annie said his father was a good man. Spencer clung to those words. His mother's own family would never have something that positive to say about her. She was *not* a good person. So how had a good man ended up producing a child with Paula Boyd? And was that one of the bad choices to which his aunt referred?

"Hey there," Lorelei said, joining him on the porch. She held a plate in her hand, and the scent of cinnamon wafted around her. "How's it going?"

Spencer gave a half smile. "Better." His eyes dropped to the lined yellow paper in his hand. "I can't stop reading it."

"I don't blame you. It's like one giant answer that comes with a million more questions."

Her words expressed exactly what he was feeling. Spencer should have known that Lorelei would understand. One of their first long talks, over a couple of milkshakes at Tilly's, they'd been two kids connecting over the shared experience of having mystery fathers. His wasn't a complete mystery anymore, but there was an endless list of things he still wanted to know.

Some answers might be found in an obit, but not others. Not the things Spencer really wanted to know. Like did his father enjoy working with his hands? Or did he ever think about coming to see his son?

"Are you going to write her back?" she asked, sitting down next to him on the swing.

The thought had occurred to him. "I don't want to make this time any worse."

"She sent the letter. She had to know someone might write back."

"But she didn't sign it 'Hope to hear from you soon' either."

"Spencer Boyd," Lorelei said, "you're that man's flesh and blood. You're part of their family. The least they can do is give you some answers."

Lorelei was right. Whatever information his mother might cough up would be half-truths and would tell him nothing about the man in the picture. Annie Ramirez was Spencer's only chance to learn more about who he was. And he deserved to know.

"Maybe in a few weeks," he said, "when they've had more time to grieve, I'll send a few questions and see if she answers." Spencer refolded the letter and slipped it back into the envelope, feeling uneasy about reaching out to the strangers with whom he felt no connection. To change the subject, he asked, "What do you have there?"

"Oh," she said, holding the plate higher. "I'm trying a new cookie. Snickerdoodles."

"I've never heard of them."

"I think they're more of a northern thing. Basically a sugar cookie rolled in cinnamon." She stuck the plate under his nose. "Try one and tell me what you think."

They definitely smelled good. "All right," he said, picking up one of the warm cookies. "Is it supposed to be all cracked like that?"

"According to the pictures online, yes."

It looked ready to crumble in his hand. Sticking the letter under his thigh, he broke the treat in half and popped one side in his mouth. He tasted heaven.

"Oh, man," he said with his mouth full. "That's awesome."

"Good." Lorelei hopped off the swing and headed back inside.

"Wait. Let me have another one."

"Sorry," she trilled. "You can't eat the inventory. These are for tomorrow."

He wasn't about to let her get away with that. "Tomorrow my ass," he said, chasing Lorelei into the house.

As the screen door slammed behind him, Spencer never saw the wind carry the letter off the edge of the porch.

By midafternoon, Lorelei had baked and packaged the twelve dozen cookies and moved on to the breads. Spencer had done more than his part, which had won him his own batch of snickerdoodles. Granny returned home from a late lunch with Pearl and stepped inside soaked. What had started as a sunny day turned overcast shortly after noon, and the rain had moved in less than an hour later.

"It's like a monsoon out there," Granny said, shaking the rain out of her gray curls as Lorelei grabbed a towel off the clothes basket near the bottom of the steps.

"Don't you keep an umbrella in the car?" she asked, wrapping the towel around the older woman's shoulders.

"It's in the trunk. I would have gotten even more drenched if I'd taken the time to dig it out."

"Not the best place to keep it then, is it?"

Granny shot Lorelei a dirty look. "It's not as if I knew it was going to do this. Not one of those television weathermen predicted rain today."

"You can't trust 'em," Spencer said from the couch, where he watched a baseball game with Champ curled up at his feet. "You'd have as much luck consulting a Magic 8 Ball as depending on those forecasters."

"I know, I know." Granny slipped off her wet shoes and walked into the kitchen. "It sure smells good in here. Is that cinnamon?"

"It is. I made a new cookie." Lorelei returned to her banana bread mixture. "Well, not new as in I invented it, but new to Lulu's Home Bakery."

"That is such a cute name." Holding the towel tight around her shoulders, Granny examined the cookies through their clear wrap. "Snow was so smart to come up with it."

When Lorelei had told her grandmother about the new name and showed off the amazing logo Snow had designed, which was the word "Lulu's" in a fun and funky font sitting on a brown oval with the words "Home Bakery" tilted on the bottom right-hand side, she'd oohed and aahed with the appropriate enthusiasm, but she'd mentioned nothing that said she understood the name's significance.

"Does the name mean anything to you?" she asked, hoping to trigger something in Granny's memory.

"It means my grandbaby has her own thriving business." A quick check of the bread batter over Lorelei's shoulder and she added, "And Lulu isn't that far from Lore—" The words stopped abruptly. "Oh, my," the older woman said. "That's what your mother called you."

Relieved she hadn't imagined the pet name, Lorelei nodded. "Yeah," was all she could say.

Granny gave her a hug from behind. "That's a good memory. We don't think about those often enough."

Lorelei agreed. This week she would ask Mike to share some stories from his high school days with her mom. She wanted to hear more about the girl Donna Pratchett had been.

"So what did you two do today?" Granny asked. "Besides turn out all these cookies."

The game went to commercial, and Spencer stepped into the kitchen with an empty beer bottle. Lorelei glanced his way with raised brows. They hadn't discussed if he intended to tell Granny about his new discovery. Since it wasn't her news to share, Lorelei stayed quiet, content to support his choice of whether to spill or not.

"I received an interesting piece of mail today," Spencer said, dropping the empty bottle into the recycle bin under the sink.

"How did you get mail on a Sunday?"

"This one came through my mother."

Granny sobered. "Oh. Was this mail good or bad?"

Leaning on the counter, he crossed his arms. "A little of both." Reaching around to his back pocket, Spencer said, "Shit."

"Now, Spencer," Granny scolded.

"Lor, where's the letter?"

"I don't know. You had it."

"I thought it was in my pocket."

"It isn't there?"

"Would I be asking if it was?"

She dropped the wooden spoon into the mixing bowl. "You don't have to get snippy. It has to be here. Where was the last place you had it?"

Spencer checked the couch, flipping the cushions to check underneath. "I was reading it on the porch swing, and then . . ." His words trailed off as they both remembered where he'd put it.

Lorelei reached the door first and barreled down toward the swing. The wind was blowing the rain sideways, spraying drops down her side.

"Is it there?" Spencer yelled over the sound of rain hitting the tin roof. She didn't have to answer, since he could see the swing was empty.

"We'll find it," she said, running back to the steps, then across the yard to the end of the porch. Spencer took a shortcut and hopped over the railing. There, drenched and stuck in the mud, was the precious envelope. Lorelei picked it up, noticing immediately that the return address had washed away. "It's just a little wet," she lied, handing it over.

"It's more than that," he said, wiping off a chunk of mud with his thumb.

"We can fix it. We need to let it dry." Taking him by the hand, she dragged Spencer back to the porch, where Granny stood near the door looking confused.

"Is that your piece of mail?" she asked, pointing to the letter in Spencer's hand.

"It was," he said.

"I'm telling you," Lorelei said, "we can dry it out and it'll be fine."

"Lorelei, the address is gone. We can't bring that back."

"Come on," Granny said, holding the screen door open and waving them both inside. "You won't be fixing anything if you get pneumonia."

Champ met them inside the door, sniffing at the envelope. "Back up, buddy," Spencer said, ignoring the water dripping from his hair. "Rosie, can you bring me a towel so I don't soak your floor?"

Granny brought them each a towel from the basket, then stepped back to sit on a stool beside the island. "What's in this letter that sent you two running out into the rain?"

Wiping down his arms, Spencer answered, "My dad."

By the time they'd shared with Rosie everything that Spencer had learned that afternoon, the envelope had dried enough to examine without shredding to bits in his hands. The return address was definitely gone, but he'd hoped the letter might be intact. As soon as Lorelei gently unfolded the yellow paper, his hopes vanished with the running ink.

"At least the picture is okay," Lorelei said. She'd apologized twice already, as if his leaving the letter on the swing was somehow her fault. Which it wasn't.

"You do look a lot like him, Spencer." Rosie held her reading glasses low on her nose as she examined the image.

"Do you remember him at all?" he asked.

Rosie shook her head. "Not the name or the face. They were rebuilding the old Franklin Street bridge around that time. Lots of young men came into town to do the work, then moved on." Handing the photo back, she added, "Sorry I can't be more help."

Spencer shook his head. "Nothing to apologize for. We're talking thirty years ago. I doubt anyone would remember him."

"There's always your mother," Rosie said. "She should be able to tell you something about him."

"She's been keeping this secret for three decades. It's unlikely she'd be willing to talk about him now. And I'm not sure I'd believe anything she told me anyway." He laid the photo on the island countertop. "What I need is his side of the story. And it's too late for that."

"It isn't too late," Lorelei said. "We'll find Annie Ramirez."

"Lorelei, the return address was somewhere in Dallas. What are the odds she's the only Annie Ramirez in that area?"

Waving his words away, she said, "We have the Internet. You can find anyone with the Internet. She's probably the only Annie Ramirez linked to a Doug Crawford."

"No."

"No what?"

"We're not tracking this woman down." The letter had not included an open invitation for contact. If the family wanted to know him, this aunt of his would have said so. Spencer's gut told him that no good could come out of pursuing this further. The man was gone and nothing was going to bring him back, especially not an unwelcome letter to some mystery aunt.

The stubborn look he knew all too well settled over Lorelei's features. "You have an entire family living in Texas. Relatives, Spencer. Blood relatives. You have to pursue this."

There was nothing to be gained by contacting his father's family, which was how he thought of them. They belonged to the stranger who'd had a fling with his mother and never looked back. They had no connection to Spencer. Now that he'd had some time to think about things, he knew hunting them down would be a waste of time. Nothing he learned would bring his father back.

"When I woke up this morning," he said, "I didn't know who my father was and thought I never would. Now I have a name and a face. And that's enough."

"But—" Lorelei started, until Rosie cut her off.

"It's his choice, Lorelei. If Spencer doesn't want to contact them, you need to let it go."

The younger woman crossed her arms as her jaw worked from side to side. Spencer appreciated Lorelei's tenacity, especially since it was on his behalf, but this time he needed her to give in.

"I'm serious, Lor. This ends here."

Her lips snapped together, and her eyebrows shot up. "Fine. You don't want to contact them, that's your call."

"Yes, it is." She was dying to argue. He could see it practically vibrating through her. But instead, she said, "I have more bread to make," and turned to wash out the mixing bowl in the sink.

Chapter 18

Lorelei tried going to sleep, but she couldn't do it. She couldn't stop thinking about Spencer and the mistake he was making by not contacting his family. Whether he agreed or not, that's what they were. The man could have siblings, or grandparents, or at least a cousin or two. After a lifetime of nothing, he deserved to know more. To feel part of a family where people cared about you. Maybe even looked like you. How could he ignore that?

Though she knew the answer to that question. What if they rejected him? What if they didn't want anything to do with the son Doug Crawford had abandoned? Or worse, what if they thought he only wanted money? Not that there was any indication the man had any, but still. There were plenty of ugly roads this family hunt could go down, and Spencer had likely thought of every one of them.

She didn't blame him. The letter hadn't really read like an open invitation, but maybe the aunt assumed Spencer was the one who wouldn't want to see them? He'd been the abandoned one, after all.

But if he made an effort, maybe they would as well. Surely they'd give him something. Medical history if nothing else. On top of finding out his mother had spent a lifetime keeping his father a secret, and then finding out that father died before Spencer could meet him, he learned that he now had a family history of something.

Cancer. Such an ugly word.

Lorelei didn't want to think about Spencer getting cancer. What would she do if she lost him?

Sitting straight up in bed, she searched the darkness for the intruder who'd put that thought in her head. When had she started thinking about a forever with Spencer? And for that matter, when had she stopped thinking about leaving Ardent Springs? Lorelei couldn't pinpoint the moment, but the idea of leaving hadn't crossed her mind in days. Maybe more than a week.

Good Lord. Had she sniffed too much flour? Lorelei threw off the covers and crossed to the window seat where she had a clear shot of Spencer's apartment. This was all his fault. Helping her find something she enjoyed doing. Getting her a job on top of that. One that she didn't hate and didn't require her to spend long hours on her feet serving ham and eggs to obnoxious drunks.

And then there was that easy charm. Spencer's sweet nature and chiseled body had wormed their way under her skin and back into her heart. Though if she were being honest, Lorelei would have to admit he'd never really left her heart. For twelve years she'd compared every man to Spencer Boyd. None had measured up. And then she'd settled, and look where that had gotten her. Homeless, penniless, and right back where she'd started.

Which wasn't so bad after all. Who'd have guessed Ardent Springs would win her back, the same as Spencer had. And he most certainly had.

Leaning her head back against the wall, Lorelei noted that a light still shone through his window, which meant he was still awake. Couldn't hurt to try to convince him that finding Annie Ramirez was the right thing to do. Since neither one of them was sleeping anyway.

Right, honey child. Tell yourself that's *why you're going down there.*

Lorelei ignored the voice of her conscience and mentally stuck to her story. This was about making Spencer see reason, and that was all.

She kept up the delusion as she slipped on a pair of pajama shorts and crept down the stairs, skipping the ones she knew would squeak beneath her weight. There was no reason to wake Granny, after all. This would be a quick visit, and Lorelei would be back in her bed in no time.

And I have a bridge in Arizona I could sell you, whispered the annoying inner voice.

"Shut up," she whispered back as she fluffed her hair in the mirror of the tiny bathroom at the base of the stairs. As soon as she realized what she was doing, Lorelei turned off the light and marched toward the front door.

Ginger meowed as if to say, "Hussy."

"Hush, fur ball," Lorelei ordered, and then she stepped out of the house, pulling the door shut quietly behind her.

Spencer had tried calling it a night, but there was no use. He'd tossed and turned thinking about his father, his mother, the family he didn't know and never would. There was still time to change his mind. He didn't doubt Lorelei was right that they could find this Annie Ramirez if they really tried. But he couldn't do it. There was no way he was invading a family in mourning.

The only real answer he'd needed had been in that letter. His father was Doug Crawford, and he'd regretted not being in Spencer's life. That little bit of knowledge made all the difference.

But that didn't mean sleep would come anytime soon, so he'd turned on one of the late-night talk shows to drown out the voices in his head, leaning back on the couch with a lap full of black Lab. The moment the interview ended and the show cut to commercial, a knock sounded on his door.

Champ hopped up, wagging his tail as if the person on the other side came bearing treats. "You're a shitty watchdog, you know that?" he said to the animal bouncing with his usual enthusiasm. "Someone ever breaks in here, you'll probably lick him to death before he can steal anything. Not that there's anything here to steal."

Spencer moved the curtain on the door an inch to the right and spotted Lorelei hovering on his porch. It was too dark to see what she was wearing, but it didn't look like much. He'd wanted a distraction, and this was a far better option than Jimmy Fallon. As he pulled the door open, Lorelei stood up straighter and tugged on the hem of the oversized gray shirt that hung precariously low off one shoulder.

He leaned his weight on the doorknob and said, "Little late for a visit, isn't it?"

Lorelei shrugged. "I couldn't sleep."

"So you climbed out of bed, crept across the yard"—he glanced down at her bare feet—"with no shoes on to tell me that?"

She huffed. "Why are you being hateful?"

"'Cause it's fun to see you get mad like that." Spencer couldn't help himself. She was so damn delicious when her temper flared.

With flushed cheeks, she cocked a hip and crossed her arms, which dropped the shirt even lower off her shoulder. By the looks of things, she was cold. Or at least parts of her were. Parts that made Spencer's mouth water.

Tapping a toe, she asked, "Are you going to let me in?"

Spencer pushed the screen door open for her to pass through. "Why not?" he said. "I'm not sleeping either."

"I know," she said, curling her toes into the carpet. "I saw your light on."

The AC in his apartment cranked from the window behind the TV, keeping the temperature inside cool enough to hang meat, which was how Spencer liked it. But when Lorelei shivered, he crossed the room to turn the unit down. "Have a seat and I'll get you a blanket."

"How can you stand it so cold?" she asked, hopping onto the brown tweed and tucking her feet beneath her bottom. "I'm surprised it isn't snowing in here."

"Careful, Lorelei." Spencer dropped an old quilt across her lap. "Your drama queen is showing."

She gave him a one-finger reply.

"Very mature." After settling himself at the opposite end of the couch, he muted the idiot box. As if he didn't already know, Spencer asked, "So what's on your mind?"

Lorelei toyed with the edge of the quilt. "I think you're making a mistake."

"And what mistake is that?" He really didn't want to get into this again. Regardless of how much she argued, Spencer had no intention of changing his mind.

"You know what mistake." Before he could shut her down, she held up her hand, palm out. "Listen for a minute. I know that the letter didn't include any mention of wanting to get to know you or have you meet the family that is rightfully yours." He opened his mouth to argue again, but she shushed him. "I'm not done. I also know that it would suck if you sent something and no one answered. If they rejected you, or worse, accused you of wanting something from them. But you still have to try."

Spencer scrubbed his hands over his face. "Lor, the man died a month ago. Less than a month before that, he announced he had a son somewhere. That's a lot for any family to deal with."

"Maybe having a piece of him there would make them feel better. You could be something good in a tough time."

"Or I could be an interloper."

She leaned an arm along the back of the couch, making the night-shirt fall off the other shoulder. "One conversation and they'd know you had good intentions." Seeing so much smooth skin showing, Spencer struggled to focus on what she was saying. "You have to stop being so stubborn about this."

Shaking the lust fog from his brain, he said, "I'm not being stubborn." In an effort to change the subject, he asked, "Do you want something to drink?"

"Not unless it's hot chocolate." She shivered again. "This blanket isn't helping." He knew one way to warm her up, but he didn't think she'd be open to his idea. "Get over here," she said, holding the blanket open for him to crawl in with her. Spencer hesitated, trying to determine if she was setting him up for something. "Come on. I know you're a damn heater over there. Help a girl out."

He could help her out all right.

Obeying the order, he scooted down the couch and put his arm around her shoulders as Lorelei settled the blanket around them both. "That's better," she sighed, cuddling in tight against his side and laying her head on his shoulder. When she dropped a kiss on his neck, Spencer pulled her in tighter.

"Lorelei?"

"Mm-hmm?" she purred.

"Did you come down here to seduce me?"

Another kiss, this time on his collarbone. "Would that be a bad thing?"

Spencer gave the question real thought. There was still a lot of fragile ground between them. She wasn't offering a lifetime or, for all he knew, anything beyond one night. But when she threw a leg over his lap, his brain function faltered, and the feel of her warm body wrapped around him squelched any ability to protect himself from harm. This had been what he wanted from the moment he'd spotted Lorelei sitting on that airport bench. What he'd dreamed about for years before that.

"Should I take your lack of argument as encouragement?" she asked, lifting off the couch and sliding across his lap until she was straddling him between her thighs.

"Yes," he said, the word coming out as a croak. Spencer cleared his throat. "I highly encourage you to keep doing what you're doing."

Lorelei shot him a smile he remembered all too well, turning his bones to putty. Well, all but one.

"To be clear, I didn't come down here to have sex with you." Her teeth nipped his bottom lip.

"I never said you did," he murmured, sliding his hands around to her bottom. "But we're not going to have sex, Lorelei."

He tried to take her mouth, but she jerked back. "We're not?" she said, eyes wide.

Spencer dipped his hands under her shirt and slid them slowly up her back, enjoying the feel of every muscle twitching at his touch. "No," he said, "we're going to make love."

Lorelei had never been a stickler for semantics, but the way Spencer said *make love* added a whole lot of meaning to something she'd thought was pretty simple when she'd climbed into his lap. No matter what she'd told herself upon sneaking out of the house, she'd wanted this. And the moment Spencer opened the door wearing nothing but black sweats riding low enough on his hips to make her breasts turn traitor, she knew they'd be naked in no time.

But unlike the last time they'd kissed in his apartment, this encounter started more like a slow burn than a flash fire. Spencer had kept his eyes locked on hers as his strong, warm hands slid down her back, and then cupped her face as if she were a fragile piece of china. Lorelei couldn't have looked away if she wanted to. When his thumb grazed her lower lip, seconds before he dropped a kiss on her forehead, her entire body felt as if she'd been shot with a tranquilizer. Heat traveled through her bloodstream and her muscles seemed to melt, while every nerve ending came alive.

As one knuckle slid down the column of her neck, raising goose bumps as it went, Spencer said, "I've been waiting for this for a long time."

She would have offered the same sentiment, but Lorelei was too focused on his touch to form words. This had definitely been a long time coming. Too long.

Fingertips danced across her exposed shoulder as he said, "You're the most beautiful woman I've ever seen." And then he finally took her mouth with his, and sparks turned into flames. Lorelei ran her hands through his hair as the taste of him, sweet and wet and oh so hot, filled her senses. She rocked against him, telling him with her body what she couldn't say with words. How had she ever given this up? And how had she waited so long to have it again?

Her movements turned frantic. No matter how she moved, she couldn't get close enough. Spencer broke the kiss to pull Lorelei's shirt over her head, an action she would have protested, but he immediately took one sensitive nipple between his teeth and all she could do was hold on. Her nails dug into his broad shoulders as he pulled her closer, angling his hips until she could feel him pressed against her core. She drove down at the same moment he bit, and Lorelei nearly exploded right there in his lap.

"We need," she panted, "less clothes."

"We'll get there," he said as he shifted to the left to give her other nipple equal attention.

The pressure continued to build as her body temperature soared. Being cold was definitely no longer a problem. Not with Spencer's mouth on her breast and his hands on her ass. When he dragged a hand over her thigh to press a thumb against her clit, she really did explode.

Her scream echoed in the tiny space, followed seconds later by Champ's deep bark. As Lorelei's forehead hit Spencer's shoulder, she was laughing, even as the currents still pulsed to her toes. "Was that a warning bark, or more a good-job-way-to-go thing?" she asked, unable to resist dropping a kiss on his moist skin.

"I'm not sure," Spencer said. Lorelei was happy to notice he sounded out of breath. "But I'll gladly say that was a good job, way to go."

Lorelei nibbled his earlobe. "You did all the work. Now I think it's my turn to help you out."

"That would be appreciated, because I'm about to die." Without warning, Spencer stood up, taking Lorelei with him. She wasn't small by any stretch of the imagination, but he didn't seem to be struggling. She wrapped her legs around his waist, locking her ankles as he said, "Stay." Presumably to the dog.

There was no need to ask where they were going as Spencer turned toward the only area of the apartment she had yet to enter. With only the light of one lamp on the living room end table and the glow from the muted television, Lorelei's quick glance behind her revealed little more than a large bed and a chest of drawers in the corner. When they reached the end of the mattress, Spencer lowered her down slowly and crawled onto the comforter with her.

"Are you still cold?" he asked. "Do you want to get under the blankets?"

What a crazy question. Surely he could feel the heat pouring off of her. With a shake of her head, she said, "You're all I want right now, Spencer. Just you."

Instead of responding, he stayed still, leaned up on his elbow, staring at her as if trying to memorize everything about her. Then he brushed a lock of hair off her forehead and said, "And you're all I want, Lor. The only one I've ever wanted."

Chapter 19

A punch of guilt hit Lorelei in the stomach as her encounter with Carrie came roaring back.

"Do you know what it's like to lay next to a man, all the while knowing he wished you were someone else?"

Stilling Spencer's hand, she said, "Did I ruin your marriage?" The words were out before she knew it, and all she wanted to do was take them back. What the hell was the matter with her?

His entire body tensed as his mouth stretched into a straight line. "What did you say?"

Lorelei grabbed the side of the comforter as she pulled away and sat up. Holding the blanket across her breasts, she said, "That's what your ex-wife says. That you wished she was me."

Spencer shook his head as he sat up. "What are you talking about? When did you talk to my ex-wife?"

"At Brubaker's," Lorelei answered. "In the bathroom."

"And she said *you* ruined my marriage? Her memory is a bit faulty considering she's the one who slept with someone else."

Scooting closer, she said, "Tell me you didn't look at her and see me. Tell me I wasn't some invisible other woman."

Lorelei needed to hear the words. After what she'd done in California, how she'd been the torpedo that blew up another woman's family, she needed to hear that she hadn't done it twice.

"This is crazy," Spencer said, running a hand through his hair.

"That's not an answer."

"What do you want from me, Lorelei?" he asked, leaping off the bed. "You want me to say I didn't miss you? That I stopped loving you? I can't, okay? But dammit, I went into that marriage knowing exactly who I was marrying, and I'd have stayed married if she hadn't cheated on me."

Not the reassuring words she needed. "And what if you were still married now? What if when I came back, you were still with her?"

Spencer threw his hands in the air. "That's a crazy question. I'm not married. I haven't been married for five years. I never cheated on my wife, with you or anyone else. And I wouldn't have, even if you came home sooner." Turning his back on her, he propped his hands on his hips. "I can't believe you'd bring this up now. Why didn't you tell me you talked to Carrie?"

How did she answer that? Why hadn't she told him the minute she returned to the table? Because she'd been afraid he'd tell her the accusation was true. That she'd been the ghost in the bedroom.

"I never wanted to hurt anyone," she said, wiping away the tear that rolled down her cheek. "I never mean to make a mess, but I do. It's like a curse."

Climbing back onto the bed, Spencer brushed the next tear away. "You didn't hurt anyone, Lor. I swear to you, I loved my wife. Maybe not the way I loved you, but that's how life works. You never love two people the same. That doesn't mean one is any less than the other."

Lorelei had truly believed she loved Maxwell. And Spencer was right, it wasn't the same way she'd loved him, but it still felt real. And it still hurt when it all fell apart.

"I wanted you to be happy. I really did." She laid a hand against his cheek. "I'd hate to think that I stood in the way of that happening."

Pulling her against him, Spencer said, "You never stood in the way of my happiness." After kissing the top of her head, he added, "Though you're kind of doing that right now with all this crazy talk."

She couldn't help but laugh. "I'm sorry. My timing was always a little off."

Working the comforter out of her grasp, he said, "I know how you could make it up to me."

"You still want to have sex with me, all snotty and red-eyed?" she asked, letting go of the blanket.

Spencer stilled. "Hold on," he said, once again leaping off the bed and returning a second later with a wadded-up T-shirt.

Lorelei eyed the shirt suspiciously. "Are you suggesting I put on a shirt?"

The man had the nerve to roll his eyes. "I don't have tissues. This is to blow your nose."

Right. Like that would be sexy. "You can't be serious."

"You owe me double now," he said, shaking out the shirt. "Here." Spencer held the cotton to her nose as if she were a three-year-old.

"Give me that," she said, snatching it out of his hand. Lorelei paused long enough to give him a dirty look before turning her back on him and blew her nose. She used the sleeve to wipe her eyes, then faced him again to hand it back. "There. Happy?"

"The hamper is next to the dresser." He indicated a tall black hamper over his right shoulder. Lorelei tossed the shirt and by some miracle made it in. "Excellent shot," Spencer said, crawling up the bed and dropping onto a pillow flat on his back.

"Um," Lorelei said. "What are you doing?"

"Waiting for you to make it up to me." Lifting his head off the pillow, he added, "Twice."

The mood was totally gone, but he did still look crazy hot. His sweats had drifted lower as he'd moved up the bed, revealing an inviting trail of light brown hair running from his belly button and disappearing behind his waistband. She could see he was no longer standing at attention, which almost felt like a challenge. Lorelei never could walk away from a challenge.

Joining him up on the pillows, she lay on her side, close enough to feel his body heat, but not so close that they touched. Lorelei leaned her head on her hand and watched him for a minute, lying with his eyes closed and a smile on his lips. He was so smug. And she didn't mind it one bit.

But she also couldn't make this too easy. "How exactly are you expecting me to make this up to you?" she asked. "Twice?"

One eye popped open. "Use your imagination."

Lorelei nodded and the eye closed again. "I could bake you some cookies."

That got both eyes open. "Not for this. This is going to require something more . . . hands-on."

"Bread then," she said. "I have to knead the dough with my hands, so that should count."

Flopping onto his side, Spencer copied her position and narrowed his eyes. "You're playing a dangerous game, Ms. Pratchett. If you refuse to pay up, I'm going to have to collect payment myself."

She lifted one brow. "I'm not afraid of you, Mr. Boyd."

Spencer knocked her elbow so her head fell onto the pillow, and he was on top of her before she could blink. "That's it," he said, pinning her hands above her head. "Time to pay up."

Wiggling her hips against his, she said, "Happily," and took his mouth with hers.

Lorelei let him think he'd been in charge, for about two seconds. He was still riding the surge of feeling her press up against him when Spencer found his back to the mattress and the woman he'd been about to ravage ravaging him. After kissing him into delirium for what felt like an hour, she dragged her lips down the column of his throat, slowly, then gave his left nipple a quick, unexpected bite.

Spencer gurgled something, but forming actual words became impossible when she slid lower, licking his abs while her hands explored well below his waistband. Though the brief interruption had cooled his body, Lorelei was driving him back to dangerous heat levels in record time. When she dragged her nails over his ribs while her other hand grasped him through his sweatpants, Spencer's body jerked hard enough to smack the headboard against the wall.

"You okay up there, big boy?" Lorelei asked, her voice sultry and low, her fingers slipping inside his pants.

"Uh-huh," he managed, lifting his hips without needing instructions. The pants landed somewhere on the floor, but Spencer couldn't have guessed where since Lorelei's breath had wisped over the head of his dick as soon as he'd sprung free. Spencer preferred to sleep naked, so he'd not bothered with underwear after his shower.

"Commando, huh? Does that mean you still sleep in your birthday suit?"

This time his only response was a quick nod of affirmation. Her slender fingers had found his balls, and any blood that might have still been near his skull rushed to join the party going on in the lower hemisphere.

After touching her tongue to his throbbing tip, Lorelei whispered, "Is this the kind of imagination you were hoping for?"

A guttural moan filled the air as she took him deep without waiting for a reply. Spencer had a faint memory of the two of them engaging in this kind of activity during their high school days, but those rushed, stolen moments in the backseat of old Beluga, or on a blanket on the riverbank, had nothing on this. This was . . . There were no words for this.

As Lorelei drove him crazy, all Spencer could do was hold on. To the sheets. To his pillow. To her hair. When he was almost there, Lorelei rose up to her knees and grasped both his hands as she took him over the edge. She rode out every spasm with him, their hands joined in a white-knuckle grip. His body was on fire, and he felt completely useless when she was done with him. If the world fell down around them in that moment, he couldn't have lifted an arm to protect them.

She'd literally sucked him dry, of energy as well as everything else. And all he could do was smile.

"You look very pleased with yourself," she said, dropping kisses along his torso as she fit her body against his side.

"Nope," he said. "I'm very pleased with you."

Her laughter felt like a prize from the gods. Spencer couldn't believe that after twelve long years, Lorelei was back in his arms. Back in his bed. As she nuzzled close against him, all he could think was that if this was all a dream, he never wanted to wake up.

Lorelei hadn't felt this content in a very long time. If the sun never again broke the horizon, she'd be perfectly fine lying here beside Spencer in an endless night, pretending that nothing else mattered outside of this apartment. That she'd never screwed up anyone else's life, and that maybe, just maybe, she wouldn't screw up Spencer's ever again.

That was probably too much to hope for, but she clung to the belief nonetheless.

"You're not drifting off on me, are you?" Spencer asked, playing with a lock of hair over her ear.

Stretching and tossing a leg over his thigh, she said, "I'm enjoying the moment."

Spencer pulled up his knee, which tugged her leg up to press against the very personal part of him she'd thoroughly explored not long ago. He was already growing hard.

Rubbing against him, she said, "Impressive recovery time."

"What can I say?" he whispered, turning until they were facing each other with her leg over his hip and his tip pressing against her shorts. "You bring out the best in me. But I've noticed a little problem."

She edged closer, dropping tiny kisses along his solid jawline, enjoying the feel of the sharp whiskers that, if she were lucky, would redden her own delicate skin before long.

A strong hand slid down the small of her back and inside her underwear behind the shorts. "You're wearing way too much right now."

Though she hated to pull away from him, the chance to let him watch her undress, even if it were only a simple pair of shorts, was too much to pass up.

"Then I'd better fix that." Lorelei rolled backward and spun so her feet hit the floor.

"Where are you going?"

"Not too far," she answered, turning to face him as she dipped her thumbs inside her waistband and pressed down. She watched Spencer's eyes as he watched her body. The television glowed brighter, letting her see his brown depths turn nearly black with desire. His reaction was like a touch, dragging her back across the bed on her knees until she was astride him once again.

"Better?"

"Perfect," he said, pulling her down for a deep, hot kiss that lasted long enough to have them both gasping for air. "I need to be inside you. We need to reach the nightstand."

Lorelei was so lost in arousal, it took her several seconds to understand what he was saying. Since she wasn't on any kind of birth control, they definitely needed what was in his nightstand. She nodded and dropped to the left, with Spencer rolling with her until he was on top. He reached into the drawer, continuing to feather kisses along her shoulder until he left her long enough to rip the package open with his teeth.

"Nice move," she said. "I can take it from here." Spencer lifted his hips to give her access, and Lorelei slid the condom home. "Now it's both of our turns." She pulled one leg high as he settled back against her, loving the feel of his weight and heat surrounding her. She may have thought she'd come home the day Spencer picked her up at the airport, but Lorelei had been wrong.

This was coming home.

Holding himself up on his elbows, he slid a thumb along her bottom lip, lying still as they stared at one another. "Thank you," he said, his mouth no longer smiling.

"For what?" she asked.

"For this," he said, running his knuckles down her arm. "For all of this."

A tear threatened again, but one of joy, not hurt or regret. The fact that this wonderful man was willing to forgive her was the greatest gift Lorelei had ever received. That he was also willing to let her back into his heart was more than she ever deserved. But she was selfish enough to take it all, and only hoped she would someday earn it.

"I told you, Lorelei," Spencer said, the corner of his mouth hinting at one of his charming grins. "Faults and all." With those words, he took her mouth in such a sweet kiss that she couldn't hold back the tear any longer. As it slid down her cheek to drop somewhere on the pillow, she kissed him back with everything she was feeling, hoping he'd understand what she wasn't ready to say with words.

His mouth still on hers, Spencer danced a hand over her breast, then lower to slip between her legs. He teased her until she was writhing off the bed, then slipped inside, but it wasn't enough. "Please, Spencer. I'm ready. Please," she begged.

Seconds later, he gave her what she wanted, driving in slowly at first, then picking up the pace. Lorelei pulled both knees up and pressed her heels into the bed as the pressure built. She met him thrust for thrust, holding tight to his neck and shoulders, their tongues mimicking the action of their bodies. When she was close to the peak, his hand shifted lower, pressing circles to the spot he knew would take her over the edge. She didn't just fall over, she flew, digging her nails into Spencer's back, pulling him closer, as if that were humanly possible.

The tremors were still pulsating down to her toes when Spencer drove hard and came apart himself. They held on to each other, their bodies wet and hot and locked together as if they might never let go. Spencer shifted as if to pull out, but Lorelei locked her ankles.

"Not yet," she whispered. "Not yet."

Spencer nodded, his breathing ragged as he dropped his forehead onto her shoulder. She could feel the smile dancing on her own lips, and imagined a rainbow glowing somewhere close by.

Chapter 20

Spencer woke to the feeling of hot dog breath on his cheek. The clock read 5:49, eleven minutes before his alarm would normally go off. Lorelei slept soundly beside him, with one lock of blonde hair tumbling over her eyes. He considered moving it, but didn't want to wake her. It was rare to see her this peaceful, and he wanted to enjoy her for a few minutes more. Especially since he had no idea what would happen when she woke up.

Was last night a one-off? Would she regret coming to his apartment? Would she grin and stretch and crawl on top of him for morning sex?

Not that Spencer didn't already have morning wood, but that thought made the condition almost painful. The sheet covering nothing from the top of her delicious bottom up didn't help either. When Champ whined, Spencer caved. The animal had to pee and so did he. Scooting off the bed as gently as he could, he managed to extricate himself from the covers, pull on his sweats, and get the dog outside without waking her.

In fact, he also managed to take care of his own business, let the dog back in, and climb in the shower as she softly snored away. It wasn't until he had put on a pair of jeans and was buttoning his shirt that she started to come around. Stretching like a cat, she rolled onto her back, revealing the body of a goddess. Spencer stopped buttoning. He lost feeling in his fingers the moment she pushed the hair out of her face and glanced around as if not sure of her location.

"Morning," he said, his voice rougher than intended.

Lorelei's head turned his way with a look of confusion, and then her eyes went wide. "What time is it?" she asked, her voice frantic enough to worry him.

Spencer checked the clock beside the bed. "Six twenty-eight. I have to leave in a couple minutes. I have an early meeting this morning."

He'd planned to wake her on his way out so she could get ready for work. He liked the idea of kissing her good-bye before leaving for his day.

"Holy crap," she said, scrambling off the bed. "Where are my clothes?"

This didn't sound like a woman happy to be kissed good-bye.

"Your shirt is probably still around the couch somewhere." Spencer walked around the bed. "Here are your shorts and panties." He lifted the clothing off the floor, and Lorelei snatched them from his fingers.

"Why didn't you wake me up?"

Opting not to contribute to her dramatics, he opened his top dresser drawer and pulled out a pair of socks. "I didn't think you needed to be up before now," he said, sitting on the edge of the bed to put his socks on. "I thought you might be tired. We didn't get much sleep."

The last time he'd seen the clock, the numbers were rolling toward three thirty.

"I can't believe I'm still here," she mumbled, dragging the panties up her legs and following with the shorts. Holding an arm across her chest, she stormed into the living room to find the shirt. "I should have been back in my room hours ago."

Last Spencer checked, they weren't kids sneaking around to have sex. Granny wasn't going to ground Lorelei or give them a speech about being too young to go so far. At least he didn't think so.

"Am I missing something here?" he asked, walking into the kitchen to fill his travel coffee cup. "Are you embarrassed about what we did last night?"

That question got her attention. Lorelei pulled her shirt over her head and looked his way. "No, are you?"

"Not at all, but I'm not the one acting like a crazy person right now. What does it matter if you go home now or if you went a couple hours ago?"

"I don't want Granny to know, that's all."

"Why not?"

Lorelei huffed. "I just don't."

"That's not an answer."

Running a hand through her hair, she said, "Granny is going to ask a bunch of questions that I'm not ready to answer. Maybe if I'm lucky, she's not up yet."

"Does that mean I shouldn't ask any questions either?" There were several running through his head, but Spencer knew how easily Lorelei spooked. This was definitely a spooking situation.

With a deep breath, Lorelei cut her eyes to the heavens as if praying for patience. Or a way out. "I don't regret last night, but I don't know what last night means long-term. What I do know is that I'd really like to repeat last night on a regular basis for the foreseeable future. How's that?"

He didn't like the avoidance of dealing with anything beyond the present, but the fact that she didn't consider the night before a mistake, and was suggesting he get more sex on a regular basis, made Spencer less inclined to argue.

Hiding the smile behind his coffee cup, he said, "You look sexy as hell right now."

She shook her head. "I'm sure I look like crap right now. I need a toothbrush and a shower."

"Now I wish I'd dragged you into the shower with me." He must have been exhausted not to have thought of *that* sooner.

"There would still have been the toothbrush issue." Lorelei dropped a kiss on his cheek and padded toward the door.

"That's all I get?"

The grin she shot him from the door brought on a new case of morning wood. "I'll make it up to you tonight," she promised, then disappeared down the steps.

Lorelei felt like a spy on a mission. She high-footed her way across the yard, running up the porch steps and pressing her body against the side of the house. She'd auditioned for a cop show once and realized that she would have felt like an idiot doing this on a daily basis. Chancing a peek through the kitchen window, Lorelei didn't see lights on or movements inside. Letting out the breath she hadn't realized she was holding, she opened the screen and tried the inside door. It was locked.

"Shoot," she murmured. Had she locked the door on her way out? She didn't think so. Lorelei hadn't intended to be gone all night, so why lock the door? Did that mean Granny was up? That she'd locked the door? "Crap, crap, crap."

The spare key. When she was a teen it had always been under the ceramic frog in the flower bed. Glancing over the rail, Lorelei was relieved to see the frog still sitting on his lily pad. "Oh, thank God."

Bouncing back down the steps, she had to step into the mulch to reach the smiling amphibian. "Would it have been so hard to grab flip-flops, Lorelei?" she admonished herself. Lifting the frog, she found nothing. This was not her morning. And if she didn't get in soon,

Spencer would catch her out here traipsing around like an incompetent cat burglar.

Climbing back onto the porch, Lorelei racked her brain to figure out where else the spare key might be. But before she came up with an answer, the inside door opened, scaring her so badly she nearly peed herself. She also screamed bloody murder.

"Was that necessary?" Granny asked, as her granddaughter held a hand over her racing heart and struggled to catch her breath.

"I didn't expect you to open the door," Lorelei panted.

"I didn't expect you to be on that side of it."

Point to Granny.

"Fine," she said. "You caught me. Now can I come in?"

Without responding, Granny walked away, leaving Lorelei staring through the screen. She'd taken a walk of shame or two in her life, but none had ever felt like this. As if she'd kicked a puppy, run over a kitten, and swiped a Happy Meal from a toddler all in one move. If Spencer hadn't been so damn distracting last night, she might have remembered to order a wake-up call. Or, if she'd been smart, she would have come home before they'd gotten to round three.

Or had that been four?

"I made a pot of coffee," Granny said as Lorelei closed the door. "Or were you planning to go back to bed? I'm guessing you didn't get much sleep last night."

Lorelei had expected twenty questions, not a VIP ticket to guilt city.

"I'll take a cup," she said, expecting Granny to pour. She'd expected wrong. "I guess I'll get it."

As she pulled a mug from the cupboard, her grandmother turned a page of the paper laid out on the island. She didn't ask any more questions, instead ignoring Lorelei completely. Though it was obvious by the set of her jaw that she was holding something in.

"Is there a reason you look ready to spit nails?" Lorelei asked.

Turning another page, Granny looked up, blue eyes glaring over the reading glasses. "What are your intentions toward that boy?" she asked.

The question took Lorelei by surprise. She'd expected excitement that they might be getting back together. Even if only tentatively. She'd expected talk of marriage and babies and forever. So why did Granny look angry? And shouldn't she have been grilling Spencer about *his* intentions toward her granddaughter?

"First of all," Lorelei said, "he's not a boy. And second, what kind of a question is that?"

"You hurt him once. And he's been through a lot more in the ensuing years than getting over teenage heartbreak. After what he learned yesterday, I can't believe you'd take advantage of him like this."

She took advantage of *him*? Really?

"Your high opinion of me is flattering." Lorelei put the mug back in the cupboard. "I'm going to take a shower."

"Don't you walk away from me, missy." Granny blocked her path out of the kitchen. "Are you staying here for good?"

Lorelei chewed the inside of her cheek. This was the question she wasn't ready to answer. Could she settle into a life in Ardent Springs? Admittedly, the town hadn't been unbearable since she'd been home, but it hadn't even been a month yet. It could get worse. It would probably get worse.

"I don't know," she finally admitted. The most honest answer she had.

"Then you better figure it out. Spencer loves you, and he always has. I know you love him. I can see it every time you're in the same room together."

"It isn't that simple."

Granny threw her hands in the air. "There you go again, making every gosh darn thing more complicated than it needs to be. Your grandfather was always right about that." Slamming her hands onto her hips, she said, "Your grandfather loved that boy, too. Told me before he died he could go in peace knowing you had a good man to take care of you."

That admission hit like a blow. "I never knew that," she whispered.

"I suppose I should have told you, but I didn't want you staying here out of guilt or obligation. You'd have turned out bitter and angry, and I watched what that did to your mother." The steam seemed to go out of her as Granny's shoulders fell. "I couldn't watch the same happen to you."

"Why was Mama so bitter?" Lorelei asked, a question she'd never had the guts to mutter aloud. Deep down, she'd always believed her own existence to be her mother's greatest regret.

Granny shook her head. "Your mother made some choices she couldn't live with, but didn't have the courage to change."

"What?" Lorelei asked. "Like the choice of having me?"

"Don't ever say that again, young lady. Your mother's mistakes were plenty, but you were not one of them." Taking Lorelei's hands, her voice gentled. "You're getting a second chance at something a lot of folks never find at all. This time around, follow your heart. That's the only way you're ever going to be happy."

Squeezing the older woman's hands, Lorelei asked, "What if I don't know what my heart is telling me to do?"

"You'll know," Granny said. "You'll know." Turning back to her paper, she added, "And next time, tell me when you're leaving the house. I nearly had a heart attack last night until I figured out where you were."

Lorelei took a step toward the stairs, then stopped. "Last night?"

"I heard a noise. Must have been you shutting the door on your way out." Glancing over her glasses once more, she said, "You're lucky I didn't come down there and drag you back. Don't think I didn't consider it."

Trying to calculate how quickly they'd gotten naked and how much her grandmother would have seen, Lorelei sent up a silent prayer of thanks that Granny had stayed in the house. "No more sneaking around," she said, giving Granny's shoulders a hug. "I do love you, you know."

"Yes," Granny said, patting her arm, "I know. Now go take a shower. You smell like sex."

Lorelei nearly choked on her tongue hearing such a statement from her grandmother. The mortification kept her silent and carried her up the stairs as fast as her feet would go.

Chapter 21

Spencer felt extremely pleased with his current lot in life. He had a name and a face for his father, and Lorelei was back in his arms. As far as windfalls went, a man couldn't ask for much more. It would have been nice to know more about his dad, but he'd meant every word he'd said to Lorelei the night before. He would not invade the man's family. Maybe someday he'd reach out and see if someone reached back, but for now he'd be content with what he had, which was a lot more than he'd ever dreamed would come his way.

"You're looking chipper this morning," Mike Lowry said, stopping near Spencer's table in Tilly's Diner. "Have a good weekend?"

Spencer had stopped for lunch, but he hadn't been seated long enough to order his food yet. The mention of the weekend widened his smile. "Best weekend I've had in a while. How about you?"

Mike nodded. "Not bad, but probably not as good as yours." Rubbing his chin, he added, "Lorelei was looking chipper herself this morning."

Now things were getting awkward. If Lorelei didn't want Rosie to know they were back together, or whatever she'd call it, then no one else could know either.

"I guess the chipper thing is going around." Pointing to the seat across from him, he asked, "Want to sit down?"

"I can do that." Mike dropped onto the red vinyl and placed his black cowboy hat upside down on the seat next to him.

Jeanne returned to the table, took their orders, and then left the men alone once more. With the news about his father, Spencer had done some math to figure out who might have been around at the time Doug Crawford was in Ardent Springs. He may not be ready to reach out to Texas, but that didn't mean he wasn't curious to learn something. By his calculations, Mike would have still been in town.

"When did you head down to Nashville?" he asked, hoping his new lunch companion wouldn't consider him nosy.

Mike crossed his arms on the table. "Thirty-one years ago this month, as a matter of fact." Shaking his head, he added, "No wonder it feels like a lifetime ago."

So Spencer's math *was* right. "You went to school with my mom, didn't you?"

"Paula was in my history class." He tapped his temple. "Or maybe it was English."

"Do you remember when they built the bridge out on Franklin?" he asked, aware that his questions were all over the place, but impatient to get to the point.

With confusion in his eyes, Mike answered, "Sure. I was part of the crew. Are you going somewhere with this?"

Flashing an apologetic smile, Spencer said, "Yeah, I am. Do you remember a guy named Doug Crawford? He wasn't a local, but I understand he might have come to town to help with the construction."

"I remember Doug. He was a good guy. Didn't talk much, but I know he spent a lot of his off time with your mom."

Spencer's heart kicked like an angry mule. He couldn't believe he'd gotten lucky on the first shot.

"Do you remember anything else about him?" Spencer asked. "Did he mention his family at all?"

Mike shook his head. "Like I said, he didn't talk much. I get the sense this isn't idle curiosity."

Tugging his wallet from his back pocket, Spencer drew out the picture. "Does that look like the man you remember?" There was no need to reveal the truth if they weren't talking about the same person.

Squinting a bit, Mike pulled the photo his way. "It's been a long time, but the eyes look the same." As if a revelation hit, his head shot up. "Same as your eyes. What is Doug Crawford to you?"

Spencer felt odd saying the words. "He's my father. I found out yesterday."

"You didn't know?"

"My mother always said *she* didn't know. She claimed it could have been any number of guys and they were all worthless, so I wasn't missing anything."

Mike handed the picture back. "How old are you? I thought Doug left town before I did."

"I'll be thirty-one next February," Spencer answered. "I guess Mom must have been pregnant with me when you left."

The usually friendly expression on Mike's face grew serious. "Then how old is Lorelei? I thought you were both about twenty-eight."

"She's two months older than I am. Didn't you see her date of birth when you hired her?"

His eyes dropped to the table, unfocused. "I had her enter her own information into the computer." Lifting his hat off the seat, Mike slid from the booth. "I need to go," he said.

"But what about your lunch?"

"Tell Jeanne to cancel the order."

With no further explanation, the business owner charged out of the restaurant like a man on a mission, leaving Spencer to wonder if he'd said something wrong. What did Lorelei's age matter to Mike? Then a thought occurred. Maybe Mike knew who Lorelei's father was as well. Spencer's mom, Lorelei's mom, and Lowry had all gone to school together.

The story Lorelei had been given was that her mom had gone on a spring break trip and had come back pregnant. No one knew the identity of the father, and the expectant mother's story was that she didn't remember a name. But maybe that wasn't true.

Spencer's mother had lied to him. What if Lorelei's mother had lied, too?

"Jeanne!" he yelled, gaining the waitress's attention where she stood behind the counter. "Cancel our orders."

"But they're already cooking."

The waitress didn't get a response, as Spencer charged through the door the same way Mike had.

Lorelei had hoped Spencer might bring her lunch. She'd been thinking about him all day, replaying the night before in her mind, which only resulted in lots of squirming in her chair. She kept catching herself grinning like a fool while alphabetizing stacks of vendor invoices from earlier in the year. Trying to wipe the smile from her face only worked for minutes at a time. At this rate, her cheeks would be sore by the end of the day.

Granny had told her to follow her heart, and right now her heart wanted nothing but Spencer. Though the bit about her mother growing bitter over her own choices still nagged at the back of her mind. What did that mean? From Lorelei's earliest memory, her mother carried a sadness about her. There were moments, when she was playing with Lorelei and maybe forgot the rest of the world, when a genuine smile would split her face. But those memories were few and far between, faded by time.

As a little girl, Lorelei didn't know what depression was. She only knew her mom was always tired, and at some point she stopped getting out of bed. Eventually, Lorelei went to live with Granny and Pops and only saw her mother a couple times a month, if that. The memories of the drunken binges were the strongest, because they'd come at the end of her mother's life. It had always struck Lorelei as ironic that the one day her mother stayed sober, for her daughter's eleventh birthday, she'd been killed by a drunk driver.

That was when Lorelei changed from the confused little girl who wanted nothing but to be with her mom, to the angry teen who didn't care about anyone but herself. And the new version had stuck around for a long time. Stubborn to a fault, with a chip on her shoulder that should have been knocked off years before. The chip wasn't completely gone, and likely never would be, but she *was* getting a second chance, and she'd be a moron to throw it away.

Maybe if her mom had gotten a second chance, she'd still be around. Maybe she'd have found a man, one worth sticking around for, and forgotten that a stranger had knocked her up on a spring break trip. Then again, with Lorelei as a constant reminder, how could she ever have forgotten that fact?

"You deserved better, Mom," she said aloud. "You deserved so much better."

Lorelei finished with the March stack of invoices, set them aside to file, and then took a potty break. Spencer was clearly not coming, so she might as well grab the sandwich she'd brought for lunch from the fridge. But before she turned the corner into the hall, her phone started playing "Macho Man," the ringtone that indicated Spencer was calling. He'd put the ringtone on himself, and she had yet to figure out how to change it. The infernal smartphone was sure as heck smarter than she was.

"Hello," she said in greeting. "Why haven't you brought me lunch yet?"

"Is Mike there?" Spencer asked, sounding out of breath. Had he really called *her* cell phone looking for her boss? After what they'd done last night, he couldn't bother with so much as a "Hi, baby"?

"No, he isn't," she ground out, tempted to hang up on him.

"Has he called you in the last five minutes or so?"

Now he was making her worry. "No. Why? Did something happen? Has there been an accident at a job site or something?"

With a loud sigh, Spencer said, "Maybe I'm wrong then."

"Wrong about what?" Lorelei dropped into her desk chair. "Spencer, you're not making any sense. What's this about?"

"I don't know," he said. "I ran into Mike at Tilly's and asked if he remembered Doug Crawford."

"And did he?" That Spencer was still asking questions meant he might still give in and contact his aunt.

"Yeah. He said Crawford didn't talk much and spent a lot of time with my mom."

"We knew that. At least the part about being with your mom. What else did he say?"

"Nothing. He asked how old I was, and then how old you are. When I told him, he said he had to go and left the diner."

"What do our ages have to do with anything?" When Spencer didn't answer right away, she prodded, "What are you not telling me?"

In a quiet voice, Spencer said, "I think he might know who your father is."

Lorelei sat up straighter. "That's not possible. Mom was on a trip. No one knows who my father is."

"But what if that's just what you were told?" She could almost see him lifting his cowboy hat to run a hand through his hair. "What if your mom lied like mine did?"

There was no way. Lorelei's mother was nothing like Spencer's. She hadn't been hateful and selfish. She'd been depressed, not evil.

"She wouldn't have done that."

After another hesitation, Spencer agreed. "You're right. She wouldn't have. I'm sure I jumped to the wrong conclusion."

And he'd put that same conclusion into her head now. What if there *was* someone a phone call away who could tell Lorelei who her father was?

What if Granny had known all along?

A stab that felt way too real pierced Lorelei's heart. This was ridiculous. Her mother had taken a spring break trip to the Gulf two months before graduating high school and had gotten knocked up by some anonymous guy who hadn't even given her his last name. No one had lied to Lorelei, especially not her own family.

But what if . . . ?

"Lor, you still there?" Spencer asked. "Hon, forget I said anything. It was stupid. I'm letting all this stuff with my mom cloud my judgment. Mike probably had an appointment he forgot about."

Lorelei knew Mike didn't have any lunchtime appointments today. And he'd known her mom. They'd gone to school together. Maybe she'd confided in him and no one else. Maybe he could give her answers he didn't know were secrets after all these years.

"I'm fine," she said. Lorelei didn't want Spencer coming to check on her. If Mike did come back, she didn't want anyone else around. "No worries. I'll see you tonight, okay?"

If she'd ever had any hint of acting skills, Lorelei hoped they'd come through for her now.

"You sure?" Spencer asked, sounding less than convinced.

"Yes, I'm sure. I've got a stack of invoices to file, and I still need to eat lunch." Staring unseeing at the papers on her desk, she added, "Do me a favor and grab the cookie trays from Snow's, would you? I need to pick up some ingredients for tomorrow, and I'd rather not backtrack to the shop."

She also intended to wait for Mike to return to the office. The week before he'd given her a key so she could go without having to wait for him to lock up. Today she would wait.

"I can do that. But Lorelei?" Spencer said.

"Yeah."

"I'm sorry."

"It's fine. Really." Lorelei added extra cheer to her voice. "I have a call coming in on the office line. Talk to you later."

After Spencer said good-bye, Lorelei dropped the cell and stared at her computer screen. The image of Mike Lowry wearing a hard hat while standing next to his company truck stared back.

"Do you know something I don't know, Mr. Lowry?"

"Yeah, I do," said a voice from behind her. Lorelei spun in her chair to see her boss standing in the doorway twisting the brim of his cowboy hat between his fingers. "We need to talk."

Chapter 22

It was a rare occasion in Lorelei Pratchett's life when she was scared speechless. But Mike's words had definitely done the trick.

We need to talk.

Was she about to find out that her dad was some loser she'd seen a million times growing up? Or maybe he was a musician who'd been playing at a crappy bar in Gulf Shores and seduced her country-bumpkin mother on a dare. Sadly, Lorelei couldn't figure out which scenario she preferred. In fact, blissful ignorance was sounding better and better by the second.

After hanging his hat on the coat rack in the back corner, Mike rolled his desk chair around the office until it was a few feet from Lorelei's. He sat down with a resigned sigh, leaned his elbows on his knees, and stared at her for several seconds. Lorelei waited for him to blurt out the news. To spit it out so she could deal and move on.

"Right," Mike said, running his hands over his face. "Where do I start?"

"I don't know, but you need to start somewhere, because if what Spencer thinks is true and you don't tell me soon, I'm going to lose my mind."

Mike sat back in his chair and crossed his arms. "What day were you born?" he asked.

"December 19, 1984," she answered, biting her tongue as she fought for patience.

"Damn," her boss said, lifting his eyes toward the ceiling. "Why didn't you tell me?"

"I put it on my paperwork when I started," Lorelei replied. And then she realized he wasn't talking to her. Everything went still as the air turned suffocating. He didn't mean . . . No way. That would be crazy.

Leaning forward again, Mike looked her straight in the eye. "Your mother was the love of my life. I want you to know that. She was my first love, my first, well, everything. And I was hers."

Frozen in place, Lorelei felt as if she'd lost touch with her body. There was nothing but a low rumble of emotions, as if they were all building into a giant wave that would crash over her any second.

"I asked her to go with me to Nashville," he continued. "She kept putting me off and wouldn't give me an answer. Then, on graduation night, Donna turned me down. Said that if I was going to chase my dream, I'd have to do it without her."

"Why?" Lorelei whispered.

"I don't know." Mike sprang from his chair. "She was scared, I guess. She'd never been away from your grandparents until that trip we all took during spring break down to the Gulf. Your grandmother hadn't wanted her to go, but Donna was eighteen and went against her wishes. Hell, it was probably the first time in her life she'd ever defied her parents. I know your grandmother gave her a hard time about it when we got back. Made her feel really guilty."

As enlightening as this all was, Lorelei hadn't been asking why her mother didn't go with the father of her child.

"I mean, why did you leave her to deal with a baby all by herself?" Lorelei's voice gained strength as her anger grew. "You left her to deal with the censure and the dirty looks. The condemnation of the only people she'd ever known. And for what? To sing stupid little songs on back-alley stages?"

Mike shook his head from side to side. "Lorelei, you have to believe me. I never knew. I had no idea she was pregnant when I left. I was so angry that Donna hadn't been willing to go with me, I tried to put her out of my head. I didn't write or call. And by the time I got over the hurt, it was too late."

"What do you mean, it was too late?"

"It had been three or four years when I ran into someone we'd gone to school with at a bar in Printer's Alley. She said Donna had a little girl." Returning to his seat, he added, "I didn't ask how old or who the dad was. I could hardly think, knowing she'd gone on with her life and I'd missed my chance to get her back."

Lorelei stayed silent, struggling to process what he was telling her. "Are you sure that you're the one?" she asked, grasping at the slim chance that maybe her mother hadn't lied to her. To everyone.

"Your mother wasn't some tramp who slept with any boy who passed by, and I won't have you talking about her as if she were. I had a crush on her from freshman year on, but she was so quiet and shy. Always with her nose in a book, and I couldn't get her to notice me. At the start of senior year, I knew I had to give it one more try, and by some miracle, she finally looked up from one of those books and gave me the sweetest smile I've ever seen to this day." Shaking his head as if to drag himself out of the past, he said, "We were together every day after. Until I left for Nashville."

If Mike Lowry was the only boyfriend her mother ever had, then Granny must have known. How could her own grandmother look her in the eye and not tell her the truth? What kind of a person could do that?

And then Lorelei remembered Granny's nagging about her working for Mike. This must have been why. Because she knew.

"I don't know what to do with all of this," she said, staring at the floor but seeing nothing. How was a person supposed to deal with meeting her father for the first time, let alone when that father also happened to be her boss? And what was the next move upon finding out your entire life was a lie? That the people she'd loved the most had kept something so important from her felt like being hit by a truck, then having the thing back up and run over her again.

"I don't know how to process it either," Mike said. "I figured this out less than thirty minutes ago, and it still feels like some crazy dream."

Whether this was a dream or a nightmare, Lorelei wasn't sure. All she knew was that she needed to talk to Granny. Mike was as much a victim in this as she had been, and they both deserved more answers. But she'd get her own first.

Pulling her purse from beneath the desk, Lorelei headed for the door. "I need to go."

"You're leaving?" Mike asked.

"Yeah, I am," she said.

Spencer was thankful to have a clear schedule for the afternoon. He never should have called Lorelei with his crazy assumption. Lorelei never called him back to say that Mike had returned to the office and shared the life-changing news of who her father was. So he had to be wrong.

This was his own mother's fault. She'd turned his life into a bad soap opera, and now Spencer was trying to do the same to Lorelei. Shame washed over him at the memory of accusing her mother and grandparents of lying to her all these years. As if he'd wish that kind of hurt on anyone.

It was time for a distraction. Something monotonous that would occupy his hands and let his mind relax. He needed time in his workshop. To feel the hum of the tools and watch the wood transform, as if whatever Spencer created had been trapped inside the whole time. If only he could shape his own life as easily.

Remembering that Buford had left him a message that the oak he'd ordered had come in, Spencer headed that way. He could get started on two custom orders and maybe get ahead of schedule for once.

As the bells chimed over the door, Spencer regretted his decision. Jebediah Winkle was standing at the counter talking to Buford, and the pair looked to be in the throes of a serious discussion. This was the last thing he wanted to get involved in today.

Unfortunately, Buford saw him before he could cut and run.

"Perfect timing, Spencer," Buford said. "The mayor and I are talking about Lorelei's idea for that fall festival."

Spencer cringed on the inside but kept his face as neutral as possible. "What about it?" he asked.

The store owner pointed at his opponent with a cookie. "I was saying how I think it's a good idea, at least better than anything we've come up with so far. Mayor Winkle doesn't agree."

What a shocker. Jebediah Winkle didn't like an idea that Lorelei proposed. If nothing else, the man was predictable.

"I didn't say I didn't agree."

Buford raised a brow. "That's exactly what you said."

"What's your problem with a festival, Mayor?" It wasn't as if Spencer was going to get out of this, so he might as well dive in. Maybe he could fend off Jebediah's arguments now and save Lorelei the trouble next week.

"There's a lot of planning involved with an event of this size," the mayor said.

Spencer tilted his head. "We don't know what size it'll be. Lorelei hasn't presented anything yet."

"It's not as if this town is new to festivals, Spencer. We know the basics of what's involved."

"That's right," Spencer said. "Which means we know exactly what it takes to put one on, and who the best people are in the community to carry it off."

"And you think one of those people is Lorelei Pratchett?"

Losing his temper with the mayor would only make things more difficult. There had been plenty of enthusiasm when Lorelei suggested the festival as a possible fund-raising event, but Jebediah had a way of swaying people to his side of an argument. That's how he'd unseated Buford and taken over running their little metropolis, and he would no doubt do the same to defeat any significant committee plans he didn't like.

"Lorelei came up with this idea on her own, Mayor Winkle. She's been tasked with presenting a proposal to the committee and deserves the chance to do so. Nothing has been voted on, and there's no reason to pass judgment until we've seen what she comes up with."

"I agree with Spencer," Buford said, speaking around the bite of cookie in his mouth. "We need to hear her out."

Though he was surprised to hear Buford speaking in support of Lorelei, Spencer didn't say so. There was little love lost between the two older men, and if the chance to piss off Winkle was motivation enough for Buford to back Lorelei, all the better.

At the sure sign that he was in the minority, Jebediah's hackles went up. "Fine," he said, "we'll hear what she has to say. But if the committee *does* decide to pursue this option, I suggest we put someone with experience in charge."

"You mean like your daughter?" Spencer asked. Becky had been helping plan the Main Street Festival since Jebediah had taken office. From what Spencer'd heard, she did little more than sit at the front of the room during meetings, delegating duties until there was nothing left on her to-do list. She was a figurehead and nothing more.

"Becky does have substantial experience planning this sort of event, yes."

Spencer let his anger seep through when he said, "This is Lorelei's project. Should we choose to go forward, she'll have the full support of the restoration committee."

Jebediah stood his ground, but his eyes lost their usual arrogance. "So you speak for the entire committee now?"

"Don't push this, Jebediah," Buford warned. "You won't win."

With a curt nod, the mayor said, "We'll see about that."

Stepping aside to let the blowhard by, Spencer waited until the door swung closed before saying, "He's going to be a pain in the ass, isn't he?"

"That's what he does best," Buford said, munching on another cookie. "These things are dang good."

The small bag on the counter sported a Lulu's Home Bakery sticker. "Are those the ones for sale over at Snow's place?" Spencer asked.

"Yep." The store owner took another bite, and a look of bliss crossed his face. "I don't know who this Lulu person is, but she bakes like an angel."

Spencer rubbed a finger under his nose to hide the smile. "I've heard that. Your message said the oak is in?"

"Wrapped and ready to go. Drive around back and we'll load it up." Wiping his hands on his shirt, Buford added, "You want one of these? I have to eat them here as the missus says I need to eat healthier. The woman cut me back to three beers a week, and she's trying to make me eat *salads*."

The last word was said as if lettuce and tomatoes were equal to crickets and worms.

"I'll pass today," Spencer said, thinking at least he had one piece of good news to share with Lorelei tonight. "Let's get that wood."

Chapter 23

Lorelei huddled in the corner of the couch staring at nothing while her mind churned through thirty years of memories. Halfway home she'd remembered that today was bridge day over at Pearl's, and she was tempted to drive over there and make a scene. But for once in her life, Lorelei chose not to be impetuous. This wasn't something she wanted to have out with an audience. Though she *was* contemplating calling Spencer. He'd been right that Mike knew who Lorelei's father was, he just hadn't guessed how well he knew him.

After all these years, to learn that her father didn't know about her either was a bit mind-blowing. Well, all of this was mind-blowing. Mike had claimed that if he'd known, he never would have gone, but was that true? He'd been a kid himself. Lorelei had essentially done the same thing her father had—run for the county line the first chance she got. Granted, she'd run a lot farther. And she'd given up Spencer to do it. Based on Mike's story, Lorelei couldn't tell if her mom had asked him to stay, or simply sent him on his way, knowing she was leaving herself to carry a burden alone.

She hadn't bothered to open the curtains that Granny kept closed during the day to keep the house cool, and the rage that had filled Lorelei's being the moment she realized Granny must have known all along faded to a low simmer the longer she sat in the dimly lit room. A tiny voice of reason kept repeating that there was still a chance Granny might have been in the dark as much as Lorelei. But then why had the older woman been so against Lorelei working for Mike? She'd said it wasn't a good idea, but wouldn't give a reason. What other reason could there be than *because he's your father, Lorelei*?

A daytime soap opera had nothing on Lorelei's life. At thirty years old, she was a failed actress who'd wasted twelve years of her life, become an unwitting mistress, destroyed a family, and returned home to a small town, where she wasn't welcome, to end up working for the father she'd never known. Her only positive thought was that things could only go up from here. And then she heard Granny's car pull into the drive and remembered there was still a chance that her farce of a story was about to get even worse.

"Lorelei?" Granny said, pushing into the house and dropping her purse and keys on a table in the entryway. "Are you okay? Are you sick?"

"I'm not sick," she said, her voice flat. There were too many emotions warring in her mind for any specific one to win out. "I got some news today."

Granny sat down on the couch, her face etched with concern. "What is it, honey? What's happened?"

"Did you know that Mike Lowry was Mom's boyfriend in high school?" she asked, opting to get right to the point.

Blue eyes turned away. "I knew they spent time together."

"Did you know he was my father?"

Her grandmother's eyes closed and her shoulders fell, but she didn't look shocked or surprised. "I suspected, but not until Mike came back last year."

Not the answer Lorelei expected.

"You mean you didn't know from the beginning?" she asked. "Mike says Mom wasn't the type of girl to sleep around. How could you not have known the boy she'd been dating was my father?"

"She told me they'd had a fight on that spring break trip," Granny said, crossing her arms. "Said she'd been reckless, had a few drinks, and had sex with a stranger. I knew those sorts of things happened when young people went off on their own. That's why I hadn't wanted her to go. But she was eighteen and that boy had convinced her she was old enough to go without our permission."

"That boy?" Lorelei repeated, rising to her feet. "You mean my father?"

"I didn't know that!" Granny rubbed her forehead. "He was long gone by the time your mother told me she was pregnant. I believed her when she said it wasn't him. And when I brought up finding the stranger from Gulf Shores, she didn't want to talk about it."

So Granny hadn't been lying all those years. But she'd said she suspected the truth for a year. And still she didn't say anything.

"What changed when Mike came back?" Lorelei asked. "Why didn't you say something? To him *or* to me?"

"I . . ." The older woman leaned back on the couch. "I don't know. I thought if Mike was your father, that he had to have known before he left. And if he was the kind of man who'd walk away from you and your mother, then he wasn't the kind of man you needed in your life anyway."

"That wasn't your decision," Lorelei snarled.

"I did what I thought was right," Granny defended. "I watched what your mother went through. The shunning and shameful looks for being one of *those* girls. Her friends turned on her, spurred on by that jealous Jebediah Winkle."

"What?" Lorelei sat down on the coffee table. "What does Jebediah have to do with Mom?"

"Oh, he always had a thing for your mother," Granny said, waving a finger in the air. "She wanted nothing to do with him, and when she chose Mike Lowry over him, he was livid. As soon as word got out that she was pregnant with you, Jebediah spewed poisonous lies about her to anyone who would listen. And those fools believed him!"

This was a revelation Lorelei never saw coming. Jebediah had made Lorelei's childhood a living nightmare, and now she knew why. He'd done his best to paint her mother with a mark of shame, and once she was gone, he ensured Lorelei carried the mark as well. But why would anyone have listened to a jealous boy? He wasn't a respected man of the community back then. This wasn't the fifties they were talking about. But then, small Southern towns did have a way of getting stuck in time.

"Did Mom ever defend herself?"

Granny shook her head. "What was she going to say? Her story was that she didn't even know your father's name."

"But why would she do that when she could have told them it was Mike?"

On a long sigh, Granny said, "I've tried to figure that out for the last year. I guess she loved him and didn't want people to think poorly of him for leaving her pregnant."

Lorelei considered that, then remembered what Mike had said. "But he didn't know."

"What?" Granny said.

"Mike says he had no idea Mom was pregnant when he moved to Nashville. He found out later that she had a little girl, but thought I was born a couple years after he left. He didn't even know how old I was until today."

With eyes wide, Granny's mouth opened and closed several times, but nothing came out.

"She didn't want to give him a reason not to go," Lorelei said, the truth dawning. "She knew he wanted to chase his dream, and telling him she was pregnant would have taken that away from him. He'd never have gone to Nashville if she'd told him about me."

"Are you saying your mother ruined her own reputation and bore the brunt of this town's self-righteous judgment so a young man could chase a singing career?"

Scooting over to join Granny on the couch, Lorelei ignored the question. "You said Mom was bitter because of her own choices. Choices she didn't have the courage to change. What did you mean?"

"I thought she regretted taking that trip to Gulf Shores. That she never forgave herself for giving in to a boy who didn't love her, whether it was Mike or some stranger."

"Did you know Mike asked her to go to Nashville with him?"

Granny's brows shot up. "He asked her to go?"

Lorelei nodded. "That's what he says. She turned him down on graduation night. Mom had to know she was pregnant by then."

"Two kids trying to make it in Nashville with a baby would have been terribly hard."

"Yeah," Lorelei said. "She did all of this for him."

Her grandmother squeezed her hand. "That's a big sacrifice for a boy who didn't love her enough to stay."

With a shrug, Lorelei said, "I didn't love Spencer enough to stay either."

"But Spencer wasn't pregnant."

"That definitely would have been a reason to stay," Lorelei said with a chuckle. "She must have loved him a lot."

With two fingers on her chin, Granny turned Lorelei to face her. "She loved you, too. And she was never ashamed of having you. I meant that this morning."

Knowing she'd been created from love and not some seedy one-night stand changed how Lorelei saw herself and her mom. Donna Pratchett hadn't been a lonely, bitter woman who fell into a bottle now and then and lived in the dark.

She'd been a woman who knew love and gave life to a daughter despite what it would mean for her future. She wasn't weak, as Lorelei had always thought. She'd been incredibly strong. And brave.

"I wish her life could have been different," Lorelei said as she leaned her head on Granny's shoulder.

"Me, too," Granny said with a sigh.

Spencer pulled the trays and boxes off his passenger seat and headed up to the house with Champ bouncing around beside him. Lorelei's car was in the drive along with Granny's. One of them must have let the dog out for him. Before he reached the porch, the front door opened and Lorelei stepped out.

"Hi," she said. Her eyes were red, as if she'd been crying, but she offered him a half smile.

He set the trays on the porch and went to her. "What happened?"

Lorelei sniffed. "Let's sit on the swing," she said, pulling him along by the hand. "I got some news today, and Granny and I figured a few things out."

Spencer's gut tightened. "Was I right about Mike?" he asked, swallowing hard as he sat down beside her on the swing.

"Sort of," she said, pulling her feet up and leaning into him. "Mike didn't just know who my father is. He *is* my father."

It was a good thing Spencer was sitting down or he'd have landed on the floorboards. "What?"

"According to Mike, Mom was the love of his life. He asked her to go with him to Nashville, but she turned him down. She never told him she was pregnant, and Granny and I think she let him go and then lied about who my father was so he could chase his dream."

A whistle escaped his lips. "I did not see that coming. But how did Mike not know?"

"He was so mad when Mom refused to go with him, he left and never looked back. A while later he heard she had a kid, but didn't think to ask how old I was."

"And now you work for him." Spencer wondered what the odds on that were. "Is that why Granny didn't want you to work for him? Did she know all this time?"

Lorelei shook her head. "I thought that, too, but no. She did start to suspect it when Mike came back last year. I don't look a whole lot like him, but something he did during a brief encounter at Brubaker's, some mannerism, she said, reminded her of me. She assumed if he *was* my father, that he must have known and left anyway. Which didn't make him a good guy in her eyes, so why bring him into my life?"

This meant that in the last forty-eight hours, both he and Lorelei had found their fathers. Except Lorelei's was still alive and well, and living in Ardent Springs. Spencer hid the unexpected pang of jealousy that hit him in the chest. That his father was gone while hers was still breathing wasn't Lorelei's fault.

"So you have a dad," he said, wanting to be supportive, but not yet sure how Lorelei felt about this new revelation. "Is that a good thing?"

She grinned. "I think so. I like Mike, so that's something."

"Are you going to let people know?" Since Lorelei's parentage had been a big issue with the townsfolk, letting them in on the truth could change the way some of them saw her.

"I don't know. I guess Mike and I have to talk about that."

Spencer wanted to find Mike Lowry and ask him, how could he have not known. Why didn't he check on the girl he left behind? If he really loved her, how did he ever walk away in the first place?

But then he remembered that Lorelei had walked away from him once upon a time. And he hadn't loved her enough to go with her. Stupidity really did run rampant at that age.

"I'm sorry," Lorelei said, her voice so low he barely heard her.

"For what?" he asked.

"For leaving you twelve years ago," she said, laying her head on his shoulder. "For having a father I can go talk to when you don't. For being a bitch in the past, and for the times I'm sure to be one in the future."

Spencer focused on the last word she said. "Does that mean you're going to stick around for the future?"

She dropped her feet to the floor, rose off the swing, and turned to face him. "How about we enjoy the present and not worry about the future for a while?" she said, taking him by the hands and pulling him close. "Twelve years ago, I spent too much time thinking about the future to appreciate what I had. I need to learn how to focus on the now, and this seems like a good place to start."

Tightening his arms around her, Spencer nodded. "I have to admit," he said, "right now *is* feeling pretty good."

"And it's about to get even better," she whispered, dropping a kiss along his jawline. "Granny made a pecan pie."

Lifting Lorelei's feet off the ground, he bellowed, "Why didn't you mention that sooner, woman?"

The delicious smell of fresh pie filled Spencer's senses as he entered the old farmhouse with Lorelei in his arms.

Chapter 24

Lorelei sat at an empty picnic table on the north side of the town square—which ironically enough was round—ignoring her basket of fries while toying with the stuffed brown dog Spencer had won for her. He'd proven he still had solid pitching skills by knocking down the six stacked bottles on his first try. As any smitten girl would do, Lorelei applauded and rewarded her beau with a kiss on the cheek.

At which point Spencer had dragged her to the back of the game tent and coaxed her into the longer, wetter, and hotter kiss he felt he deserved. Lorelei obliged willingly, as she'd been doing a lot of in the last four days.

It had been an odd week. So different from the many, many weeks before. Lorelei was getting to know Mike as her father, which would have been weird on its own, but she was also spending her nights in Spencer's bed, enjoying a rather satisfying form of getting reacquainted. In some ways, they were once again teenage lovers, in a rush to rip each other's clothes off and get to the good stuff. But as adults, they were also enjoying the quiet moments, lying together after the lovemaking, content to cuddle and talk with no need to break apart and race home to make curfew.

The freedom lent a leisureliness to their moments together. Lorelei had set out to live in the now, and the now was definitely holding her attention. There were moments when she thought about the future. About spending her life in Ardent Springs, building a home and a family with Spencer. But then her chest would grow tight, as if the air were being squeezed out of her, and she'd distract her mind with memories of the night before. Or even the morning hours, when they dressed and readied for their day in perfect harmony.

It hadn't taken long for Lorelei to move her necessities into Spencer's bathroom. There was no reason to scurry back to the house in the wee hours of the morning when the garage apartment offered a perfectly good shower. Especially when the apartment also held a rather sexy man willing to help wash her back.

And her front.

"That's an awfully big smile on your face," Mike said, stepping up to the table and taking a seat across from Lorelei. "Almost as big as the one you walked into the office with this morning."

"I'm a happy girl, I guess," she said with a wink, which was completely out of character for her. She blamed Spencer for the change. "A little hungry there?" she asked, watching Mike maneuver a cheeseburger and fries, funnel cake, and giant soda onto the table.

Mike tucked a napkin into the collar of his dark blue T-shirt. It was odd to see him looking so casual, since he wore Western button-up shirts to work every day. They'd had dinner on Tuesday evening to talk about their newly discovered connection, and discussed whether or not to share the information publicly.

Both had agreed that keeping the truth to themselves would be best until they'd gotten to know each other better. Though Mike had been less adamant about keeping the secret, Lorelei had convinced him that the locals might start treating him differently if they found out. She wouldn't let that happen.

And in the end, it was really none of their business.

"At my age," Mike said with a fry in his mouth, "a man can't eat like this often unless he wants to buy stock in an antacid supplier. Festivals and fairs are the only times I let myself splurge, and if I'm going to suffer, it might as well be worth it."

"You make yourself sound ancient." She didn't want to think of Mike as old. That implied she might not have much time with him, and she'd lost too much already.

Taking a large bite of the burger, his eyes closed as a look of ecstasy crossed his features. "So good," he murmured, once he'd swallowed. "I've still got a good bit of years left in me, but you'll learn soon enough. At a certain point, you can't eat like a kid anymore. At least not all the time."

Lorelei eyed the fries in front of her. She'd gone without the bad-for-you stuff for years out in LA. Heaven forbid she put on a pound, or get a pimple the night before an audition. There were no auditions to worry about now, and if her chance to enjoy some edible decadence was running out, then she'd better take advantage of the time she had left.

After dipping two fries into the dollop of ketchup, Lorelei popped them into her mouth. Mike was right. Splurging now and then was totally necessary.

"So why are you sitting here all alone?" Mike asked, looking around the area. "Shouldn't you be eating with Spencer?"

She hadn't mentioned what was going on between her high school sweetheart and herself, but everyone seemed to know anyway. It could have been the fact that they'd spent the last two nights taking in the festivities while barely keeping their hands off each other. Their public displays of affection had earned them some hard looks, but others appeared genuinely happy for them.

"Alas," she said, "Spencer is answering the call of duty. He's working the Ruby Restoration booth trying to recruit new members to the cause."

"Speaking of that, did you ever come up with a good fund-raising idea?"

"I did." Lorelei dipped two more fries in the ketchup. "I suggested we throw one of these," she said, waving the fries to indicate what was going on around them.

"A festival?" he asked, wiping a drop of mustard off his cheek.

"Yep. But this one in the fall and located at the Ruby. I still have to put a presentation together, but I can practically see it all in my mind." Wiping her hands on her napkin, Lorelei propped her elbows on the table. "I'm hoping to bring in a performer from Nashville. Someone who could draw a crowd, but that we could still afford without losing all the money we manage to raise. You have any connections that could help me out?"

Mike sipped at his drink while contemplating her question. "I could make some calls, but the only acts you could afford are likely to be unknowns. Which means they won't pull in much of an audience."

Not the answer she'd been hoping for. "That wouldn't do us much good then. No better-known-but-partially-retired types?"

Her dinner partner's face lit up. "There's Wes."

"Wes who?" Lorelei asked.

"Wes Tillman. He lives up here now."

Lorelei's jaw dropped. "*The* Wes Tillman lives in Ardent Springs? How have I not heard about this before?"

"Technically, he lives outside the town limits, but still in Robertson County. He married Harley Dandridge last year and moved up this way."

"A country singer married our small-town radio DJ?" Come to think of it, that wasn't such a big surprise. "I guess that makes sense, but how did they meet?"

"Wes played the county fair last August. I guess they'd known each other years before, at the start of his career, so it's a bit of a reunion story."

Kind of like Lorelei and Spencer. So maybe a second time around could work out.

"I jammed with him a couple times this past winter. He does an acoustic set at Second Chance Saloon once a month. Harley's cousin owns the place, so Wes brings in the occasional crowd and gets a chance to dust off the cobwebs."

"Color me impressed." Her father played music with Wes Tillman. The long, tall cowboy of country music. Not that Lorelei was a huge fan of the genre, but everyone knew who Wes Tillman was. "Do you think he'd do it?"

Mike shrugged. "He wouldn't have to go far, and seeing as it's for charity, I don't see why not."

"Could you call him for me? It would be incredible if I had a go from a big-name performer when I give the presentation." She could picture Jebediah Winkle swallowing his own tongue when she received approval from the committee. No way would they turn down the idea if she already had a top headliner ready to play.

"I'll give him a call tomorrow," Mike said, digging into his fries.

In a fit of excitement, Lorelei hopped out of her seat and rounded the table to throw her arms around Mike's shoulders. As he gave her arm a squeeze in return, she couldn't help but smile. She'd have hugged him no matter what at the news that he would help get Wes Tillman for her festival, as she'd begun thinking of it, but the fact that she was also hugging her dad was pretty cool, too.

"I knew it," screeched a voice from somewhere behind Lorelei.

She and Mike both spun around to find a seething Becky Winkle pointing an angry finger and barreling in their direction.

Life was good. Or so Spencer thought, until he spotted Mayor Winkle heading his way, with Grady Evans right behind him.

"We need a word with you, Boyd," the mayor said as he reached the Ruby Restoration booth.

"Yeah, that's right," Grady said, like some kind of lapdog cheerleader there to wave pom-poms behind his trusty leader's head.

As he was speaking to a possible new recruit for the committee, they would have to wait. "One minute, gentlemen." Taking his time, he continued explaining to Jacqueline Forbes, a woman who looked to be in her midthirties who'd recently returned to town, the mission of the committee. Though tentative and somewhat shy, she showed interest and agreed to attend the next meeting.

Spencer didn't have time to enjoy the small victory as the Bobbsey twins were waiting impatiently when he turned their way.

"How can I help you, Mayor?" he asked, ignoring Grady completely.

"We have an issue with this fund-raising festival Ms. Pratchett has proposed." Jebediah locked his hands on his hips, and Grady imitated the stance behind him. Spencer struggled not to roll his eyes.

"Mayor, we've been over this. There hasn't been an official proposal. How can you have an issue with something that doesn't exist yet?"

"Well," Winkle started, nodding toward his brainless puppet, "Grady has brought it to my attention that a fall event could conflict with our county fair. That fair is a big earner for our local 4-H club, and we don't want to cause them to lose out for a restoration that might never happen."

Good to know what little faith the mayor had in their efforts. "The county fair covers ten days in September. The festival would last two days, according to Lorelei's suggestion last Friday, and I'm sure there wouldn't be a problem scheduling it around the fair to prevent any conflicts."

The two men looked at each other as if searching for another point to argue.

"We're not moving the fair," Grady said, as if Spencer had suggested they should.

"Didn't expect you to," Spencer replied. "So the issue is settled then. Now if you'll excuse me." Turning to an older couple standing near the far corner of the booth, he dismissed the pair from his mind. Only they didn't take the hint.

"Now wait a minute," Jebediah said. "What about parking?"

This time Spencer did roll his eyes before turning back around. "What about parking?"

"Where are people going to park?"

Leaning his hands on the table between them, Spencer lowered his voice. "I'm going to say this one more time. The official presentation for the festival has not been seen or heard yet. If you want to ask questions at the meeting once Lorelei has shared the plans, that's fine." Staring hard into Jebediah's eyes, he added, "But if you think you're going to run interference on this idea simply because you have some ungrounded grudge against the person who came up with it, you won't only find yourself off this committee, but I'll do everything in my power to get your self-righteous ass out of office. Do we understand each other?"

A flash of comprehension crossed the mayor's face. He knew Spencer wouldn't make an empty threat, and he also knew he lacked the popularity he'd enjoyed at the beginning of his term. The economy was down, and contrary to his campaign promises, Jebediah had done nothing to change that. The people would tolerate his lack of action for only so long before looking for another potential savior.

"You can't do nothin'," Evans said, but Winkle shushed him.

"I'll bring up any questions I have at the meeting then," Jebediah said. "If we're going to do something of this size, I simply want to make sure all the details have been addressed ahead of time."

With a nod, Spencer agreed. "Then we'll be happy for your input to make the event a success."

Grady didn't look happy as the town leader led him away. Spencer wasn't happy either. He'd planned to let Lorelei handle the presentation on her own, but there was no way he'd throw her onto Jebediah's mercy in front of the entire committee. And regardless of the older man's willingness to back down today, Spencer held no illusion that the fight was over.

Once the two men disappeared around a cotton candy stand, Spencer turned back toward the couple who'd been lingering moments before, only to find his ex-wife standing in their place. This night kept getting better and better.

Carrie shuffled from one foot to the other, crossing and uncrossing her arms before sliding her hands into the front pockets on her jeans. "So you're back together?" she said. No *hello*. No *how are you doing?* Fine. He wasn't in the mood for pleasantries either.

"No thanks to you," he said, straightening a stack of committee fliers.

"So she told you." Neither of them needed to expand on what Carrie meant.

Gathering all the patience he could muster, Spencer said, "I married you, Carrie, because I loved you. Not because I was trying to find a stand-in for Lorelei."

"I'm sure that's what you tell yourself."

Spencer gnashed his teeth together so tightly he wouldn't be surprised if one chipped. "Did I ever once say her name when we were together?"

Carrie looked away. "You told stories about when you were in high school. Every time the old school chums got together, that's all I heard about. How wild and fun Lorelei was. The skinny-dipping or water-skiing or racing down the back roads."

"Those were stories about all of us. About Cooper's souped-up cars. Or Bobby mooning Principal Rivers. Yes, Lorelei was part of those stories. Were we supposed to edit her out because you had some groundless jealousy we knew nothing about?"

"I wanted to feel like *I* was a part of things." Carrie shoved a hand through her hair. "I saw your face whenever someone mentioned her. You didn't look at me like that. You never did."

He couldn't win this. Carrie had created something in her head that Spencer didn't put there, but that didn't mean it wasn't real to her. Maybe if he'd known back then, things would have turned out differently. But there was no going back now.

"I don't know how I looked at you," he said, "but I know how I felt. I wanted to have children with you. Doesn't that mean anything?"

"We both know how I screwed that up."

"Don't do that, Carrie. Losing Jeremy wasn't your fault. I thought we were past that."

She rolled a shoulder. "I guess I'm getting a do-over. We'll see what happens this time."

Grabbing a napkin from the table behind him, Spencer held it out to his ex-wife. "Make sure the doctors know what happened with Jeremy. They'll keep an eye on you so it doesn't happen again."

Carrie took the napkin and blotted a tear off her lashes. "Yeah. They know." She wiped her nose, then said, "I guess everything is working out the way it was supposed to. You and Lorelei together and all. I'm sure you two will be happy."

Before Spencer could respond, the frail woman he'd once vowed to love and honor 'til death did they part walked away. He couldn't pretend he still loved her or wanted her back. The humiliation had been the toughest part about what had gone down between them. Half the town knew she was running around with Patch long before anyone told Spencer. But that all felt like ancient history now. Carrie's parting words didn't carry a lot of sincerity, but there was nothing he could do about that. If she had regrets now, that was her problem.

And he really did hope for the best where the baby was concerned. Carrie would be a good mom, he had no doubt about that. He didn't wish Patch Farmer as a father on anyone, but again, not much he could do about that either. She'd made her choices, and now she had to live with them.

Chapter 25

"You scheming bitch." Becky hurled the words at Lorelei before she'd reached the table. "One man isn't enough for you?"

"You've lost your mind, Winkle," Lorelei said, vowing not to become notorious for yet another scene at a Main Street Festival. "Calm down and stop embarrassing yourself."

"You're the one who should be embarrassed. Boffing your boss? Isn't that too clichéd, even for you?"

Mike intervened. "No one is boffing anybody," he said, though how he phrased his rebuttal made Lorelei giggle.

Which made Becky fume even more. "You think this is funny? This town was happy to see you go, Lorelei Pratchett. And nobody wants you back."

Now she was going too far. "Back off, Becky. You don't want to push me."

"Why not?" the blonde asked, an evil smirk on her face. "You can't do anything to me."

"I said don't push me." Lorelei stepped forward, but Mike caught her arm.

"This is ridiculous. For heaven's sake, Becky, I'm only a year younger than your father. I've told you before and I'll tell you again, I'm not interested." He looked around at the crowd gathering and lowered his voice. "We've created enough drama for one evening, don't you think?"

Becky ignored Mike, aiming her hatred at Lorelei. "You think you can collect men like knockoff purses, don't you? First you took Spencer for yourself, and now this."

Wait. Took Spencer for herself? Did Becky want Spencer? "I'm starting to see the light now," Lorelei said, amazed the truth hadn't dawned on her long ago. "You hated me long before I dated Spencer, but that was the last straw, wasn't it? You wanted Spencer and I had him."

The crowd had thickened now, setting a buzz in the air. Lorelei wasn't the one screaming and acting like a lunatic. Not this time. Becky was far enough gone that it seemed almost unkind not to push her the rest of the way.

"You never deserved him," Becky growled. "Like mother like daughter, that's what they always said. The slut and her bastard child."

Before she could think about what she was doing, Lorelei pulled back her arm, her hand fisted tight, but Mike caught the punch before it connected with Becky's nose.

"You listen to me, little girl. Donna Pratchett was a better woman than you can ever hope to be." The Stetson came off as Mike crowded Becky, who couldn't retreat thanks to the onlookers behind her. "People like you, with your high and mighty ways, made her life miserable, and for what? For doing what everybody else was doing at the same time? I knew your parents, and I can promise you the holier-than-thou Deacon Winkle didn't wait for his wedding night to take a roll in the hay with your mama."

Wow. Lorelei did not see that coming. Mike certainly hid his temper better than Lorelei ever had. Then again, he'd had more years to practice. Pride welled in her chest at his defense of her mother. He really *had* loved his high school sweetheart. And the way he stepped in front of Lorelei said maybe he was beginning to care for her, too.

"How dare you besmirch my mama," Becky squealed, her eyes wild with anger, and maybe a little fear. "You don't know what you're talking about."

"Have you ever stopped to think about the hatred you throw around?" Mike asked. "What it does to other people?"

Becky pushed backward, forcing the crowd to part around her. "I won't be insulted for speaking the truth," she defended, fear definitely winning now.

"You ain't perfect, missy," yelled a woman behind Lorelei.

Were the locals taking up Lorelei's defense, or were they simply tired of the Winkle tyranny? Either way, she was relieved the stones weren't cast in her direction for once.

Shoving an innocent woman who'd gotten in her way, Becky yelled, "This isn't over, Pratchett."

Lorelei held her tongue. The heightened tension that had surrounded them dissipated as Becky stomped off. Several people gave Lorelei an approving nod, as if to say they were with her. Maybe opinions could change in this town. She returned the nods with smiles of appreciation and even accepted a couple pats on the back.

As Mike slid his hat back on, she said, "Thank you."

When he turned, she was surprised to see the hurt in his eyes. "You have nothing to thank me for. If I'd been here from the beginning, all of this would be different."

What he said was true, but there was no changing the past now. Lorelei had lived there long enough, running on anger about things she could do nothing about. She'd vowed to live in the now, and the now was too good to let Becky Winkle mess it up.

"You were here tonight," she said. "And that means a lot."

"We need to tell them. I'm tired of your mother being thought of this way."

Oh, no. Her mother had sacrificed too much to keep Mike out of the fray. Lorelei would not have that sacrifice be for nothing now.

"We agreed, Mike. It's how she wanted it."

He returned to the picnic table. "But we can fix it for her."

"And have them all turn their judgment on you? What if the high and mighty decide they don't want to do business with a man who cut and run on his pregnant girlfriend?" she whispered. "You know they won't care about the details. Who knew what and when. Honor our agreement," she said. "For her."

Mike shook his head, then sat down at the table and dropped his face into his hands. Lorelei returned to her seat across from him. After several seconds, he looked her way. "I hate this."

She nodded. "Me, too." With a smile, she tilted her head. "Is that true about Becky's parents?"

A dark brow shot up. "I shouldn't have said that, but yeah. People seem to forget we were all kids in the 1980s, not the 1880s. Becky's mom is the daughter of a preacher. Those girls were always the fastest."

"No," Lorelei said, the word heavy with shock. "Mrs. Winkle, the queen of the cardigan and pearls, was a fast girl?"

Her father narrowed his eyes. "Remember what it's like to have your mom talked about, Lorelei. Don't go doing the same to someone else."

Sobering, she tried to wipe the smile off her face. "I didn't say I was going to mention it to anyone. But still." The smile won out. "Mrs. Winkle?"

"Lorelei."

"No, you're right." She made the motion of locking her lips and throwing away the key. "You won't catch me repeating anything."

"Good," Mike said. "Now how about helping me with this funnel cake?"

Lorelei pulled the paper plate her way. "I thought you'd never ask."

226

Fifteen minutes after Carrie had walked away, Spencer settled in his rickety metal chair, taking a break for the first time in more than an hour. The couple who'd come to the booth while Jebediah and Grady had monopolized Spencer's attention had returned. As luck would have it, they'd spent their first date at the Ruby, and many more after that. As the theater had played such a significant role in their romance, Mr. and Mrs. Handleman were happy to join the cause. That made four new members on the night, including the Forbes woman, and Haleigh Rae's mom, who'd stopped by the booth with her daughter to say hello.

Spencer had been tempted to ask Haleigh if she'd seen Cooper, but he couldn't think of a reason she would. Cooper had loved Haleigh from afar for years, long enough that the woman should have figured it out by now, but if she hadn't, Spencer wasn't going to be the one to let the cat out of the bag. Of course, if Coop would man up and ask the woman out during one of these visits, he might actually get somewhere. This stupid notion that a doc wouldn't want anything to do with a mechanic was all in the man's head, but Spencer had given up trying to change his friend's mind several years ago.

"You can't say I didn't warn you, Spencer," Becky Winkle said, appearing to his left.

Glancing to the heavens, he wondered what he'd done to deserve this much harassment in one evening.

"I'm really not in the mood, Becky." After his divorce from Carrie, Becky had kept him supplied with casseroles and the occasional Bundt cake. None of which she'd prepared herself, of course. He'd spent three months dodging her hints until the day he moved into the garage apartment at Rosie's. It was as if the Pratchett house was surrounded by an invisible fence that the scheming woman couldn't get through. Or wouldn't. Either way, he'd been relieved to be rid of her, and she hadn't shown any interest in him since.

"She was never good enough for you, but you were too blind to see it."

Lorelei. Of course this was about Lorelei.

"I'm not blind to anything. Between the two of us, I'd say you're the one with the cloudy judgment."

Becky's jaw worked as if she were trying to dislodge it. "You've been humiliated by a woman once, Spencer. I'd think you wouldn't let the same thing happen again."

Why would she not give this up? "I told you, I'm not in the mood for your lies and innuendos. When are you going to learn to get your nose out of other people's business?"

"And when are you going to realize that Lorelei Pratchett is a two-timing slut like her mother?"

If there hadn't been a table between them, Spencer might have actually put his hands on the woman. "When are you going to realize that this petty jealousy only makes you look like a pathetic fool? There's nothing you can say to me that is going to change anything, Becky. Give it up."

"I saw them," she mumbled, struggling to maintain eye contact. A dead giveaway she was spewing one more baseless lie.

"You saw who?" he asked, curious to see how far she was willing to go.

"Lorelei and Mike Lowry." Becky crossed her arms, looking around as if making sure no one else could hear. "They were in the alley behind Snow's shop and they were making out. I saw them with my own eyes."

It was as if not a day had passed since high school. He actually felt sorry for her. The hatred she had for Lorelei said a lot more about Becky than the adversary she was determined to destroy.

"No, you didn't," he said, refusing to play into the drama.

"Yes, I did," she screeched, her voice hitting an octave he hadn't heard before. "The image is burned into my brain. It was disgusting."

With a sigh, Spencer said, "I'm sure it's a dark and unhappy place in that head of yours, but there's no way you saw Lorelei and Mike doing anything in an alley." He walked away from her then, collecting the fliers and information cards spread out along the opposite table.

As he assumed she would, Becky marched around the outside of the booth, joining him on the other side. "Like there was no way your wife was sneaking around with Patch Farmer, making a joke out of you?"

She was pushing his buttons on purpose. Trying to get a reaction. Spencer counted to ten, reminding himself that history was not repeating itself. Of that he was certain.

"Go home, Becky."

"Why won't you listen to me?" she pleaded, as if she were asking for help and he refused to give it.

"Because I know you're lying."

"I'm telling you, I know what I saw."

"And I'm telling you, you didn't see anything of the kind."

"Yes, I did," she said, stomping a foot. "Why don't you believe me?"

Out of patience, Spencer slapped his hands on the table, leaning forward until they were nearly nose to nose. "Because he's her father!" he yelled.

Becky's eyes went wide, and in an instant Spencer realized what he'd done. How could he be so stupid? Becky was trying to push his buttons, and somehow he'd let her do it. Only Becky had had no idea which button she was about to hit. Short of turning back time, there was nothing Spencer could say that would undo the damage he'd just done.

Dammit to hell, what was he going to tell Lorelei? While he contemplated the mess he'd made, Becky stared with her chin nearly on the pavement. Then, without a word, the blonde turned on her heel and disappeared into the darkness. He called her name, but there was no point.

Spencer had just unleashed a shit-storm of epic proportions for Mike and Lorelei, and Lorelei was never going to forgive him.

Chapter 26

Brushing powdered sugar from the front of her shirt, Lorelei crossed Main Street on her way back to Snow's store. She'd been helping out, as they'd agreed she would at the beginning of the month. Lulu's Home Bakery had supplied twice as much product today, and Lorelei was enjoying hearing festivalgoers wax poetic about her treats.

Though her baked goods had sold out nearly every day since they'd appeared in the store, Lorelei had never actually seen anyone enjoy them. She hadn't realized how cool the experience would be, especially when some of those raving were people who'd never said anything nice about *or* to her.

Which reminded her of the way the locals had sort of taken her side against Becky. Now that had been fun to watch, though not as fun as watching Mike take the wicked witch of Ardent Springs down a notch.

If only they'd had a bucket of water to throw on her.

"I only stopped to say hello," came a frantic female voice out of the darkness. Lorelei scanned the street for the source. There weren't any large parking lots around the town square, so anyone attending the festival had had to find a spot along the side streets.

"What have I told you about talking to him?" said a male voice, anger clear in his tone.

"Patch, please," the woman replied. "Don't do this. I swear it didn't mean anything."

Wasn't Patch the name of the guy who'd married Spencer's ex-wife? How many men named Patch could live in the area? Lorelei walked farther up the street, pulled by the fear in the woman's words.

"You're mine now, you hear?" The sound of a slap accompanied the words. "Don't make me tell you again."

Lorelei spotted the couple in time to see Patch's hand connect again with Carrie's cheek. "Hey!" she yelled. "Leave her alone."

"Mind your own business, bitch," the man ordered, grabbing his wife's elbow tight enough to make her wince.

"I said leave her alone." Lorelei stepped close enough to be seen in the light from the streetlamp. Carrie gasped before Patch jerked her hard behind him. In that moment, Lorelei knew she had to get the woman away. "Why don't you pick on someone your own size, asshole."

"I said this is none of your business." Patch tried to tower over her, but Lorelei had learned a thing or two about taking care of herself while working overnight shifts in LA.

"I'm making it my business," she said, then kicked Patch hard enough in the balls to send him to his knees. "Come on, Carrie." Lorelei took the sobbing woman's hand and ran across the street, dodging between vehicles, then headed for Snow's shop. She didn't know how long it would take Patch to recover, but they needed to find a hiding place before he did.

"What are you doing?" Carrie asked, but she kept up and didn't try to break Lorelei's hold on her.

"I have no idea," Lorelei said, out of breath from the sudden sprint, which was a good indication she should probably start working out. "But I couldn't let him hit you like that."

Carrie didn't answer as they charged into Snow's shop, sending the bells over the door jingling as if someone were trying to rip them down. Three ladies perusing the jewelry section turned their way, causing Lorelei to stop in her tracks. She nodded and tried to look as if nothing weird was going on.

Putting Carrie in front of her, she pushed her toward the back of the store, hoping to find Snow and slip into the back room to catch their breath. The groin kick had been spontaneous, but Lorelei realized this was a serious situation. They had to figure out what to do next. All she knew was that Carrie was not going back to that man.

"You're back," Snow said, confusion etching her face as she took in Carrie's red face and Lorelei's heavy breathing. "Looks like I missed something."

Nodding toward the back room, Lorelei said, "I'll tell you in here."

Snow followed the pair into the brightly lit storage room, where Lorelei put Carrie into one of the chairs at the metal table in the corner, then took the one next to her. Bending over, Lorelei put her head between her knees.

"Are you okay?" Snow asked.

Lorelei held up one finger. Carrie didn't speak, but she didn't seem to be as breathless as her rescuer. Damn, she was out of shape. First thing Monday morning, Lorelei was looking into a gym membership.

After maybe ten seconds, she sat up and glanced over to Carrie, who was no longer crying. She looked like a deer caught in the lights of an oncoming bus. Lorelei couldn't blame her, considering what had happened.

"Seriously," Snow said. "I'm dying here. What's going on?" Glancing at the wide-eyed stranger, she said, "Do I know you?"

Carrie shook head. "I don't think so."

"She's Spencer's ex-wife," Lorelei said. "Carrie, meet Snow Cameron. Snow, this is Carrie Farmer."

Snow dropped into a chair, looking from one woman to the other. "So Spencer's ex-and-now-current girlfriend just ran into my shop with Spencer's ex-wife. Do I have that right?"

When she said it that way, it did sound strange. "This wasn't planned," Lorelei said, which didn't really explain anything. "Carrie was in a bad situation, and I got her out of it." She didn't feel right telling someone Carrie didn't know that her husband was beating her in the street. "We needed a place to figure out what to do next."

"I see," Snow said, and the look on her face said she could guess the part that Lorelei didn't say. Then again, the red mark on Carrie's cheek was enough to tell the story without words. "Take all the time you need. There's tea in the pot, and bottles of water and soda in the fridge." Smiling at Carrie, she added, "It's nice to meet you, Carrie. Let me know if I can help, okay?"

Lorelei had already considered Snow a cool person, but in that moment she was promoted to freaking awesome.

"Thanks," Carrie said, speaking for the first time since they'd entered the store. "I appreciate that."

Snow offered an understanding smile, then left them alone. Lorelei didn't say anything right away. Though Carrie clearly didn't have a great life, by kicking her husband and then dragging her away, Lorelei had probably made it about a hundred times worse.

"Do you have anywhere you can go?" she asked. "Family you can call?"

Carrie shook her head. "Mama moved to Louisville a couple years ago. For a man," she added. "And Daddy isn't much different than Patch. He'd tell me to go home to my husband like a good wife should."

"No siblings?"

"An older sister. She lives in Albuquerque and doesn't have much to do with anything back here." That was a diplomatic way of saying the older sibling had gotten out and wasn't interested in helping her little sister do the same. "My little brother is in the military. I think he's somewhere overseas right now."

"Right. Well," Lorelei said, "you can't go back to your house, so you'll have to come home with me."

"What?" Carrie sat up straighter. "Did you say home with you?"

"Yes." Lorelei rose from her seat. "You want something to drink before we go find Spencer?"

Carrie's head shook from side to side as if she were watching a high-speed Ping-Pong match. "Spencer wants nothing to do with me. I can't go to him with this."

"Spencer is my ride, and that means he's your ride, too, now. And if you think he wouldn't help you in this situation, then you never really knew him at all."

Snatching two bottles of water from the fridge, Lorelei muttered, "I need something a lot stronger than this, but it'll have to wait until we get home."

"Why?" Carrie said as Lorelei set one of the bottles in front of her.

"Why what?" Lorelei asked.

"Why are you helping me?"

Excellent question. Lorelei searched for an answer, but only one came to mind. "Because you were in trouble. I couldn't let that jerk knock you around and not do something about it."

"But you're offering me a place to stay."

"Not forever." Lorelei opened her water and took a drink. "We'll find you another option tomorrow. But tonight you'll have a hot shower and a warm bed." Looking Carrie in the eye, she added, "You'll be safe."

Looking as if she were holding back tears, Carrie stood. "I was wrong about you," she said. "A lot of people were wrong about you."

The frail woman before her could have no idea what those words meant. With a half smile, Lorelei said, "Come on. As much as I hope your idiot husband is still puking on the curb, I'm sure he's recovered by now. How are you at sneaking around in the dark?"

"Lead the way," Carrie said. "I'll keep up."

The crowds thinned, and Spencer knew that Lorelei would show up soon, ready to head home. He knew he had to tell her right away. If someone asked her about Mike being her father before Spencer could confess what he'd done, getting her to forgive him would be even more difficult.

But Lorelei knew what Becky was like. She'd know he never meant to say the words, that they'd just come out. And telling her tonight would give her the chance to call Mike and warn him. Then again, maybe Spencer should do that himself. Mike wasn't as adamant about keeping the secret as Lorelei was. He might help her come around to see that this wasn't the end of the world.

Right. It wasn't as if Spencer had slipped and blurted her shoe size. He'd announced to Lorelei's sworn enemy the identity of her father, and without the chance to explain the details to save Mike from the assumptions people were sure to make.

If only there was a way to find Becky and make her keep quiet. Barring sewing her lips shut, he couldn't think of any way to do it.

"Spencer!" Lorelei called in a loud whisper, if there was such a thing. He turned to see her shuffling through the shadows behind the tents to his left. Why wasn't she walking on the street? She was going to trip over something back there and hurt herself.

"Lorelei, we need to talk."

"Yes, we do," she said, stopping at the corner of the tent next door. "But we need to get out of here first."

"What?" he asked, as she frantically waved a hand for him to come to her. Maybe someone had already asked her about Mike. They probably wouldn't say how they heard, which meant she'd have no way of knowing he'd been the source. "Hold on."

He loosened the two knots that held the front and side flaps of the booth up, letting them fall to the ground. Slipping out the back, he used the same ropes to tie the flaps back together at the bottom so they wouldn't blow up in the wind. After making sure the entire booth was secure, he hustled over to where Lorelei remained in the shadows.

"I need to tell you something," he said, and then spotted his ex-wife lurking behind Lorelei. "What's she doing here?"

"She's with me," Lorelei said, taking him by surprise. "Or rather, with us for now. I'm taking her to the house, and we need to go." Turning her back to Spencer, she nudged Carrie back in the direction they'd come.

"Hold on one minute." Since when did his ex-wife and Lorelei have slumber parties? "What do you mean you're taking her to the house? To her house?"

He couldn't be sure, but Spencer would have sworn that Lorelei rolled her eyes. "No, to my house. Would you come on?"

As he stood in place, watching the two women disappear into the night, Spencer struggled to understand what was going on. Why would Lorelei take Carrie anywhere near her house? As far as he knew, they'd only ever talked the one time in Brubaker's bathroom, and that hadn't been a friendly exchange, based on what Lorelei had told him.

"Come on, Spencer," she hissed in the distance.

Realizing he wasn't going to get any answers standing still, he broke into a jog to catch up. "Why are we in such a hurry?" he asked.

"I'll tell you once we reach the truck." Lorelei stayed close to Carrie, as if protecting her from something. When Spencer turned to slide between two booths to reach the light of the street, she whispered, "We need to stay over here."

"Lorelei, you're not making any sense. What's going on?"

"I said I'll tell you at the truck." She tugged on his sleeve. "Would you please hurry?"

Carrie had yet to say a word, nor had she looked Spencer in the eye when he found her standing with Lorelei. He didn't know when they'd entered some crazy spy movie, but he was willing to keep the questions in check until they were all three inside the Dodge.

"Now," he said as soon as they were buckled. "Explain."

"While you drive," Lorelei said, waving a hand toward the steering wheel.

Spencer dug deep for patience. Once the truck was rolling down South Margin, he asked again. "Now?"

Lorelei looked to Carrie on her right, who nodded yes to whatever unspoken question was being asked.

"I found Patch smacking Carrie around on the street not far from Snow's place. So I kicked him in the nuts and we ran."

"Patch hit you?" Spencer exploded, leaning around Lorelei to see his ex-wife.

"Watch the road!" Lorelei screamed, slamming a hand on the dash. Turning back to the windshield, Spencer jerked the wheel to keep the truck from driving onto the sidewalk.

With anger and adrenaline pumping in his ears, Spencer squeezed the wheel in a white-knuckle grip as he asked, "Does he know you're pregnant?"

"You're pregnant?" Lorelei burst out.

With her eyes turned toward the passenger window, Carrie answered both questions. "Yes and yes, but it hasn't changed . . . things like I'd hoped."

"Why didn't you tell me?" Spencer asked, turning right onto Fifth Street.

"I'd think the answer to that would be obvious."

Carrie had him there. But still. She couldn't think he wouldn't have helped her. Then he remembered Lorelei's part in the evening's adventures.

"And what were you thinking?" he asked the woman pressed against his side. Patch Farmer wasn't a small man. Besides the fact that he deserved a kick in the balls for laying his hands on any woman, Spencer didn't like the idea of Lorelei putting herself in harm's way. "Why didn't you find a cop or something? They're all over the festival."

"It's not as if I had time to think," Lorelei said, sarcasm dripping from every word. "I saw the slap and reacted. And I hope the moron is still trying to pull his sack out of his windpipe."

Spencer took off his hat and tossed it onto the dash, then ran a hand through his hair. "Don't you think he's going to come looking for her at your house?"

Lorelei turned to Carrie. "He doesn't know who I am, does he?"

Carrie shook her head. "I don't think so. He's not originally from here, and I've never mentioned you."

"Then we're good." Though she sounded confident, Lorelei's quick glimpse behind them revealed her concern.

Silence loomed for nearly a mile before Spencer asked, "So what happens tomorrow?"

The women exchanged another look. "We haven't gotten that far yet," Lorelei answered.

"Great." Spencer ran his hand through his hair again. He still needed to tell Lorelei what had happened with Becky, but he didn't want to have the conversation in front of Carrie.

No one spoke the rest of the way home. Once Spencer cut the engine, Lorelei had to wait for Carrie to climb out first. They rounded the truck and headed for the house.

"Lorelei, I still need to talk to you."

Both women stopped, and Lorelei said, "Go on up to the porch, Carrie. I'll be right there." Once his ex was out of earshot, she said, "Can it wait until tomorrow?"

In all likelihood, the news wouldn't spread too far by morning. And if Lorelei was dealing with Carrie's mess, she wouldn't be encountering any locals before then.

"I guess so." Taking her hand, he asked, "Do you know what you're doing?"

She shook her head with a half smile. "As usual, I have no idea."

Dropping a kiss on her knuckles, he whispered, "Thanks for saving her."

Lorelei offered a kiss on Spencer's cheek in return. "So far, I only saved her for tonight. I have a feeling this is about to get very messy."

That was probably the understatement of the night. Patch didn't seem like the type to let Carrie walk away without a fight. He only hoped they could find a solution that would keep her safe.

After watching Lorelei disappear with Carrie into the house, Spencer climbed the stairs fighting the temptation to walk back to the truck, go find Patch Farmer, and do what he'd wanted to do for the last five years. There was certainly more than reasonable grounds to do it now. But then he couldn't talk to Lorelei first thing in the morning if he were in jail for assault and battery.

At least he had the night to figure out how he was going to tell her.

Chapter 27

Carrie stopped four feet inside the door looking as if she might bolt. "I really don't want to be a burden. Maybe I should go to a motel."

Lorelei pulled two glasses from the cupboard. She would have liked a tall glass of wine, but they'd have to settle for sweet tea. "You're not going anywhere tonight. Pull up a stool," she said, indicating the backless wooden stools on the far side of the kitchen island.

"But I—"

"Carrie," Lorelei said with force. "Sit. Down."

With a quick nod, the younger woman did as ordered. "What are you going to tell your grandmother? She lives here, too, right?"

"She does." Granny and Pearl had been playing bingo at the festival the last Lorelei knew. They'd probably close the place down. "My grandfather built this house in 1965, and Granny has been here ever since." After sliding a glass Carrie's way, Lorelei sipped her own with a hip resting against the counter. "I'll tell her only what you want me to tell her."

Running a finger around the rim of the drink, Carrie kept her eyes down. "I never had any grandparents, really. My dad's parents were hard people. The only thing I remember about visiting them was the immediate threat of being beat if we even considered acting out of line."

"What about on your mom's side?" Lorelei asked.

"They didn't like Dad, so we rarely saw them." She lifted the tea to her lips saying, "They died before I was old enough to go to school."

Setting her glass on the island counter, Lorelei leaned on her elbows, considering the woman across from her. She'd clearly been living with abuse her whole life, if what she said about her father being like Patch was any indication. Life with Spencer must have felt like landing in paradise. Yet she'd thrown the safety and security of a good man away, only to land back in hell.

Questions danced on the tip of Lorelei's tongue, but she and Carrie were still mostly strangers. Saving her from a beating didn't mean Lorelei had any right to pry into her life or her psyche.

"How far along are you?" she asked, choosing to stick with the present situation.

"Not quite three months." Settling a hand on her stomach, she added, "I'm starting to show already. They say that happens with your second pregnancy."

So much for staying in the present. Did Lorelei have a right to ask about the child that Carrie and Spencer had lost? She'd never asked Spencer, and he hadn't brought it up. Not that she expected him to. In fact, the few times they'd talked about a future together in the last several days, neither had mentioned kids at all.

"I thought having a baby would make Patch happy," Carrie said, closing the window of opportunity to ask about the first pregnancy. "But I was wrong."

Unable to hold in the one question she most wanted answered, Lorelei said, "Why didn't you leave before? When the abuse first started?"

Carrie rubbed her cheek on her shoulder, met Lorelei's gaze for half a second, and then returned to staring at her glass. "No place to go," she said. "No job, so no money of my own. I'm sure it sounds insane to you, but at least with Patch I have a roof over my head and food to eat. That's important, especially with the baby now."

The explanation did sound insane to Lorelei, but then the only reason she'd finally agreed to come home from LA was because the alternative was being homeless. Maxwell had been paying her bills until his wife walked into the picture. Pride had kept her on the West Coast for longer than was rational, and though she didn't say as much, pride likely played a role in Carrie's decisions as well. Lorelei would be a hypocrite to condemn this damaged woman for a fault she had a more than passing experience with herself.

"Tomorrow, then," she said, standing up again. "We'll research shelters in the area, look into your legal options, and make a plan. Do you want to contact your mom? She's in Louisville, you said?"

"I called Mom a couple weeks ago. Going there isn't an option."

Lorelei took a second to process that statement. What kind of a mother refused shelter to her pregnant, abused daughter? But again, none of her business.

"Right." This definitely called for something stronger than tea. Lorelei stepped into the pantry and returned with a large Tupperware container. "Have a cookie," she said, pulling the teal lid off the bowl.

Carrie hesitated, but succumbed to sugary temptation. Biting into a chocolate chip cookie, she caught a crumb that fell from her lip and said, "These are delicious."

Considering how much of Carrie's personal life Lorelei had invaded this evening, she gave the woman a bow. "Lulu's Home Bakery, at your service," she said with a flourish.

Light blue eyes went wide. "You're Lulu's Home Bakery?"

"That I am." Lorelei popped a piece of a cookie into her mouth. "But I am swearing you to secrecy. I keep this bit of information quiet for a reason, which I'm sure you can guess."

"The only thing I've ever been good at is pie," Carrie said. "And that took me years to get right." Swallowing the last of her cookie, she added, "After what you did for me tonight, you can consider your secret safe with me."

"Good." Lorelei collected the crumbs from their snacking into her hand and brushed them off over the garbage can under the sink. "Come upstairs and I'll show you where you'll be sleeping. I don't know when the guest room was last used, but other than some dust on the furniture, it should be clean enough."

"I can sleep on the couch," Carrie said, following Lorelei to the stairs. "I really don't want to put you out."

"What's the point of having a guest room if you're going to put a guest on the couch?" Running into Ginger at the foot of the stairs, Lorelei said, "This is Ginger. She's mean." Carrie bent down and the cat came right to her, purring up a storm as the newcomer rubbed behind her ears. "Okay," Lorelei said. "She's only mean with me. Good to know."

Halfway up the stairs, Carrie said, "I really appreciate all that you're doing, and I hope I can repay you someday."

"This is probably going to get worse before it gets better," Lorelei said, brushing off any talk of repayment. "Let's wait and see if you're still thankful in a few days."

Carrie didn't respond. For now, Lorelei could provide a warm bed for the night and a good breakfast in the morning. What would happen after that was anyone's guess. This could work out with few bumps, or they'd all be living in a crazy Lifetime movie within the week.

But one thing was for sure. The next few days would be anything but boring.

Spencer barely slept as guilt and fear warred for supremacy in his mind. Though he wanted to believe that Lorelei would forgive him, a sliver of doubt hovered low in his gut. He still couldn't believe he'd let Becky push him so far. The run-in with the mayor had affected him more than he realized, and Spencer hit a breaking point when Becky kept insisting on something he knew was false.

There was only so much slandering of Lorelei that Spencer could tolerate, and he'd apparently hit his limit.

By the time the sun broke the horizon line, Spencer was dressed and anxious, but he knew better than to expect Lorelei to be awake at the crack of dawn. If his guess was right, she and Carrie had spent time talking before the night was over. Something about which Spencer wasn't sure how he felt.

He shared a complicated past with both women, and he intended to spend a complication-free future with one of them. Did this new development mean the pair would become friends? That Carrie would become a regular part of his life again? Spencer didn't hate his ex-wife, and after what he'd learned last night, he felt more protective of her than he had in years.

But he also didn't want to sit around over coffee reminiscing about the past.

Once the clock on the back of the stove glowed eight thirty, Spencer slid on his boots, but he left the cowboy hat on the table. He didn't need it for this particular mission. As Spencer's foot hit the last step, a pickup truck came flying up the driveway, throwing gravel in every direction and bouncing through the potholes hard enough to give whoever was driving a bad case of whiplash.

The green Ford had barely stopped before Patch was out of the truck and charging Spencer's way.

"Where's my goddamn wife?" Patch said, grabbing the front of Spencer's T-shirt.

"Get off me, Farmer," he said, shoving the man back. But Patch's reason had left him.

"She ain't got no place else to go, so I know you have her." A drop of spittle dangled precariously on the edge of Patch's bottom lip. "She's mine and I want her back."

Spencer broke the man's grasp on his shirt for the second time. "I don't have your wife." Which was true. Carrie wasn't with him. "Now get out of here before you do something you'll regret."

"I'm not afraid of you," Farmer said, shoving up his sleeves. "You can't keep her from me."

"Why'd she run from you, huh, Patch? What did you do to her to make her leave?" Provoking the already furious man wasn't the best idea, but Spencer had passed mildly pissed himself. "Maybe you should pick on somebody your own size."

Patch's eyes went wide with fury as he lunged at Spencer again, but before the two men locked together, a shot rang out from the porch. Both turned to see Rosie Pratchett marching toward them carrying a shotgun pointed at the sky.

"Get off my property right now," she yelled at Patch. "You're not welcome here. Now go."

Farmer had the sense to throw his hands in the air. "I only come for my wife."

"Spencer doesn't have her. Now go on, before I fire at something other than the clouds."

Keeping his eye on the older woman, Farmer climbed into his truck and backed out of the driveway, leaving Spencer standing next to Rosie, dazed and confused.

"Since when do you keep shells in that gun?" He knew Rosie had a gun in the house, but as far as he knew, she hadn't bought ammunition for it in years.

Rosie kept her focus on the retreating Ford. "I had one left in a box in the pantry."

Which meant two things. She'd been bluffing when she'd threatened to shoot Farmer, and Rosie kept live rounds next to the baking soda and pancake mix.

Once the truck disappeared from sight, she turned to Spencer. "Are you all right?"

Straightening the front of his shirt, he answered, "I'm fine. Are you?"

Dropping the gun onto her shoulder, she said, "Fit as a fiddle. Come in and have some breakfast."

⌒

By ten o'clock, Lorelei was still reeling from the fact that Granny had chased off Carrie's husband with a shotgun. She'd been sleeping until she'd heard raised voices outside her window. By the time she reached the window seat, Granny had fired the shot and was charging across the yard like a geriatric angel of vengeance.

Lorelei had stayed up the night before, waiting for Granny to get home to explain why Spencer's ex-wife was sleeping in their guest room. In typical Granny fashion, she'd declared that Carrie would stay with them as long as she needed and no man would lay a hand on her again.

So it was no surprise that her grandmother had put herself into the fray, but pulling a gun on a man shot past protective and into crazy territory. Then again, Lorelei had kicked the man in the groin, so who was she to judge?

"We need to talk," Spencer said, joining Lorelei at the sink where she was loading the dishwasher. Carrie and Granny were sitting in the living room looking at old photo albums. Granny never passed up the chance to show off embarrassing pictures of Lorelei riding her rocking horse in nothing but a diaper.

"Are you sure you're okay?" she asked, still shaken by the thought of what Patch could have done to him. Not that Spencer couldn't hold his own, but Carrie's husband was already nuts. Add in uncontrollable rage and there was no telling what he might have pulled. What if he'd had a gun of his own?

She shuddered to think of how bad the morning could have been.

"I'm fine," he said, taking her hands. "This is important."

Before Lorelei could answer, her cell phone went off. "Hold that thought," she said, sweeping the phone off the table near the house phone. "Hello?"

"Lorelei, it's Snow."

"Hey. Is it getting busy over there already?"

Snow dropped her voice. "Not yet. Mrs. Mitchner was in here with her daughter a few minutes ago."

"So Haleigh Rae *is* in town," Lorelei said, remembering how Cooper had reacted when Spencer had mentioned her at the bar. Maybe they could all get together before she headed back to Memphis.

"Right. Haleigh." Snow spoke to a customer, then returned to the call. "I heard them talking to the mayor's wife, and I wouldn't have paid much attention, but I heard Mrs. Winkle say your name."

Lorelei was not surprised to be the topic of gossip, especially considering the source. "That's nothing new," she said, holding up one finger to Spencer, who looked agitated.

"*This* was new." Snow's voice dropped so low that Lorelei could barely hear her. "Mrs. Winkle said that Mike Lowry is your father."

Dropping into a chair, Lorelei said, "What?"

"Mrs. Mitchner didn't seem to believe her until she said that her daughter had heard the truth directly from Spencer Boyd, so it had to be true." Snow told a customer she'd be right with them before whispering again. "Anyway, I don't know if it's true or not, and I'm not asking, but I thought you'd want to know."

Locking eyes with Spencer, she said, "Thanks, Snow. I'll talk to you later."

Disconnecting the call, she rose from the chair and said, "Outside. Now."

Chapter 28

He knew the second she looked at him that she knew. Why the hell hadn't he stopped her from taking that call? Dammit, he'd wanted to be the one to tell her.

"Lorelei, let me explain," he said as soon as they reached the porch.

"You told Becky Winkle?" she demanded, turning on him. "Why?"

"I didn't mean to." Spencer took her by the arms, but she shook him off. "The words just came out."

Running her hands through her hair, Lorelei looked incredulous. "What, were you two talking about the weather and the words 'Mike Lowry is Lorelei's dad' came flying out of your mouth?"

"Of course not."

"Why were you even talking to Becky?" she asked. "Of all the people . . ."

"She found me at the Ruby tent. Becky was all worked up and said she'd caught you and Mike making out in an alley or something."

"That's bullshit," Lorelei said.

"That's what I told her. I knew she was lying, and I called her on it."

With a muscle ticcing in her neck, she said, "You called her on it by telling her that Mike is my father?"

"No." This was all wrong. He needed to make her understand. "Not at first. I kept telling her she didn't see anything of the kind, but she wouldn't admit she was lying. She wouldn't give up, and I lost it and said it couldn't be true because Mike is your father."

As the hurt crossed her face, Spencer said, "She was trying to drive a wedge between us, to make me believe that you were seeing Mike behind my back. She even had the nerve to say that you were making a fool of me like Carrie did."

"And your ego couldn't let her get away with that," Lorelei said, her voice even, monotone. "You had to set her straight."

"I told you," he said, reaching for her again, "I didn't mean to tell her. Dammit, I'd give anything if I could go back and change what happened, but I can't."

Lorelei stepped back. "No, you can't."

"Lor, don't pull away from me. I'm sorry."

"I need to go back in." She moved around him.

"We can talk inside."

"No." Lorelei stopped at the screen door. Without turning around, she said, "You need to leave."

"Darling, please—"

"You couldn't stand it, could you?" she said, turning on him fast enough to force Spencer a step back.

"Couldn't stand what?" he asked.

"That my father is still alive. That he never abandoned me. That he wanted my mother."

Hot anger danced at the base of his skull. "You're going too far," Spencer said. "You know I'm happy that you and Mike found each other."

"Right," she snorted. "So happy that you had to blab it to the one person who would make it sound tawdry."

"Listen to what you're saying, Lorelei. You know I wouldn't do that."

"At least I was conceived by two people who loved each other," she yelled.

Spencer closed his eyes, the words hitting like a blow.

When he opened them again, he said, "And I'm the unwanted accident of a casual fuck. Thanks for the reminder, Lorelei. I'd almost forgotten."

Turning on his heel, Spencer walked down the porch steps with his head high. He'd known Lorelei would be angry and disappointed, as she had every right to be. But he'd never imagined she would lash out at him, striking a blow to his very core.

And he'd had no idea how much it would hurt when she did.

By dinnertime Saturday evening, Lorelei had found only one shelter for battered women within fifty miles, and the facility had no beds available. The caseworker she'd finally reached suggested filing a police report, requesting a restraining order, and said a shelter in East Tennessee might be Carrie's best option.

She'd also explained that restraining orders were practically useless, and that if they could get the victim to relatives out of state, that was likely the safest way to go. But Carrie'd made it clear that staying with her mother wasn't possible, and she refused to call her sister.

Lorelei was half tempted to inform the woman that she didn't have the luxury of holding on to her pride, but then she saw the determination in Carrie's eyes and kept the thought to herself. So other than hiding the pregnant lady in the attic, they hadn't come up with anything viable.

At which point Granny suggested Carrie might like to learn how to crochet. The younger woman looked surprised, but also as if she didn't want to offend her hostess. When Granny said she could make a baby blanket, Carrie nodded and followed her into the sewing room to pick out some skeins of yarn.

Lorelei took the opportunity to consider the last twenty-four hours. Seconds after she'd watched Spencer walk away, still riding on anger, she'd called Mike to let him know their secret was out. He sounded almost relieved, as if Spencer's big mouth had done them a favor. Lorelei didn't feel quite as charitable. Every time she thought about Becky Winkle telling everyone in town that Mike was her father, likely adding her own details, like Lorelei's mother had gotten pregnant to trap him, she wanted to scream.

Oh, how Becky would relish the idea that Donna Pratchett hadn't been able to leg shackle a man, even when she was expecting his child.

As if Becky "divorced-three-times-by-age-thirty" Winkle was any better.

Now that Lorelei was alone for the first time all day, the tears came. She crossed her arms on the table, dropped her forehead onto them, and let go. Yesterday morning she'd woken in Spencer's arms, feeling as if something good had finally come her way.

How had she said such horrible things to him? She might as well have put a bullet through Spencer's heart. There would be no coming back from this. No rainbows on her horizon. No Spencer loving her, faults and all.

As Lorelei sniffed and reached for a tissue, Granny's ancient computer in the corner of the living room dinged to alert that an e-mail had been received. Lorelei hadn't owned the address for long, less than a week, which meant she never got messages. Wiping her nose, she crossed the room to sit at the desk and checked her inbox.

There on the second line was a message from the last person she'd expected. And above it, a subject line revealing a plane ticket confirmation. It looked like Lorelei would be heading back to the airport.

Spencer was supposed to work the Ruby Restoration booth again on Sunday, but he'd called Buford to let him know he wasn't coming. Though he wasn't the type of man to wallow in self-pity or hide from his mistakes, the thought of leaving his apartment made him want to get in his truck, point it toward the state line, and never look back.

Champ never left his side, the animal sensing that his master was injured, even if the wound wasn't visible on the outside. Spencer didn't eat. He didn't shower. To keep his mind occupied, he tried working on the paper that was due on Tuesday, but after reading the same paragraph four times and not comprehending a word it said, he gave up and closed the file.

The television stayed on, but he paid it little mind. Until a story on the news caught his attention.

"Police are investigating the death of a Robertson County man last night at a bar in Gallatin," the announcer said. Spencer recognized the green Ford pickup in the inset picture over the woman's right shoulder. "Patrick 'Patch' Farmer reportedly got into an altercation with another patron. Witnesses say he was severely intoxicated and continually repeated a statement to the effect that he wanted his wife back. The Sumner County Sheriff's Office is working with Robertson County officials to locate Mr. Farmer's wife, whom authorities haven't been able to find. Anyone knowing the whereabouts of Caroline Farmer is asked to contact the Robertson County Sheriff's Office."

Dragging a shirt over his head, Spencer didn't bother with shoes. He was at the front door of the house in seconds. When Rosie opened it, she said, "Spencer, Lorelei is sleeping, but I don't think she wants to see you."

"I'm not here for Lorelei." He pulled the screen door open and brushed past the older woman. "Where's Carrie?"

"I'm right here," his ex-wife said, entering the living room with a ball of yarn and a long needle in her hand. "What's going on?"

"Have you seen the news?" he asked.

Carrie shook her head. "No. Why do I need to see the news?"

Shock had carried him this far, but Spencer hadn't thought about how he would say the words. Crossing the floor to stand in front of her, he said, "It's Patch."

The yarn and needle hit the floor. "What about him?" she asked.

"He got in a bar fight down in Gallatin." Running a hand through his hair, he spit out what he knew. "Patch is dead."

The color drained from Carrie's face seconds before she crumbled. Spencer caught her before she hit the floor and carried her to the couch. As Rosie joined them with a cold washcloth, Lorelei stepped out of the stairwell.

"What's going on? What are *you* doing here?"

Spencer didn't look up from dabbing Carrie's forehead and cheeks with the rag. "I had to tell Carrie something."

Lorelei charged over to the couch and looked down at the unconscious woman. "What the hell did you tell her that made this happen?"

"Patch Farmer was in a bar fight last night." Meeting Lorelei's eye for the first time, he said, "Her husband is dead."

Spencer stuck around long enough for them to revive Carrie and then contact the authorities, but he was gone before the sheriff's deputy arrived. It was going to be hard enough for Patch's wife to explain why she'd been so hard to find. Explaining why her ex-husband knew her whereabouts when her current husband did not seemed like an unnecessary conversation to have with the police.

But then Patch was now Carrie's former husband as well. Her reaction to the news had been a clear indication of how she'd felt about the man whose baby she was carrying. For all his faults—and from what Lorelei had learned, Patch had many—his wife still loved him. In fact, she insisted he had a tender side and could even be romantic when he wanted to be.

Unfortunately, he could also be a real SOB, and he chose to be that more often than not.

By nightfall, Carrie looked exhausted and had said more than once that she felt overwhelmed. She could return home now, since the danger that had kept her at the Pratchett house had passed—literally. But Lorelei had grown to like the expectant mother, and Granny looked ready to adopt her. Together, they convinced her to stay one more night, though they did make a quick run to her double-wide for some personal items and a fresh change of clothes.

She'd been borrowing pieces of Lorelei's, but as Carrie was a good four inches shorter and twenty pounds lighter, even at three months pregnant, than her fashion benefactor, she was in desperate need of something that didn't make her look like a castaway.

"I can tell you one thing," Snow said while tapping a nail on the dining room table, "this town always had its drama, but things have gotten a whole lot more interesting since you walked into my store."

Lorelei wasn't sure if the statement was a compliment, but she did know she couldn't take credit for everything. "I had nothing to do with what happened to Carrie's husband."

"Well," Snow said, "you did kick him in the nuts and take his wife."

"I didn't know that would make him get roaring drunk and take on three guys in a fight."

The police had shared more details than Spencer had gleaned from the news coverage. Patch had run into some coworkers in the bar in Gallatin, and they apparently weren't his friends. When one of them asked where Patch's pretty little wife was, Farmer snapped and jumped him.

No one knew for sure who broke the beer bottle that killed Patch, as the incident happened in the parking lot and none of the men were being very cooperative, but all three were currently being held in the Sumner County Jail as authorities continued to investigate.

"This is true," Snow said, glancing at Carrie, who sat with Granny in the living room. "I feel so bad for her. Talk about a crappy weekend."

Lorelei propped an elbow on the table and dropped her chin into her palm. "From what I've gathered, she's had a crappy life. While the threat of being backhanded is gone, she still has a baby coming. With Patch gone, not only is there no father, but now she has no income."

"Do you think he had life insurance?" Snow asked.

Patch Farmer hadn't seemed like the kind of guy to have his own insurance agent. "Maybe they offer something through his work. I'll make sure Carrie looks into it."

Tilting her head to the side, Snow said, "That girl is lucky you found her when you did. But doesn't your shared connection with Spencer make this somewhat . . . complicated?"

Mention of Spencer brought Lorelei's anger back to the surface. Deep down, she knew he would never have intentionally spewed her secret to Becky, but she also didn't understand how something so important could just slip out. Unable to reconcile her feelings one way or another, she'd pushed the whole topic out of her mind.

"I wouldn't know what to do if things weren't complicated," Lorelei replied. And she was telling the truth. The good came with the bad. Her mother had sacrificed and suffered, but she'd also known real love. Carrie had endured more than her fair share of crap, but she remained sweet-natured and still had a new little one to look forward to.

And Lorelei had more than a complicated relationship with Spencer, to say the least. If they had any relationship at all at this point. She was still too mad to even think about forgiving him. And after what she'd said, she doubted he was feeling very forgiving in her direction either. Spencer may have been an endlessly patient man who'd seen past the attitude and bravado and declared that he liked her, faults and all, but they'd both crossed a line this time.

"Lorelei?" Snow said. "Where did you go?"

Shaking her head, Lorelei apologized. "Sorry. What did you say?"

"I was lamenting that the store isn't busy enough for me to give her a job. Not that what I could pay would be enough to support her and a baby, but it would be something for now."

Talk of giving Carrie a job planted an idea in Lorelei's mind. "I may be able to help her in that area."

"You know someone who's hiring?"

"The position is currently filled, but that will be changing very soon."

With narrowed eyes, Snow dropped her voice. "I admit, I haven't known you very long, but that look is pretty universal. You're up to something."

"Like you said yourself," she answered with a smile. "I do like to keep things interesting."

And it was about time Lorelei used her powers for good.

Chapter 29

Spencer didn't see Lorelei on Monday or Tuesday. He knew she'd been helping Carrie clean up the mess Patch had dropped in her lap. As much as he hated to think ill of the dead, he couldn't help but be pissed at the man who'd slept with his wife, taken her for his own, then been irresponsible enough to get himself killed while Carrie was carrying his baby.

The fact that he'd abused her would have been enough to keep Spencer's blood boiling, but he also couldn't ignore his own part in pushing Carrie in the jerk's direction. Yes, they'd been young and hurting and neither knew how to deal with losing a child, but maybe if he'd tried a little harder. If he'd put in more effort or talked through it instead of keeping it all inside.

Ironic that second-guessing the mistakes he'd made with Carrie had pushed Spencer to do something about what was going on between him and Lorelei. He wasn't about to lose another woman due to stupidity or pride or out-and-out pigheadedness. In fact, losing Lorelei was an experience he intended *not* to repeat.

On Tuesday afternoon, Spencer had stopped by Snow's shop on a mission. Lorelei liked sparkly things, and Snow had no shortage of items to fit that description. He'd asked the proprietor if she knew of any piece in particular that Lorelei had her eye on. After he'd convinced the store owner that his intentions were in the right place, she showed him a ring that Lorelei had been drooling over since her first time in the shop.

There was a large stone in the center, with ten triangular rubies or garnets—Snow wasn't sure which—set around it, giving the effect of a ten-point star. Surrounding the deep red stones were half circles of tiny diamonds, and the whole piece looked like an expensive flower planted atop a solid gold band.

Snow explained that she was no antique dealer, but she guessed the ring had been made in the first half of the twentieth century. The owner, who had given the ring on consignment, wished to remain anonymous, but Snow had received explicit instructions regarding the minimum amount she could accept. That amount was three hundred dollars less than the little tag said, and Spencer walked out of the store with the token safely encased in a navy-blue velvet box tucked in the shirt pocket over his heart.

Exactly where it belonged until he could slide it onto Lorelei's left hand. Which he would do today.

At exactly nine o'clock on Wednesday morning, Spencer walked into the office of Lowry Construction with his heart in his throat and sweat soaking his palms. But as he rounded the corner into the main area, Lorelei's desk was empty while Mike sat behind his own reviewing a set of blueprints.

"Where's Lorelei?" Spencer asked.

Mike looked up with raised brows, clearly surprised by the unexpected visitor. "She isn't here."

Spencer could see that much for himself. "Then where is she?"

Rising from his chair, Mike said, "She doesn't want you to know that."

After Spencer had broken the news about Patch's death, he'd left the women to handle details with the police and called Mike to request a meeting that afternoon. To his relief, Mike hadn't been nearly as angry about his slip to Becky, and in fact completely understood how the busybody in question could push a man to his limits.

This made the uncooperative response a surprise. "Mike, I need to find her."

"Well, you won't find her here anymore."

"What?"

"She quit," Mike said. "She's giving her job to Carrie Farmer, though I'm still not sure how she convinced me to agree to that."

The blood drained from Spencer's brain. This couldn't be happening. Not again. Her car wasn't in the driveway at the house when he'd left. If she didn't go to work, then where was she?

"Why'd you let her do that?"

Mike gave a humorless laugh. "If anyone knows that there is no *letting* Lorelei do anything, it should be you, Boyd."

That was true, but dammit, he didn't have time for this. "You said she doesn't want me to know where she is. That means you know."

Dropping back into the chair, Mike said, "I've never been good at subterfuge. I shouldn't have said even that much."

Spencer was running out of patience, and the panic coursing through his gut was making it hard not to drag the older man over the desk. "Where *is* she?" he asked one more time.

With resignation in his eyes, Mike said, "She went to the airport."

Lorelei had left Ardent Springs an hour earlier than necessary, afraid traffic might cause her to be late. As luck would have it, the drive had been free and clear, as if the commuter gods knew how important this was. Walking down the long, glass-encased walkway from the parking area, she rethought her choice not to tell Spencer about this.

He was going to be furious when he found out. Maybe. After the horrible things she'd said to him, there was no way to be sure. Though there wasn't a doubt in her mind that he wouldn't approve of her decision, she had to hope he'd eventually see that this was the right thing to do.

The flight was on Delta, and Lorelei found the monitors in the main area leading to the terminals to make sure it hadn't been delayed. Flight 1772 was listed as on time. Thank goodness. Her nerves wouldn't hold up to waiting any longer than she had to.

With time to kill, Lorelei grabbed a coffee and a brownie at Starbucks. The caffeine was needed since she'd barely slept since Saturday. Every time she closed her eyes, Spencer's face loomed in the night, torturing her with the stricken look he'd worn when she'd heartlessly thrown out that conceived-in-love bullcrap. She'd been so angry with him for sharing her secret with Becky Winkle that Lorelei had lashed out without thinking.

Which was further proof that Spencer was better off without her. At least now he'd probably agree with her.

When it was time, she disposed of her garbage and headed for concourse B, but before she approached the entrance, a voice called from behind her.

"Stop right there, Lorelei." She spun to find the source and was shocked to see Spencer running her way. "I can't believe you were going to do this without telling me."

For crying out loud. Could no one of her acquaintance keep a secret?

"You would have found out," she said.

"I shouldn't have to *find out*," he answered. "You can't make decisions like this without me. Whether you like it or not, this affects me, too."

Lorelei tried to defend herself. "Of course this affects you—" she said, but Spencer cut her off.

"I'm not letting you do this."

She bristled at his tone. "It's a little late for that now."

"No, it isn't," he said, taking her by the elbow. "You're not on a plane yet, and you won't be getting on one anytime soon."

That didn't make any sense at all. Lorelei wasn't . . . then the truth dawned. He thought she was leaving. And he'd driven all the way from Ardent Springs, likely committing numerous traffic violations, to stop her. Lorelei's heart melted as renewed hope soared through her system.

"Why won't you let me get on a plane, Spencer?" she asked, struggling to keep the smile from her lips.

"Because I love you, you crazy woman, and I'm not letting you walk out of my life for a second time. Not without a fight."

"Oh, Spencer," she said, cradling his face in her hands. "I love you, too."

Suspicion crossed his handsome features. "You do? Then why were you leaving?"

"I wasn't leaving."

"You weren't?"

Lorelei shook her head. "Nope."

Taking in their surroundings, Spencer said, "Then why are we at the airport?"

"I've come to pick someone up, not fly out." Though she knew the answer, she asked, "Why are you at the airport?"

"I'm here because I thought you were leaving me again. Mike said you quit your job and had gone to the airport."

So Mike was the blabbermouth this time. From now on, anything Lorelei wanted to keep to herself would not be shared with the men in her life. Not that she planned to keep any more secrets.

"I have no intention of leaving you ever again," she said, meaning every word with all her heart. "But I wasn't sure you'd ever want me back after the things I said. I'm so sorry. That was unforgivable, and I wouldn't blame you at all if you never talked to me again."

Spencer slid one hand around her back while brushing the hair off her face with the other. "I told you once that you could never stay mad at me, Lorelei. That goes both ways. Cutting you out of my life would be like cutting off my own arm. I let you go once, and it damn near killed me. I don't ever want to do that again."

Pure, unmitigated happiness lifted Lorelei onto her toes so she could kiss the man she would never deserve or ever give up. As his arms tightened around her, she was lifted off the ground and swept into a kiss that showed her exactly how Spencer felt. When her feet returned to the ground, she knew she must be grinning like a fool.

As he trailed a thumb along her jawline, Spencer's brown eyes danced over her face as if they'd never seen her before. And truth be told, they had never seen her quite like this. Lorelei didn't need a mirror to know that she was glowing with something makeup couldn't create or hide.

Spencer asked, "So who are you here to pick up?"

"Oh, my gosh," Lorelei exclaimed, turning around to scan the crowd exiting the terminal. A dark-haired woman who looked to be about Mike's age was also scanning the area. She matched the description from the e-mail perfectly, wearing jeans and a red shirt as the message said she would be, and once her eyes caught Lorelei's, the truth was evident.

The woman approached them, stopping a few feet away. "Lorelei?" she asked shyly.

Threading her arm through Spencer's, Lorelei said, "Yes, ma'am. And this is your nephew, Spencer."

Spencer sat transfixed while his father's sister spoke with Lorelei as if they'd known each other all their lives. When a question or statement was directed his way, he nodded or gave a brief one- or two-word answer. It was the best he could manage under the circumstances. His aunt was sitting across from him in an airport coffee shop. A blood relative with eyes much like his own.

"I haven't told your little sister about you," she was saying, as she toyed with the cardboard wrapper on her cup. "She's still dealing with your father's death, and Gabby isn't the easiest child to handle even on a good day. I thought it best to give her a little more time."

"Of course," Spencer found himself saying.

"How old is Gabby?" Lorelei asked.

"Eighteen going on thirty-six," Annie replied. "Doug doted on her, I think because he was so much older when she was born and thought he'd never have children." The dark-haired woman paused. "I'm sorry, I mean *any more* children."

Spencer pushed the surreal nature of the situation out of his mind. *I have a sister.* "That's okay. I know what you meant. So she's spoiled?"

"And then some. Her mother and Doug divorced when she was ten, but he took her every chance he got. They did rodeos and shopping sprees." Annie shook her head. "He even bought her a horse, which she adored for all of a month before her attention strayed somewhere else. Doug had to sell the poor thing so it wouldn't go on being neglected."

"Are there any cousins?" Lorelei ventured. "Aunts or uncles?"

"Doug and I were it, so I'm your only aunt. At least on this side of the family." Annie leaned forward on the table. "I have three kids of my own: one in college, one in high school, and the youngest in middle school. My husband isn't used to taking care of them alone, which is why I can only stay until Sunday."

Even if she'd had to get back on a plane in an hour, this was more than Spencer had ever hoped for.

"What about grandparents?" Spencer asked.

Annie's mouth turned up in a sad smile. "You look a lot like Doug, but you're the spitting image of our father. Marshall Crawford was wiry like you, but no one messed with Daddy. He had a presence about him.

Men listened when he talked. If he hadn't been so devoted to his cattle, I have no doubt he would have gone into politics."

"That sounds a lot like you," Lorelei said, nudging him with her shoulder.

"Yeah, it does." Since the description had been in the past tense, learning about yet another male relative he would never meet was bittersweet. "And your mom?"

"Mom died of cancer back in the seventies. I sometimes wonder if Doug might have made different choices had she still been around." Annie twirled her drink. "Doug and Mom were close, and he was never the same after she died. She'd kept him on the straight and narrow, but once her influence was gone, Doug's wild side took over."

Odd how Spencer had been raised with the complete opposite—no father and a mother who could best be described as a bad example—yet he'd never developed a "wild side," as Annie had called it.

His aunt drained her cup, and Lorelei said, "I suppose we should go. You didn't fly all this way to spend your visit in the Nashville airport."

"Are you sure I shouldn't get a hotel room?" Annie asked as Lorelei threw their trash away. "I couldn't resist the invitation to come meet Doug's boy, but I don't want to be a burden to anyone."

"Of course you'll stay with us," Lorelei said. "Right, Spencer?" For the first time since he'd caught her in the main area, Lorelei looked worried.

"Yes, she'll stay with us," he agreed, not sure how Lorelei planned to explain that "us" didn't live in the same house. At least not technically.

As they walked the long glass corridor toward the garage, a million questions churned through Spencer's mind. He wanted more than the number of cousins and a list of deceased relatives. He wanted to know about his dad. To hear stories, learn how he saw the world, and what he'd told his sister about the son he never met. If he told her anything at all.

"We had a bit of a mix-up," Lorelei said. "Spencer and I are here in separate vehicles, so you can ride with him and I'll follow."

An hour alone with his newfound relation sounded nerve-racking. But it also felt like a gift.

Spencer was happy to see a smile finally reach Annie's eyes. "I'd like that very much," she said. "It'll give me a chance to get to know you."

It had somehow never occurred to Spencer that she might have questions for him as well. But then, she hadn't flown all this way to fill in the blanks that could have been easily answered in a call or e-mail. She'd come to see him. To meet her brother's boy, as she'd called him.

Dragging his aunt's small carry-on behind him, Spencer sent up a prayer of thanks to whatever entity had brought him this new fortune. Then he squeezed Lorelei's hand, grateful that she'd been the angel to make it happen. And that she wasn't leaving him after all.

Chapter 30

Lorelei was ready to puke.

The restoration meeting would start in less than ten minutes. Enough time for her to cut and run. Spencer knew the proposal as well as she did. He could present the plan and probably convince them to agree much better than she ever could.

The thought must have shown on her face as she stared at the exit.

"Don't even think about it, Pratchett," Spencer said, stepping up beside her. "You are not getting out of this."

"My throat is swelling shut and I can feel my heart pumping in my ears." Shaking her hands at her sides, she asked, "What are the signs of a stroke? There's a word to remember them, but I can't remember what that word is. Wait, is forgetting a simple word a sign? I'm having a stroke."

"You are not having a stroke," he said, waving at an older couple who'd just entered the room. "We've been over this proposal with a fine-tooth comb. Every detail has been planned out and every possible objection has a counterargument. Now breathe and smile. You're the epitome of confidence."

Spencer had made it clear that if Jebediah saw even the slightest weakness, he'd go in for the kill. It was of the utmost importance that Lorelei *not* give him that chance. And he was right about the details. They'd gone over the plan forward and back, nailing down specifics that wouldn't even need to be addressed until the proposal was approved and an event committee formed.

"You're right," she said, letting his words buoy her. "I can do this. It's an excellent idea, and if they vote it down, they're idiots."

"True," Spencer agreed. "But don't actually call them idiots. Insulting your audience is not the way to win votes."

Now he was being a brat. "I'm not going to insult anyone but you, if you keep that up. How is Annie?"

"Good, I think. Carrie and Snow are entertaining her out in the restaurant."

Lorelei giggled. "Does she know she's having dinner with your ex-wife?"

"I explained on the way over. She was surprised that we were still friends. I guess Dad didn't manage to remain civil with any of his exes."

It made Lorelei smile every time Spencer referred to Doug as Dad. At first he'd called him "my father" or by his given name, but after the trip from the airport with his aunt, the more personal title had become the norm. He would never get the chance to shake hands with the man who'd help create him, but there was a real person filling what had been an empty void for way too long.

For once, Lorelei's impetuous nature and refusal to take no for an answer had paid off. She could only hope that her presentation would go half as well as Spencer's family reunion.

Spencer would never admit it, but he was as nervous as Lorelei. She'd come so far in the short time she'd been home. Moved beyond the public tantrums and screw-you attitude. But putting herself out there, taking the lead on something so important, was Lorelei's chance to be seen as an important part of the community, instead of the rebellious teen who couldn't wait to get out, or the cowed woman who'd returned with her tail between her legs.

After tonight, she would be taken seriously as a citizen who cared about her community and was willing to give her time and energy to make it better. And Spencer couldn't be more proud.

When Buford stepped to the podium to call the meeting to order, Lorelei gave Spencer's hand one last squeeze and took the seat he pulled out for her. Five minutes later, she walked to the front of the room with her head high as he passed out the printed proposal copies they'd made for everyone to follow along.

Mike had suggested they create a PowerPoint presentation, but Lancelot's banquet room wasn't equipped for A/V.

"Good evening," Lorelei said, her voice wobbly. She glanced his way, cleared her throat, and began again. "Good evening, everyone. As you know, I'm here to present a plan for holding a fall festival as a fund-raiser for the theater. The handout Spencer is passing around is the full proposal, so you can follow along. I'll be happy to answer any questions you may have."

Flipping open her own copy, she said, "I propose we hold a two-day event between the end of September and the middle of October to avoid conflicting with the county fair, Labor Day festivities, and Halloween events held on Main Street. Because the festival would involve closing a small area of Fourth Street, I suggest the event be held on a Saturday and Sunday."

Spencer had argued with her to present the information as "I propose" instead of "We propose" as she'd wanted to do. Yes, he'd helped a great deal with the details, determined to cut off any argument Winkle might make, but the idea was all hers, and she deserved the credit.

"As you can see on page three, I've mapped out a suggested layout, which would be discussed and perfected by a planning committee should the proposal pass, that shows vendor booths offering non-edible products from the corner of South Margin down Fourth toward the theater. Closer to the Ruby parking lot would be the food vendors, either in booths or their own trucks, if applicable.

"Then, in the parking lot would be a children's section in the far corner, with a main stage set up against the back wall of the building. How often the stage would be active will depend on how many acts are booked, but as of right now I have a solid commitment from Wes Tillman to be our headliner."

That revelation sent a buzz throughout the room. Spencer ventured a glance at Jebediah and was almost jubilant to see his cheeks turn red. The mayor had to know there would be no swaying the committee to his side with Wes Tillman already on board.

Mike more than came through on that one.

"There will be a small fee for anyone wanting to host a booth or food truck, and all festivalgoers will also pay a small admittance fee. With the right advertising, we should be able to raise a significant amount of money for the restoration. Are there any questions?"

The room seemed to hold their collective breaths, much like the attendees at a shotgun wedding when the preacher reads the "speak now or forever hold your peace" part.

"How much do we have to pay Tillman to perform?" Jebediah asked, honing in on the one aspect that could make or break the proposal.

Without missing a beat, Lorelei answered, "Mr. Tillman is donating his time as well as supplying all PA equipment for the festival. Free of charge. In addition, he's offering a cash donation to be used toward advertising the event."

The buzz returned, louder this time. But Jebediah wasn't giving up yet.

"And parking? If you intend to bring in substantial crowds, they'll need someplace to park."

Again, Lorelei had a ready answer. "I've contacted all the churches along Church Street. All have agreed to let us use their parking lots. Between the Catholics, Methodists, Protestants, and Baptists, that's six large lots. If those fill up, we'll still have curb parking." Jebediah opened his mouth to speak again, but Lorelei didn't give him the chance. "Stallings Hardware has also offered to supply shuttle transportation from Main and Bridge Streets if it becomes necessary for attendees to park that far away."

Winkle shot Buford a hard look, to which the former mayor only grinned.

"Anyone else?" Lorelei said, but no one raised their hand. She turned to Buford as she stepped back from the podium, her job done and the fate of the proposal in the hands of the committee members now.

The vote took only seconds, and with a smack of the gavel, the Restore the Ruby fall festival was approved.

She'd done it. By some miracle, she'd pulled it off. And with only two easy questions from Mayor Butthead. What were the odds?

"I told you you could do it," Spencer said for the third time. The man really did enjoy being right.

"*We* did it," she argued. "The parking thing was your idea. How did you know he'd ask that?"

"Jebediah and Grady Evans showed up at the booth last Saturday evening full of fire and vinegar about the festival. I kept telling him nothing had been proposed yet, but he continued to fire arguments, and the parking was one of them."

"Thank you, annoying mayor, for being stupid enough to give us advance warning." Lorelei followed Spencer into the restaurant. Granny and Pearl had already gone in. Annie and Granny had hit it off right away, and the older woman was dying to introduce Spencer's lovely aunt to her best friend, Pearl.

When they finally reached the party, Lorelei was surprised to find enough chairs for all of them and a bottle of sparkling wine on the table. "You were so sure this would work, you ordered something for a celebration toast?" she asked.

"We'll be toasting something, I hope, but it isn't the festival proposal."

Pulling out her chair, Spencer waited for Lorelei to sit, then shifted the chair next to her. Only, instead of sitting down, he cleared the chair out of the way and dropped to one knee.

"Holy crap," she said, her hands covering her mouth. This could not be happening. Spencer pulled a box out of his pocket and her heart stopped. *This was totally happening.*

"Lorelei," he said, his face solemn and serious. She hoped he didn't expect her to match that look, because she was feeling anything but solemn or serious. He opened the box to reveal the diamond-and-ruby ring from Snow's shop. The one she'd longed for since the moment she saw it. "Will you marry me?"

And once again, her throat threatened to swell shut. Blood pumped in her ears, creating a roar that blocked out the dinner noise around them. Though if she'd had eyes for anyone but Spencer, Lorelei would have known that everyone in their vicinity had stopped eating, watching with rapt interest.

He didn't know everything yet. Lorelei had yet to explain what had happened with Maxwell, and Spencer deserved to know. To understand exactly what kind of woman he was considering spending the rest of his life with.

She tried to answer, emitting little more than a squeak. Happiness was drowning out the doubts, stealing her ability to form words.

Spencer had professed that he could never stay mad at her. Surely he would understand once she explained.

"Can I take that as a yes?" he asked, his face growing more animated.

Lorelei nodded so hard she was afraid her head might pop off and roll into the kitchen. And then she was up and in Spencer's arms and he was kissing her and nothing had ever felt so right in all her life. This was her chance to make up for all her bad decisions of the past.

When the kiss finally ended, she was surprised to find that they were receiving a standing ovation from the other guests. Tears were streaming down Granny's cheeks, and Pearl, too, was dabbing at the corners of her eyes with her napkin. If anyone found it odd that the groom-to-be's former wife had enveloped his future wife in a tear-filled hug, no one said so.

Once all hugs were exchanged and congratulations granted, Spencer popped the cork on the sparkling wine, and everyone toasted to the couple. Everyone except Carrie, who settled for a glass of sparkling cider, but she clinked with the rest of them, as if her drink were no different.

An hour later, Spencer led Lorelei to his truck, where Lorelei took the opportunity to come clean about what had happened before she'd left California.

"I need to tell you something," she said, pulling up short as Spencer reached to open her door, "and I'd prefer if you weren't driving when I do."

Spencer looked concerned, but said only, "Okay then. Do I need to be sitting down?"

She considered the question. "Yes. This might be easier if we're sitting down."

This was a make-or-break moment, after all. She may have been wearing a ring, but they'd been through this routine before and not made it to the altar. If he was going to marry her, he needed to know everything.

"Is this another one of those bad timing things on your part?" he asked as he lowered the tailgate. "Because I'd much rather be home celebrating our new status. Preferably naked."

"We'll see how you feel after this," Lorelei mumbled, lifting herself onto the truck and waiting for Spencer to have a seat. Her heart told her he'd understand, but her head wasn't so sure. After several seconds of chewing on a nail, she decided to start with some backstory. "Shortly before I left LA, I was seeing someone."

"I'm not going to like this story, am I?" Spencer asked.

Lorelei answered honestly. "Probably not, but I hope you'll hear me out."

Nodding, he said, "Go on."

"His name was Maxwell Chapel. I waited on him right before my shift ended one night, and after I clocked out, I joined him in his booth and we talked until dawn. The connection was instant. He said all the right things and was the first guy who showed an interest in a long time. Well, the first guy with a job and money and who wasn't selling drugs or taking them."

"Lorelei," Spencer said, "I was married during our years apart. I never expected you not to have dated someone during those years. The fact that you're here and not there is all I need to know."

"No, it isn't." She turned to face him, holding eye contact. "Maxwell and I were together for nine months, and I thought he was the one—until someone paid me a visit. It was his wife."

Brown eyes narrowed. "You were seeing a married man?"

"I was," she admitted, "but I didn't know it."

"What do you mean, you didn't know it? How do you not know someone's married?"

"LA isn't like Ardent Springs," Lorelei said, the words coming out faster in her need to explain. "It's huge and if someone wants to live two or even three lives, they can do it. If I'd known he was married, I never would have gone out with him. And I broke it off that day. Unfortunately, that meant losing my apartment, since Maxwell had been paying for it."

Spencer grew still. "You let him pay for your apartment? Did he live with you?"

"Not technically, though he did stay often. There were signs I should have picked up on. I couldn't call him, I could only text. I could never see his place because he had roommates that were messy." She hopped off the truck in agitation. "I mean, what thirty-three-year-old man has messy roommates?"

Spencer seemed to catch on that the question was rhetorical and held silent.

"And he traveled, of course," she continued. "That's like the age-old lie, right? I wouldn't see him for a week or more at a time because he had to be out of town on business." Lorelei jammed her left hand into her hair, which got caught on the new ring. "Ouch," she yelped.

"Hold on." Spencer extracted the hair from her ring. "You okay?"

"See?" she said, spinning the ring as if trying to take it off. "It's a sign. Your wife cheated on you, and I helped a man cheat in California. That means I'm no better. And you deserve better. Much better."

"You said you didn't know."

"But I should have known. Blind ignorance isn't much of an excuse."

"Lorelei," he said, taking her hands to stop the spinning. "You didn't willfully hurt anyone. If anything, you were as much a victim of that jerk's infidelity as his wife was. None of this changes the fact that I want to marry you. If anything, I'm thankful that he turned out not to be the one for you."

Lorelei let Spencer pull her into a hug and squeezed him tight, thankful she'd fallen in love with the most patient man ever. "I should have known," she repeated. "You were always the one for me, Spencer. The only one." Pulling back, she asked, "But are you sure you want to be stuck with me forever? Faults and all?" she added with one raised brow.

"Faults and all," he agreed. "I wouldn't have it any other way."

After a long kiss to seal the deal, Lorelei traced her thumb along his jawline.

"Now do you understand why I didn't want to think I'd spoiled two marriages?" she asked. "I know I'm not the best person in the world, but that would have been too much, even for me."

"The fact that it matters so much to you is proof that you're a better person than you think. And then there's always the fact that you took in my pregnant, abused ex-wife when most people would have looked the other way."

"There was no choice," Lorelei argued. "I couldn't leave her to be beaten, or abandon her when she had no place else to go."

"Exactly," he said, dropping a kiss on her nose. "Some would, but you couldn't. That's why I love you, Lorelei. Because deep down you're just a softie with a heart of gold."

Shaking him, she said, "If you tell anyone that, I'll never forgive you. I have a rep to protect."

Spencer laughed. "Then how about I take you home so you can show me what a bad girl you are?"

Unable to hold in her own laughter, she said, "Spencer Boyd, that's the sweetest thing you've ever said to me. How fast can you drive?"

"Pretty fast." Spencer dragged her toward the passenger-side door. "But if we can't wait," he said, lifting her onto the seat, "we can always find a secluded place to park." Wiggling his brows, he added, "I've got blankets behind the seat."

Before Lorelei could reply, he'd closed her door and was running around the front of the truck to his own. How had she ever thought to put this man out of her life? Clearly a case of temporary insanity. Thank goodness she'd been cured, because she never intended to endure another day without him.

Epilogue

The first Saturday of October dawned warm and clear, relieving a smidgen of the anxiety Lorelei carried for the day ahead. Ardent Springs had endured massive storms for several days, threatening to drown out her big day. After all she'd been through, Lorelei would scream if Mother Nature put the Restore the Ruby Festival underwater.

In three months, the five-person planning committee of Lorelei, Nitzi Merchant, Jacqueline Forbes, Mabel Handleman, and Carrie Farmer (with the help of several minions, as Lorelei liked to call them) organized what was sure to be a highly successful event.

Or so Lorelei hoped.

Along the way, Lorelei had outed herself as Lulu, but only to her small group of committee members. She was determined to sell her treats during the festival, and instead of reserving a booth anonymously, she revealed herself as the mysterious baker. To her relief, the confession was met with support and encouragement. She only hoped the festivalgoers—meaning her fellow Ardent Springs residents—would react the same way.

"You're robbing me of the bestselling product I carry," Snow said as she surveyed Lorelei's booth twenty minutes before the gates were scheduled to open.

"It's only for this weekend," Lorelei replied, spreading her pumpkin spice cookies around the ceramic pumpkin that would hold the cider. "And you don't even sell my stuff on weekends."

Once Carrie had taken over at the construction office, Lorelei had used the time on her hands to up production to five days a week. Sunday through Thursday she turned out a wide variety of cookies, brownies, and breads, which Snow then sold Monday through Friday. Thankfully, the locals could not seem to get enough.

"I plan to in the spring," Snow said. "In fact, I'm giving you an entire section of the store. It'll be Lulu's Home Bakery inside Snow's Curiosity Shop. Kind of like when they put a coffee shop in a bookstore."

Lorelei stopped what she was doing and looked up. "Are you serious?"

"Yes, ma'am. We may have to renegotiate the split, but there's plenty of time for that."

Ignoring the issue of money, Lorelei said, "So I'd have my own counter that I'd man myself? I could even have a display case?"

"We could set up tiny tables, too, for people to sit down," Snow said with a grin.

Not only would Lorelei have her own business, but now she'd have her own place to operate that business. She could maybe even rent an entire space all her own someday.

"I've seen that look," Spencer said as he joined them at the booth. "What evil schemes are you planning?" he asked, snatching a cookie off the tray she'd painstakingly arranged.

"Spencer Boyd, you touch another one of those and you're going without for a month. And I don't mean without cookies." Lorelei shifted others to fill the void he'd created. "I was thinking about the future," she said, unwilling to speak her dream aloud quite yet. Maybe when they were home and could talk about it in private. She didn't want Snow to know she was thinking of abandoning her before they'd even gotten started.

"Does that mean you're ready to set a date?" he asked, hope alight in his eyes.

Lorelei hadn't been able to decide if she wanted a spring or fall wedding. She'd also been too busy planning the festival to wrap her brain around planning their nuptials. It wasn't as if it mattered. He'd put a ring on her finger and agreed to keep her forever. To Lorelei, that was as good as any vows spoken in front of a preacher.

"One event at a time," she said, leaning forward for a kiss to appease her fiancé. "I'll make up my mind by Christmas. I promise."

Spencer took the offered kiss as Snow said, "Whatever you do, don't go to Vegas. That was not a good idea."

Lorelei and Spencer locked eyes before Lorelei asked, "Snow, are you married?"

"What?" she said, jerking her focus from the cookies to the cookie maker. "Why would you ask that?"

"Um . . ." Lorelei hedged. "You just said going to Vegas *wasn't* a good idea. As if you knew from personal experience."

Snow's cheeks grew pink as she shifted from one foot to the other. "No, I mean that's what people say. You run off to Vegas and the next thing you know you're at some little chapel taking vows and the next morning you wonder what the hell you were thinking." Waving her hand around as if she were being flip and nothing more, she added, "That's what I hear, anyway."

The explanation revealed an important truth about Snow Cameron. She was a horrible liar.

"Okay," Spencer said into the awkward silence. "We were thinking of something more local, so no worries about running off to Vegas." Turning to Lorelei, he said, "But if you don't agree on a date soon, I *will* drag you out there and find one of those chapels."

"You don't have to look far," Snow said. "The dang things are every-where."

Definitely a terrible liar.

Squirming like a four-year-old forced to sit through a long sermon, Snow said, "I'd better get up to my own booth." She glanced at her phone. "Ten minutes and this place is going to be packed."

"That's the hope, anyway," Lorelei said. Mention of the gates open-ing sent butterflies swirling through her stomach. "Good luck, lady. And thanks for buying a booth."

"Happy to do it," Snow said, giving a quick wave as she walked off.

Waiting until she was out of earshot, Lorelei turned to Spencer. "She's totally married. Or was once upon a time and doesn't want to talk about it."

"If she is married, I wonder where her groom is?" Spencer said. After Lorelei scooted a slice of nut bread an eighth of an inch to the left, he stilled her hands with his own. "Hon, you need to relax. You've seen to every detail of this festival, and if something does go wrong, there are plenty of people ready to fix it."

"You think something will go wrong?" she asked. As if she weren't nervous enough already, now Spencer believed the whole day would be a bust.

"That's not what I'm saying. Breathe, Lor. It's all good."

She did as ordered, even if he hadn't meant the words literally. Breath-ing in through her nose, she let the air exit over her lips as she closed her eyes. It took two more tries to quell the panic rising up her esophagus.

"Better?" he asked when she looked at him again.

"It's always better when you're around," she admitted. A sappy statement she never would have uttered three months earlier. Being hopelessly in love and happy had done wacky things to her brain. Or maybe it was her heart. "Now go walk around and make sure every-thing is good. Especially the stage. I don't want any issues when the entertainment starts this afternoon."

They'd lined up enough local acts, as well as unknowns from Nashville looking for any chance to play for an audience, to fill six hours before Wes Tillman would perform at eight. Mike had been instrumental in filling and creating the lineup. For once, Lorelei was relieved to be wrong about something. No one batted an eye when they'd learned Mike was her father. Some even remembered Mike and her mother being an item, and admitted they never thought she was the kind of girl that some had portrayed her to be.

Even that small measure of support had meant a lot to Lorelei.

She watched Spencer make his way through the food vendors, stopping to chat with each one. All gave a smile or a nod, shaking his hand and welcoming the visit even though they were busy preparing for the impending crowd. It wasn't the first time Lorelei had noticed how much Spencer was respected in the community. If she wasn't careful, someday she might end up as first lady of Ardent Springs.

Wouldn't that be something? The girl who'd once told the entire town to go to hell sitting at the top of the Ardent Springs hierarchy. She'd hate it, of that she was sure. But for Spencer, she'd play the part with as much class as she could muster. That's what a girl did for the man she loved. And how she did love him.

Spencer progressed farther down the lane, and then Lorelei caught a glimpse of something in the distance and couldn't believe her eyes. Arching directly over the Ruby Theater was a gorgeous rainbow. If that wasn't a sign, she didn't know what was.

Today was going to be just fine. And so were the rest of her days.

Don't miss
Our Now and Forever,
the next Ardent Springs
novel by Terri Osburn

Coming Fall 2015

Chapter 1

The moment of reckoning had come.

Snow Cameron's heart sped to a dangerous level as fear and joy lit through her system like lightning slicing through an ancient oak. The fear was no surprise, but the joy was so unexpected she was forced to grip the edges of the cash register on the counter in front of her to keep her balance.

In stunned silence, she stared into the face she'd been avoiding for nearly eighteen months. *How had she ever forgotten how beautiful he was?*

Caleb McGraw was tall and lean. The perfect combination of Greek god and good old boy, his perfect jawline was made for marble, while his eyes were the shade of a blue clear sky. She'd like to say the eyes were the first thing she'd noticed when she'd nearly tripped over him at a New Year's Eve party nearly two years ago, but the shoulders had been the first draw.

Snow had always suffered a weakness for a strong set of shoulders, and Caleb's were broad and strong. Perfect for holding on to while they . . .

Sex is what got you into this mess, young lady. Do not go there.

"You're a hard woman to find," Caleb McGraw said with the soft drawl of a Louisiana native.

Glancing around, partly to break the spell but also to gauge their audience, Snow was relieved to see few customers present, and none seemed to notice the handsome stranger in their midst. At least not yet.

"Well," she said, "my name *is* over the door." Snow evoked every ounce of control to remain calm, hoping the panic shooting up her spine didn't show on her face. "What are you doing here?" she asked, which may have been the most idiotic question ever, but she couldn't think of anything else to say.

Except maybe, *How did you find me?* Or, *Why didn't you love me?*

Though Snow had spent endless hours contemplating exactly what she'd do were this unwelcome reunion to occur, she hadn't considered how her brain cells would scatter and her knees would threaten to cease working. Thankful to have the counter between them, she waited for his answer with growing dread.

Crossing his arms, Caleb smirked. "I'd think that was obvious."

Snow studied his face, struggling to read his thoughts. Neither anger nor pleasure showed in his features. Though he loomed above her, six feet three inches of solid muscle, as she knew all too well, his stance didn't feel threatening. If she'd spent as much time learning his mind as she'd devoted to studying his body, maybe interpreting his expression wouldn't be so difficult.

With shaking fingers, Snow swiped a wayward curl off her forehead and was reminded that she was wearing a hat. A very pointy hat, along with a tight black dress, red-and-white-striped knee socks, and platform Mary Janes.

Why did he have to find me on Halloween? she thought.

The downtown vendors of Ardent Springs held a trick-or-treating event for area children every year, which would start in less than an hour. Snow had donned the witch costume to show her town spirit, as there were still several locals who never let her forget that she was a newcomer, regardless of being a resident for more than a year now.

From her left, Snow spotted Lorelei Pratchett headed toward them from the back of the store, looking intent on learning the identity of the man staring at Snow with unblinking blue eyes.

"I'm really busy right now," she said, hoping Caleb would agree to continue this conversation at a later time, preferably in private. Not that she wanted to be alone with him, but if anyone learned exactly who he was . . .

"Who do we have here?" Lorelei asked once she reached the end of the counter.

"Nobody," Snow said, at the same time Caleb introduced himself.

"Caleb McGraw," he offered, repeating his name for a second time, as Snow had spoken over him the first. "I'm here to see Snow."

Giving her friend a you-lucky-girl look, Lorelei said, "You two know each other?"

"It's been a while," Snow answered, determined to keep the details slight.

"Seventeen months, three weeks, and four days," Caleb said, shocking Snow into silence.

He'd kept track down to the day. Had he been looking for her all that time? She knew he'd eventually seek her out, as they had business that would someday need to be resolved, but since she'd mattered so little to him, Snow assumed there'd be no rush.

Unless . . .

"If you don't mind," she said, coming out from behind the counter, "Caleb and I need to discuss something. Could you watch the register for a few minutes?"

Lorelei's brows shot up, but she didn't ask any more questions. "Happy to, sure. Yeah." Making a shooing motion, she added, "You two take all the time you need."

"Follow me," Snow said to Caleb, then hurried through the store to the back room. Once inside, she opted not to offer him a seat, since she didn't expect this to take long. "What do you want?"

"You know the answer to that," he said, crossing his arms and leaning a shoulder against the wall to his left.

"No, actually, I don't." She had a guess, and the thought made her nauseated. Another unexpected reaction.

Instead of pulling out the papers she assumed he'd want her to sign, he said, "You left." Two words that felt like a one-two punch.

"Yes," she said, her voice weak. There was no reason to deny the truth. "Why?"

Tapping into unknown depths of bravado, Snow answered, "Mistakes were made. I didn't see any reason to keep making them."

Straightening off the wall, Caleb said, "After all this time, you think that's a good enough answer?"

What did he want from her? Some tearful explanation of how he'd hurt her? A deep, philosophical discussion about the negative effects of making spontaneous, emotional decisions and why there's a reason the brain should have more sway than the libido?

Snow had some pride left. Even if she was having this conversation looking as if she belonged behind a cauldron and should have green skin. There was only so far she was willing to go for town acceptance, and goopy green makeup was beyond that line.

"I have a business to run here, and the kids will be arriving soon expecting candy at the door." He didn't need to know the fun didn't start for another forty minutes. "If you have more to say, you'll have to come back at closing time when I'm free."

"When is that?" he asked.

She'd hoped her lack of cooperation would result in him storming out and never coming back. The idea of having a round two of this set up a pounding in her temples.

Tempted to lie, something told her to stick with the truth. "Seven."

"I'll be here at six forty-five." With a nod, he strolled back into the store as if they'd done little more than chat about the weather. Caleb should have been fighting mad. He should have been making demands and refusing to be tossed into the street after eighteen months of nothing.

If he ever loved her, he'd be doing all of those things. His lack of feeling wasn't a revelation, but having the reality confirmed so clearly felt as if the betrayal had happened all over again.

Worried that Lorelei might stop him on his way through the store, Snow hustled to catch up and intercept any further interrogation. Though she'd been back in her small Tennessee hometown for less than six months, Lorelei Pratchett had regained the tendency to grill any strangers who dared step inside the Ardent Springs city limits.

"So how long will you be with us?" Lorelei asked as Caleb reached the table near the door where her nosy friend was straightening a perfectly organized china display.

Cutting his blue eyes toward Snow, he said, "That depends on my wife."

Another subtle nod and Caleb exited the store, leaving bells jingling in his wake and a gaping Lorelei, shocked speechless for what Snow guessed to be the first time in her life.

"Did he say—"

Snow held up her hand, palm forward, to cut off the question, and dropped into the yellow brocade chair behind her.

Stepping up beside her, Lorelei leaned down and whispered, "Vegas?"

Surprised by the question, she asked, "How do you know about Vegas?"

Lorelei squatted, crossing her arms on the side of the chair. "You pretty much gave yourself away earlier this month, at the Restore the Ruby Festival. Spencer and I were talking about a wedding date, and you vehemently preached against the evils of getting married in Las Vegas."

Pulling off her hat and twisting the wire-trimmed brim in her hands, she said, "Was it that obvious?"

To Lorelei's nod of affirmation, Snow sighed. "Then yes. That's Vegas."

Acknowledgments

I prefer to set my stories in places with which I'm familiar, and this new series is no different. In my early twenties, I found myself at a crossroads in life, as one does in her early twenties, and made the spontaneous decision to move from Pittsburgh, Pennsylvania, where everyone I knew and loved was close by, to Nashville, Tennessee, where I didn't know a soul. To me, it was a great adventure. To everyone else, it was insanity.

In hindsight, it was a little of both.

I spent three years in Nashville, and of all the places I've lived (five states in all), it's the one city to which I'd return in a heartbeat. The area is beautiful, the people are friendly, and, of course, there's the music. And not just country. There's a vibrant culture and diversity in this central Tennessee town that might be surprising to outsiders.

And so, I want to acknowledge the area that gave me a new start, which has come full circle to provide a jumping-off point for my fictitious Ardent Springs. I also need to thank Franklin, Tennessee, for geographic inspiration. If you glance at a map of Ardent Springs and one of downtown Franklin, you'll see many similarities.

I am neither a cook nor a baker, but I did spend my childhood in a home filled with both, thanks to my grandmother, Lillian "Mickey" Bates.

She could make absolutely anything, and did. If my mother will ever hand over the ancient steno pads in which she kept her recipes for everything from spaghetti sauce to nut rolls, there will be a *Nanny's Cookbook* let loose on the world. And thanks to her inspiration, Lorelei's business, Lulu's Home Bakery, is a work of love.

As always, I could never do this without my writing buddies, who listen to me whine, talk me out of corners, and constantly remind me that I *can* do this. To my editor, JoVon Sotak, you've proven yourself to be a gift already, and I look forward to many years together. To my developmental editor, Krista Stroever, you are awesome. That is all. Of course, my agent, Nalini Akolekar, who is a godsend and my fairy book godmother. As the dedication of this book says, I have no idea what I'd do without her.

Thanks to my street team, Team Awesome, for being so supportive and patient when I disappear on deadline, and last but not least, my daughter. It isn't easy being a teenager. It's doubly hard being the child of a single parent. She gives me strength, love, and undying faith every day. She makes me laugh, she makes me mad, and she makes me want to be a better person. You can't ask for more than that.

About the Author

Photo © 2012 Crystal Huffman

Although born in the Ohio Valley, Terri Osburn found her true home between the covers of her favorite books. Classics like *The Wizard of Oz* and *Little Women* filled her childhood, and the genre of romance beckoned during her teen years. In 2007, she put pen to paper to write her own. Just five years later, she was named a 2012 finalist for the Romance Writers of America® Golden Heart® Award, and her debut novel released a year later. You can learn more about this international bestselling author by visiting her website at www.terriosburn.com.